Peter Michael Rosenberg███████████████████████
outstanding talent. His first █████████████████████
Glass, was the runner-up in ██████████████████████
Awards and received widesp████████████████████
subsequent novels, Touched███████████████████d
Because it Makes My Heart Beat Faster.

Also by Peter Michael Rosenberg

**KISSING THROUGH A PANE OF GLASS
TOUCHED BY A GOD OR SOMETHING
BECAUSE IT MAKES MY HEART BEAT FASTER**

Daniel's Dream

Peter Michael Rosenberg

TOUCHSTONE BOOKS
LONDON . NEW YORK . SYDNEY . TOKYO . TORONTO . SINGAPORE

First published in Great Britain by Simon & Schuster, 1996
This edition first published by Touchstone, 1997
An imprint of Simon & Schuster Ltd
A Viacom Company

Copyright © Peter Michael Rosenberg, 1996

The right of Peter Michael Rosenberg to be identified as author of this work
has been asserted in accordance with sections 77 and 78 of the Copyright
Designs and Patents Act 1988

This book is copyright under the Berne Convention
No reproduction without permission
All rights reserved

Simon & Schuster Ltd
West Garden Place
Kendal Street
London
W2 2AQ

Simon & Schuster Australia
Sydney

A CIP catalogue record for this book is available from the British Library

ISBN 0 684 81728 4

Printed and bound in Great Britain by Caledonian International Book
Manufacturing, Glasgow

This book is a work of fiction. Names, characters, places and incidents are
either the product of the author's imagination or are used fictitiously. Any
resemblance to actual events or locales or persons, living or dead, is entirely
coincidental.

This book is dedicated to the memory of Vicky Allen (1958–80)

Acknowledgements

I would like to express special thanks to my editor Clare Ledingham for all her help with this novel. I would also like to thank my agent Christopher Little, my partner Sara Colclough, my parents Jack and Janet Rosenberg, Lucy Ferguson at HarperCollins and everyone at Simon & Schuster for their continuing support. Thanks too to Karen Bennett, wherever she may be.

1

On the morning of the sixth of May, exactly six months after the accident, Daniel awoke from a dream unlike any he had had before. Ever since his premature return from India, trussed up like a chicken with his right arm in a sling and his neck in a brace, sleep – or more particularly, the opportunity to sleep comfortably – had eluded him. For the first two months, the sheer physical discomfort of his injuries had tormented him, and snatching anything more than a quarter of an hour of restful sleep had been impossible. This made him testy and irritable, but he had resigned himself to the fact that, until his collar-bone had mended, his bruises had healed and the osteopathic manipulation that he underwent every week had taken effect, he had no choice but to grin and bear it. That he did so with ill grace was not something that could be mentioned without rousing Daniel's wrath. Many of those around him during the weeks after the accident believed that, considering he had almost lost his life, a little insomnia was a small price to pay. However, if anyone so much as hinted at this, Daniel swiftly disabused them of the notion.

But then none of them, except his wife, Lisanne, knew about the nightmares. Even when the sling had long been abandoned, his nights were still plagued with misery. And although the osteopath no longer took his head in an arm-lock and jerked it until his neck made a sound like a walnut being cracked, his recurrent, tormented visions ensured that, for half a year, he had not yet woken from a decent night's rest.

This recurring dream – a classic, hallucinatory rollercoaster ride – never differed, in either content or intensity, and was both numbing and exhausting in its regularity. In the dream, Daniel was alone in his bedroom, caught up in a continuous cycle of somersaults, rolling over and over round his bedroom floor, slamming periodically into the walls and furniture, the forward, circular momentum propelling him indefinitely, the room twisting and turning; a dizzy, sickening motion that never ceased. No sooner had he slammed into one wall with an urgent, rib-cracking thud, than he was off again, unknown forces bending him double and sending him hurtling, head over heels, into another wall, a door or a wardrobe.

Over and over.

Only when morning broke was Daniel released from this agony. For six months he had woken, every morning without fail, covered in a cold, clammy sweat, his body trembling, his head spinning. The night-time exertions left him parched, his throat dry and harsh like cracked, sunbeaten leather. Desperate for rehydration, he would reach across to the bedside table for the glass of water

Daniel's Dream

– a constant fixture these days – and drain its contents in one.

And when he wiped the perspiration from his forehead, neck and chest, he invariably used the same towel to dry his eyes and tear-moistened cheeks. No matter what the hour, there would be no more sleep for Daniel, and he had become used to lying awake in bed, quietly, staring at the ceiling, waiting for the sun – and the rest of the world – to rise.

But not on the morning of the sixth of May. On that morning, Daniel awoke from his dream with a clear mind and a dry, cool forehead. He was neither dizzy nor anxious, nor did his throat feel as if it had had to contend with a sandstorm during the night. Even his neck, which was usually sore – the muscles tense and knotted like an intricate piece of macramé – felt relaxed, as if he had just had a deep massage, and there was an easy mobility when, from force of habit, he reached for the glass of water.

He sat upright in bed, glass in hand, but did not drink. He felt curiously calm and refreshed. It was a little after dawn and a cool, early light filtered through the gaps in the curtains, the thin, sparse white shafts fingering the walls, the carpet and the furniture with an innocent caress. He gazed round the bedroom as if seeing it clearly for the first time in ages. Even though nothing had changed – the wardrobes had not moved, the digital alarm clock still blinked myopically on the bedside table, and his clothes still tumbled chaotically from the chair – there was something different about the room, a sense that it had changed in some intrinsic, organic manner which he could not identify.

And then it became clear, for just a moment. Not a clear image or vision, just a sense that there was, of all things, a tree, in the room – an old, gnarled olive tree, its branches curled and twisted – growing straight out of the carpet at the foot of the bed. Daniel peered into the space ahead. Whatever he had seen or sensed, it was no longer there. A trick of the light? Or something left over from his dream, perhaps, lingering like the faint aroma of freshly ground coffee, persisting in the air long after the beans have been ground.

Daniel breathed in deeply, and savoured the smells of the bedroom as if they were something new and exotic rather than the usual amalgam of stale air, the remnants of deodorant and sweaty socks. He was sure that, among the familiar smells he could detect a hint of mimosa and pine. Had Lisanne been using an air-freshener? It didn't seem likely. He had, much to her relief, stopped smoking in the bedroom some months ago, so there would have been no need to perfume the room artificially. He sniffed once or twice; it was fainter now, but still there, the merest hint of fragrance, of otherness; it was strangely intoxicating.

Even more potent than the curious vision and strange smell were the unusual sounds that echoed inside his head, like the last remnants of a dream. None of the usual noises of late-twentieth-century London intruded into the bedroom. There was no traffic, no roar of motorcycles revving up, no coughing, spluttering diesel engines, no cries of children or screams of drunks. Even his home, a late-Victorian terraced house that usually creaked and crackled with a comforting familiarity, was oddly silent, and the only sounds he could hear were the exotic timbres and fading harmonics of the final notes of a haunting melody, vaguely oriental, played on what could only be a bouzouki.

Since the nightmares had become a regular part of his life, Daniel had taken to keeping a record of his impressions and feelings in the vague, and thus far vain, hope that they might assist him in his enforced convalescence. It was not a diary – Daniel did not possess the necessary discipline to keep a diary on a regular basis – but its contents were none the less revealing. It had been Dr Fischer's idea, and although Daniel was at first reluctant to use it, over the months he had found a certain, if remote, solace in being able to commit to paper some of the dread of his night-time excursions into the dark.

Daniel grabbed the cheap, faint-lined, spiral-bound notebook and pen from the bedside table and, turning to a fresh page, scribbled down a few words which, he felt, most accurately represented his visual impressions, now fading swiftly: *hot, sunny, blue, bouzouki, olive tree?* He drew a line across the paper and underneath wrote a few remarks: *sound of ocean, smell of pine needles, not a soul to be seen.* He did not know what any of it meant, but as he had developed the habit of writing even his most obscure thoughts in the notebook, it seemed the right thing to do. Besides, it made a refreshing change from the macabre and depressing thoughts and intentions that were usually committed to paper at that hour of the day.

What was the matter with him? he wondered. What exactly had he been dreaming about? Perhaps it had something to do with the sleeping tablets? For the first time in weeks he had not taken the barbiturates the doctor had prescribed. He had become fed up with their inefficacy and the sickening side effects that ensured, come what may, sleep or no sleep, he would greet the day with an abominable hangover.

And now, having cut them out for just one night, instead of waking depressed and anxious, he felt relaxed and clear-headed. Without further thought, Daniel grabbed the bottle of barbiturates off the bedside table and threw it into the waste bin beneath the window, where it landed on the heap of used paper tissues and irredeemably torn tights with a dull thud.

Wide awake now, albeit still a little baffled by the remnants of his dream, Daniel decided to get up. It was a small, simple decision, but even so it was out of keeping with his recent behaviour, and he knew it. It was weeks since he had bothered to get out of bed before Lisanne. Even on the rare occasions when he woke to find her beside him, he usually turned over and buried his head in the pillow, preferring to fake sleep and stay in bed rather than rise to a house that had yet to show signs of life.

This morning, though, without disturbing Lisanne, he slipped out from between the sheets and put on the white towelling robe that, like a security blanket, was never far from hand. Of late he had been living in loose, casual clothing, sometimes not even progressing beyond the bathrobe. Without work his days had become unstructured and meaningless; he had sometimes not bothered to dress properly or even shave. After all, what was the point of making an effort to look presentable when he wasn't going to leave the house? He knew that this slovenliness upset Lisanne, but he could do nothing about it. Besides, in one way or another, *everything* he did these days upset Lisanne, so what difference would one extra annoyance make?

Downstairs in the kitchen Daniel filled the kettle, fished

Daniel's Dream

a tea-bag out of the box, located a clean mug, tossed the tea-bag in the air and caught it successfully in the mug. Then he smiled. It was a long time since he had caught himself acting so capriciously; he rather wished that Lisanne had seen him.

He fetched a pint of milk from the refrigerator and set it down carefully beside the mug, then waited patiently for the water to boil. Once again he became strangely aware of a change in his overall mood, as if a terrible curse had been lifted from him during the night and no one had told him about it. There could no longer be any doubt. It wasn't just the sleeping tablets. Something had happened, something important.

He reached across to the radio and switched it on. It was tuned in to a local radio station that played a non-stop selection of hits from the sixties and seventies, songs that Daniel had grown up with, songs whose words and tunes were so familiar that he barely noticed what was being played. It was only as he was pouring the boiling water on to the tea-bag that he realised with a start he had stopped singing Bob Dylan's 'Lay Lady Lay' and, for several bars, had been crooning along with the Everly Brothers' 'All I Have to Do is Dream'.

Of course, thought Daniel.

It wasn't simply a case of having dreamt something new. In fact, the contents of the new dream might even be irrelevant. What was different was that he *hadn't* had the nightmare; he hadn't spent a long, lonely night turning endless somersaults and crashing into brick walls.

In its place had been . . . what? What exactly had he dreamt? He tried to concentrate but realised within moments that the process of remembering the contents of a dream had nothing to do with active thinking or hard concentration. In fact, both were probably self-defeating. Dreams didn't work like that. Daniel was not an expert, but he knew it required more abstract methods to bring dreams back from wherever it was they resided once you had woken up. Daniel had once read a book all about how to train yourself to recall your dreams, but, typically, he could not now remember any of its contents.

Save for a few of his own, slightly unconventional theories, like much of the population of the Western world Daniel saw dreams as an adjunct to life, essentially meaningless and relevant only when they played up. Like one's appendix.

At least, that was how he felt most of the time. In moments of quiet reflection, however, he was prepared to entertain other, more weighty ideas; ideas brought about, more often than not, by the contents of one of his own dreams. For example, he had no ready explanation for what he called his 'creative dreams'. Though these particular dreams occurred only occasionally, they were amongst the most baffling and – by extension – most interesting experiences Daniel had ever had. In one such dream, it seemed to him that he had composed an entire movement of a classical symphony. And yet he could not read music. Not a single note.

How did one explain such things? Unable to read music or to play a musical instrument, Daniel had been unable to transcribe any of the music into a form that might be recognisable, and before the day was out, the glorious melodies and harmonies he was sure he had created had disappeared. It was a wonderful, if ephemeral, taste of a world that he knew nothing of in waking life.

Daniel's Dream

And then there was the scene from the 'missing Shakespearean drama' that Daniel had written one night while asleep. He was no Shakespeare scholar, but there was no doubt in his mind when he woke from the dream that he had written – and watched in performance – a snatch from a hitherto undiscovered masterpiece.

Though such dreams were anomalies and could, no doubt, be dismissed as hallucinatory or hysterical, for Daniel they had happened: the works *had* existed, albeit briefly and only in a dream. But did that make them any less real? Were you any less terrified by a nightmare than by a 'real' horrifying event? Daniel knew, to his chagrin, that nightmares could be much more frightening than the most terrifying of real-life events. Even the accident – shocking and harrowing as it was – could not compete, in sheer terror, with the worst of his nightmares.

Daniel sat down a the kitchen table with his mug of tea and, for a few moments, stared aimlessly through the window. Out in the street the world was coming to life. A few early birds were already making their way to work, hurrying along in the cold post-dawn light, their faces pale, their movements automatic, their eyes glazed over. Poor sods, thought Daniel, as he brought the mug of hot tea to his lips. Still, at least they have jobs to go to; at least they have work.

Daniel gazed across at the framed photograph that hung on the wall next to the clock and sighed.

Daniel's photographic career had been triggered by events during his university days when, disenchanted with the rather sterile, academic content of his degree course in engineering, he searched for something more vital and creative to occupy him. He was a bright individual who, rather than applying himself to a single pursuit, preferred to flit from one interest to the next like a peripatetic butterfly, never settling on any one subject long enough to master it but always capable of grasping the salient features *en route*.

In this manner, while pursuing his uninspiring degree, Daniel flirted with subjects as diverse as sociology, biochemistry and developmental psychology. Along the way he was side-tracked for several weeks by a near-obsessional fascination with comparative religion – even now he liked to think of this as his 'searching phase' – and at one point he approached the Dean of Studies with a proposal to change his major. Most of the alternatives interested him initially, but he soon became bored or restless and before long he would, inevitably, find himself back on the trail, looking for some discipline, some branch of knowledge, or just something of substance that could occupy him not for just a term or two but for life.

In the end a severe toothache was his salvation. Although Daniel had a tendency to ignore the various messages his nervous system sent him concerning body-maintenance, he was never able to postpone the inevitable for long when it came to his teeth. And it was while thumbing through a copy of *National Geographic* in the dentist's waiting room that he struck gold. An extraordinary photo-essay on the roaming tribal peoples of Rajasthan in north-west India captured his senses and fired his imagination. The pictures showed a wonderfully exotic selection of brightly coloured nomads with their camels in various locations; set off against sun-baked deserts, seated around sparking fires by night or just engaged in their daily duties. The images

Daniel's Dream

were so beautiful, revealed such detail and delight, that for several minutes, while he studied the photographs and allowed himself to be drawn in by their seductive mix of mystery and majesty, he forgot about the raging pain in his corroded molar. Such was the impact of the photographs that in one fell swoop they simultaneously alleviated Daniel's itinerant subject-hopping, staunched the flow of existential angst caused by his lack of focus and direction, and provided the means by which he would clothe and feed himself for the rest of his life. From that moment on, Daniel knew what he wanted to do. It was simple. He would travel the world and capture it on film.

The fact that the closest he had ever come to any serious camera work was having his passport photo taken in an automatic booth was neither here nor there, and for Daniel certainly no obstacle. Photography was a skill, therefore it could be learnt. Artistry – which he never doubted he possessed – would express itself later, once he had mastered the practical aspects of the medium. In the meantime he would equip himself with all the necessary skills to be able to take perfect photographs in all and any conditions.

He laid his hands on a reasonable single-lens reflex camera – a sturdy if rather unwieldy East German Praktica – which he purchased second-hand using an indecent chunk of his grant. With sketchy knowledge but boundless enthusiasm, he loaded the camera with fast black-and-white stock and took to the streets, intent on discovering if (without the aid of the experts to whom he would inevitably refer) he had 'an eye'.

By the time Daniel received his third roll of film back

from the developers it was clear that here was something at which he was not merely adept but manifestly skilled. Even in those early shots, naive, repetitive and sometimes over-exposed, it was apparent that he had a natural talent for composition. Frames were filled, shapes unearthed, textures explored. Without consulting the required texts he had already chanced upon a few of the laws of composition, such as the 'intersection of thirds', whereby images frequently impact most dramatically if points of interest are located not in the centre of the frame but a third of the way from the edges, giving dynamic balance to what might otherwise be stilted or stultified compositions.

He had no notion then of how he would make the great leap from happy, enthusiastic amateur to hardened professional, but he knew that sooner or later the day would come.

Daniel learnt everything he could from the fanatics at the university's society, and the rest of the world now beckoned. After showing a portfolio of his best black-and-white work to the editor of a local rag, he fulfilled his first photographic assignment, covering a Remembrance Day parade in Brighton, for which he was paid fifty pounds.

His images – quirky and offbeat but oozing potential – caught the eye of the owner of the town's only photographic gallery and he was invited to exhibit in the following year's summer exhibition. It was the big break he had needed.

Daniel's freelance work garnered great admiration from many quarters, and before long he was making a decent living, particularly from magazines looking for exotic overseas shots. He took to foreign travel as easily as a duck to water, and his crowning glory came when, aged twenty-six, he received a commission from *National Geographic*. In just six years Danial had made the transition from viewer to contributor, and his professional reputation was made.

A sudden, sharp twinge in his left shoulder made him wince reflexively, a cruel reminder that he was still not fit enough to return to the job he loved. Damn the accident, he thought, angrily. How much longer do I have to suffer?

In the bedroom upstairs Lisanne was still fast asleep. It was about now – just after dawn, an hour before the alarm clock shocked her into consciousness – that her own dreams were at their most vivid and most bizarre. She did not suffer from nightmares – at least, not the sort of dramatic descents into hell that seemed of late to have characterised Daniel's night-time journeys – and yet there was always something puzzling and disturbing about her dreams. She assumed this was only natural; whenever she spoke to other people about dreams they described similar experiences. For Lisanne, the most disturbing and distressing aspects of dreams were not the specific contents (although she had once spent an entire night in the company of nothing but dead babies and animals) but the way in which dreams metamorphosed from one scene to the next without any logic, how visions changed randomly from one set of indecipherable images to another, and how people came and went without apparent reason or purpose, their intentions never clear. It was this nebulous, random character of dreams that most disturbed her. In real life one thing led to another and effect followed cause in a prescribed manner, but in dreams nothing ever seemed to follow from anything else, and you could be whisked from one incomprehensible scenario to another without rhyme or reason. It was very unsettling.

Still, as she had concluded on numerous occasions, she would rather suffer these unnerving discontinuities than experience, night after night, the sort of torments that Daniel had to undergo.

As Daniel was finishing his second mug of tea, Lisanne woke with a start, the disturbing images from her most recent dream still in her mind's eye, though fading fast, descending back into her unconscious, disappearing like a footprint cast in wet sand.

She rolled over and stretched out her arm in order to caress, gently, her husband's brow, as she had done every morning since the accident. It was a habit now, ingrained through months of repetition, and perhaps no longer carrying the unsullied, unconditional care and tenderness that had originally motivated the gesture.

Every morning for six months she had woken to the muffled, pathetic sighs of a man in distress. She knew the misery that Daniel suffered, knew the details of his nightly ordeal. Her caresses had always calmed him, reduced his whimpers to a soft moan, and she had persuaded herself that this small gesture, this gentle caress which reached across the boundary between wakefulness and sleep, in some way helped to ease his distress. Of course, she did not know for sure if it did; she just had to believe that in some way this simple human act brought an element of reality, security or comfort into the surreal, repetitive world of Daniel's dream.

But this morning when she reached out, her hand met only cool, ruffled pillowcase. She opened her eyes and

Daniel's Dream

was alarmed to discover that her senses had not been fooling her and that Daniel was not in bed. Her immediate response was panic. She sat up abruptly, rubbed her eyes and gazed anxiously around. Her gaze was drawn swiftly to Daniel's bedside table, and she recognised immediately that something was wrong, that something had changed. There was the glass of water, which, like some magic flagon in a fairy-tale, was always being drained but was somehow never empty. There too was the spiral-bound notebook that Daniel, on the instructions of Dr Fischer, used to record the contents of his dream.

Lisanne peered at the table top with mounting apprehension. Where was the bottle? The bottle that contained his sleeping tablets?

In that moment her worst fears – dormant for the past few months, but always lying just beneath her conscious thoughts – rose to the surface. She scrambled across to Daniel's side, leant half out of the bed and frantically searched the floor around the bedside table. Nothing. She leapt out of bed and ran to the door, stubbing her toe on the way.

'Daniel!' she yelled. 'Daniel!'

She waited anxiously for a response which, although it came no more than seconds after her call, seemed to take for ever.

'I'm down here!'

Lisanne closed her eyes, steadied herself against the door jamb and took a deep breath. He would be the death of her. She bit her bottom lip; her toe was agonising. She looked down; no blood, but the beginnings of a bruise for sure.

What was he playing at? He never got up before her, never; at least, not during the last six months. And where were those blasted tablets? It wasn't that she thought Daniel would ever do anything as silly as . . . well, she did not actively think about it. It was just that Dr Fischer had told her she had to keep an eye on him; she had to be alert. His behaviour would be unpredictable, the doctor had told her; all manner of things were possible. He had had a traumatic experience; he was suffering from terrible fears, even worse guilt, misplaced or otherwise. It was all real to him, and there was always the chance that he might take it into his head to . . .

Oh God, thought Lisanne. Why had Fischer said that to her? Why hadn't he kept it to himself? Life was difficult enough as it was, living with a clinically depressed husband, without having to contend with the possibility that at any moment, for any reason, he might top himself. Fischer was a good man, and had been her family doctor ever since she was a little girl. She had no doubt that, even though he was getting on a bit now, he was a first-class doctor. But why had he mentioned suicide? It had made her life hell; absolute hell.

'Daniel!' she called out again. 'What are you doing?'

She heard his heavy footsteps on the stairs and waited patiently until he appeared. She could see the top of his head as he plodded relentlessly from one step to the next, his head bowed as if in penitence. As he rounded the top of the staircase he looked up and saw her standing there, naked, leaning against the door. He smiled weakly.

'Very tempting. Is this a new ploy?'

'What?'

Daniel made a brave attempt to look her up and down approvingly, but Lisanne wasn't interested in playing this particular game. Apart from anything else, it wasn't funny any more. They hadn't made love since the accident, had barely touched each other. Initially this had been perfectly understandable; Daniel's injuries had precluded any activities that might aggravate his neck condition. There *were* certain exercises that his osteopath had recommended, but none of them involved the sort of movements normally associated with making love. For the first three months Lisanne had been understanding about this, but recently she had come to the conclusion that there was more to Daniel's lack of interest in sex than met the eye. He had, for the most part, studiously avoided any physical contact with her save for the occasional kiss, and even then the kisses had been singularly lacking in passion. The doctor had suggested that sex was no longer proscribed, but Daniel had not taken this particular piece of advice to heart. Lisanne avoided thinking too much about the possible reasons why Daniel was avoiding her, as the prospect of having to contemplate rejection on top of everything else was too much to bear. She had entered a little pact with herself, which involved avoiding the subject rather than confronting Daniel with it. In time, she was sure, things would revert to normal. Of course they would. They had to.

'What are you doing up? I woke up and you weren't there.'

Daniel was clearly nonplussed. 'Oh. Sorry,' he muttered, his brow creasing, bemusement contorting his expression into a question mark.

Lisanne was not to be appeased so easily. 'You never get up before me,' she said, rather more petulantly than she intended. Her toe was still sore, and she considered it Daniel's fault.

Daniel frowned. 'What can I tell you? I woke up, I felt like getting out of bed. I haven't broken any by-laws, have I?'

Lisanne realised that her complaint sounded foolish, but she knew she was not being stupid, that she had genuine reasons for concern. She wondered whether she should ask him about the sleeping tablets, but decided against it for the time being. She would have a good look round before sounding the alarm; there was probably a perfectly good, perfectly simple explanation.

She sighed. 'I'm sorry,' she said after a short pause. 'I'm being silly.' She attempted a conciliatory smile, which elicited a small response in kind.

There followed an awkward silence as they stood there, opposite each other, neither of them sure what to do next. It was the sort of awkwardness that one might have witnessed between two adolescents on a first date rather than between two adults who had been married for five years and known each other even longer.

It was Daniel who broke the impasse. Unable to sustain eye contact and silence simultaneously, he allowed his head to fall forward, as if he had dropped something on the floor and needed to find it. There was something irredeemably sad about the gesture, and Lisanne, who both felt her own pain and isolation and also sensed Daniel's deep anxiety, felt her heart go out to him. She wanted to reach out to him, to put her arms around him, to tell him how much she still loved him. But she knew the gesture would make him bristle with discomfort, and for all her sympathies she didn't think she could cope with that additional snub just now.

Daniel's Dream

'I'll, uh . . . I'll put the kettle on,' said Daniel, pleased to find an excuse to get away.

Lisanne nodded. 'I'll be right down,' she said, and turned back towards the bedroom. Suddenly, and quite against her better judgement, she found herself calling out after him, saying out loud the question that had been circling around in her head since she had woken up, the question she so desperately wanted to ask.

'Daniel, where are the sleeping tablets?'

Daniel stopped in his tracks. He looked up, expecting to see her hanging over the banister, but she was not there, her voice, disembodied, echoing between the walls on the landing.

He knew immediately what this was about, understood that, despite its casual delivery, the question was anything but innocent. He frowned, unsure whether to feel angry at the intrusion and its implication or touched by her concern. Sadly, in most matters, he had ceased being moved by his wife's concern weeks ago. Which, even more sadly, left him only one response.

'The tablets? Oh, I uh . . . I swallowed them. The whole lot.'

That did it. In a flash she was there, peering frantically over the banister, her light-brown shoulder-length hair falling forward from her face so that he could barely see the desperation in her eyes.

'Just kidding.'

'Daniel!'

'Well honestly, Lisanne . . . what did you think?'

'I was just—'

'They're in the bin,' he interrupted curtly. 'I threw them out. They just give me headaches. Okay?'

Lisanne wasn't sure whether to smile or scream. The knowledge that Daniel might have died in the accident still made her feel sick. That he might attempt to take his own life made her feel even worse. So it was with desperate irony that she had to concede there were times when she could, quite frankly, kill him.

Lisanne had first met Daniel at a dinner party, hosted by mutual friends with the express intention of introducing this mismatched pair of workaholics to each other. As the hosts would have happily admitted, it was a shot in the dark. Although they were both fine people in their own right with many virtues to recommend them, neither Lisanne nor Daniel was, at that time, a particularly sociable individual. 'Difficult' was the word that most readily sprang to mind when any attempt was made to explain why two such interesting, intelligent and attractive people were incapable of sustaining relationships with individuals of the opposite sex for longer than about three weeks.

In Lisanne's case this was more to do with her work than any personality problem. Since graduating from university she had been immersed in the world of books and literature, caught up in the commercial side of a business that was notorious for taking over one's life. By the age of thirty she was running her own literary agency and had since had a significant measure of commercial success, particularly in the notoriously fickle arena of fiction. Under her guidance and direction, two complete unknowns – writers who had come to her in her early days with dog-eared well-thumbed manuscripts of first novels – had reached the best-seller lists. Such was the financial success of these two protégés that since then she had not looked back. Others – less fêted perhaps but still successful in real terms – had followed in their wake and before long the Lisanne Cokely Literary Agency had established a reputation in the business as a small but promising firm that could sniff out good, easy-on-the-intellect fiction for the mass market.

Her established best-sellers had ensured that she could afford a holiday each year in the Caribbean and have a comfortable home to return to when, at the end of her increasingly long hours, she finally decided to quit for the day. This, of course, had been her biggest problem; Lisanne was wedded to her work. She loved words, loved books, loved the ins and outs of contracts and negotiations, felt duty bound always to get the best deals for her authors and, as a result, had not established the sort of boundaries that all self-employed individuals must draw if they are ever to live lives of their own. Friends had tried to talk to her about it but Lisanne had proved stubborn, and it soon became clear that the only thing that would shake her out of her rather extreme lifestyle was if she fell in love.

This was where the problems started, for Lisanne was such a severe, headstrong individual that only someone equally extreme could possibly have any effect on her. After several attempts to pair her with perfectly charming and eligible men had failed dismally, two of her dearest friends, John and Antonia, finally hit on the perverse idea of introducing her to a similarly difficult, headstrong and uncompromising character.

They had known Daniel since university, and agreed that someone of his peculiar psychological profile might just be able to shake Lisanne from her own preoccupations. After all, there was no reason why they should not be attracted to each other. Lisanne was lively and attractive and, once away from work, as relaxed and charming a companion as one could hope to meet. Could it work? they wondered that evening, as they brought these two lumbering beasts with their twisted psyches together for the first time.

They did not have to wait long to find out. Whatever chemistry was at work that evening – physical, emotional, intellectual – there was no question in the minds of those looking on that their two most complex and complicated friends had found a common bond.

Conversation at the dinner table that evening buzzed and crackled like an electric storm, with the two protagonists pitting their wits against each other to sparkling effect. Daniel had just returned from the north-eastern provinces of India, where he had been sent by *National Geographic* to capture the fading remnants of tribal civilisations that had only recently emerged from the Stone Age. He had come back laden with the sort of stories that usually graced the pages of adventure magazines, and held them all captive that evening with tales of danger and derring-do and of adrenalin-rush exploits reminiscent of the Indiana Jones films.

These stories, with their excitement, vivid descriptions and strong narrative drive, were like a drug to Lisanne, who thrived on such material. She interrupted and interposed at pertinent moments and, in her own clever yet subtle way, managed to shape the stories as they emerged from his lips, as a good editor might shape words upon a page. Daniel was aware of and impressed by this unusual ability, and warmed to her immediately. With Lisanne there he felt both completely at ease – as if he were telling his stories to a close friend – and oddly

Daniel's Dream

excited, as if such tales were part of some sophisticated mating ritual, the outcome of which would determine his future. She had a potent effect on him and as the evening progressed he became more and more entranced by her.

Lisanne too was transfixed. Here was someone with passions as strong as hers, who lived life on the edge, barely impinging upon normal, everyday society. Combined with his energy and acceptable good looks, she found the mix very appealing.

So it came as no surprise to their mutual friends when they discovered, two weeks later, that Lisanne and Daniel had been seen out together several times and that there was even talk of the two of them moving in together.

Within a year they were married. Despite the forebodings of those who thought neither of them capable of sustaining a long-term relationship, it turned out to be a good match. Daniel's presence gave Lisanne something other than words and books to preoccupy her. Love (and there was never any doubt that it was the real thing) helped curb her work-oriented obsessions and made her both more available and easier to deal with socially. This was seen all round as a good thing.

As for Daniel, Lisanne's influence was notable, as her greater gentleness, tact and caring nature slowly began to smooth over Daniel's more abrasive tendencies, making him an altogether more pleasant person. These changes, pronounced though they were, seemed to act only for the good and in no way detracted from their personalities. Daniel and Lisanne remained as interesting – both individually and collectively – as they had always been, guaranteed to spice up the most lethargic of parties and never short of an opinion or two. And there seemed no danger of their getting in each other's way, as Daniel's work still took him abroad every few weeks, thus guaranteeing the all-important 'personal space' they both needed. It worked perfectly. Five years on they were still together, still an item: still married.

But for how much longer?

In the bedroom, Lisanne slipped on her dressing gown and, determined not to let this latest contretemps boil over into something more unpleasant, went down to join him.

'It's still very early,' she said as she entered the kitchen to find Daniel sitting at the table, head in hand. A fresh cup of tea sat on the table opposite him. She sat down and reached for the cup, keeping her eyes on him the whole time. There was something about him this morning, something about his pose, the way he sat, that disturbed her. She didn't like it one bit.

'Daniel?'

'Hmm?'

'I'm sorry . . . for being silly.'

Daniel looked up and attempted a smile, not very successfully. He reached out across the table and took Lisanne by the hand.

'You don't need to apologise to me. You have absolutely nothing to apologise for. We both know it's me, we both know that I'm the one who is acting like a complete bastard, and if it wasn't for the fact that I've had to say "I'm sorry" so many times in the last six months that I'm sick to death of the words, I would be apologising again.'

Lisanne squeezed his hand tightly. They had been through this same scene several times lately, repeated the

Daniel's Dream

same dialogue with minor variations, the same excuses and reasons. Sympathies had been exchanged, words of tenderness and understanding spoken, declarations made . . . and nothing had changed.

Six months previously while covering the Hindu/Muslim riots in northern India for a major news and current affairs magazine, Daniel had been involved in a serious road accident in which a colleague and friend, Alex, a very promising young journalist, was killed.

There was nothing Daniel could have done about the incident. He had not been responsible for the vehicle they were travelling in, for the vehicle's driver, or for any of the series of small, individually insignificant events that conspired to turn a simple cross-town journey in an open jeep into a fiery maelstrom. He was not Alex's guardian or keeper, yet for reasons that neither Lisanne, Dr Fischer or the 'knuckle-headed shrink' Daniel had seen shortly after the accident had been able to divine, he held himself responsible for Alex's death.

It was such a sensitive issue that Lisanne could barely bring herself to talk about it these days. Daniel's own injuries were serious but not life-threatening; some severe burns, a few broken bones and – the legacy of this whole affair – chronic damage to his spine which meant that he was still unable to lift anything much heavier than a cup of tea and was certainly in no condition to travel around Asia wielding metal-bodied cameras, heavy glass lenses and a tripod which, thanks to its use of especially dense metals, was as sturdy as the Rock of Gibraltar.

But somehow even these injuries paled into insignificance when compared to the emotional damage the accident inflicted on Daniel's troubled psyche. In six months he had been transformed from a young, energetic and slightly wild maverick to a sad, pathetic and purposeless sap, drifting without direction, apparently doomed to wallow in guilt and self-pity with little hope of escape. God knows they had tried everything; even the professionals had all but given up hope. Only Dr Fischer – last of a dying breed, a product of the old school with his homilies and anachronistic methods – retained any faith that Daniel would, eventually, recover. However, even Lisanne, who was deeply fond of the doctor, had to admit that his prescribed remedy seemed to fall short of the mark. 'Ah Lisanne,' he would say to her when despair was starting to get the upper hand, 'never forget; time heals.' It was not much, by way of either therapy or comfort, but in the absence of any alternatives, she had tried to maintain faith in the old man's prognosis.

To add the final insult to the list of injuries, at the back of her mind Lisanne could not but be a little suspicious about the circumstances of the accident, especially considering the devastating effect it had had on Daniel. Lisanne had never met Alex, but it was well known that, in addition to being fun, talented and adventurous, she had also been an exceptionally attractive young woman.

They drank the rest of their tea together in silence. After a few minutes Lisanne returned upstairs to ready herself for work. Daniel waited impatiently for her to complete her complicated preparations – showering, cleansing, deodorising, dressing, making-up – oddly anxious to get out of the house himself. He could not account for why he should be in such a hurry to see the outside world after all this time. It was a pleasant morning, admittedly, but no different from a dozen or so that had graced them that summer. Nevertheless, he felt a strong urge to be on the move, even if it was just on foot through the local neighbourhood.

'See you later then,' said Lisanne, leaning over the kitchen table to kiss him on the cheek.

'Sure,' said Daniel. Then, almost as an afterthought, 'Shall I cook tonight?'

Lisanne tried not to appear shocked. Daniel was a good cook, on occasion exceptional, and until the accident they had shared kitchen duties on a more or less fifty–fifty basis, yet in six months he had not offered to do so much as boil an egg. Consequently they had been surviving on takeaways, occasional restaurant meals and numerous packages of chilled, prepared meals from high-street stores. Only at weekends did Lisanne have either the time or the inclination to cook a meal or two.

'That'd be lovely,' she said, trying not to sound either too surprised or two enthusiastic. She knew that Daniel's moods were particularly capricious these days, and that too positive a response to his occasional suggestions could just as easily put him off as encourage him. 'I'll be back around six-thirty.'

'Okay. I'll do something nice; something different.'

'I'll look forward to it. Bye.' And she kissed him again, on the forehead this time, before heading for the front door.

For several minutes after she had left Daniel sat there stupefied. He could not imagine what had prompted him to offer to cook. He had no interest in cooking these days, had not cared two figs for food since the accident and, in direct contrast to his usual attitude, had taken only minimal pleasure in its consumption. And yet, just as Lisanne had crossed the floor to kiss him, he had suddenly been assailed by the sight and smell of a dish that he had eaten several times but never prepared in his life. So vivid was the image, so potent the odour, that he felt compelled to go out into the streets, purchase the ingredients and spend the rest of the day if necessary preparing it. It was an immensely curious sensation, but no less real for that.

Only one problem remained: how exactly did one make moussaka?

A few moments later Daniel was showered and dressed. He looked at himself in the mirror, keenly aware of his improved appearance. He had always been good-looking, with a fine physique, and strong, well-defined features: people who met him for the first time felt almost obliged to comment on the unusually intense colour of his eyes, a deep, cobalt blue that put one in mind of some semi-precious stone. Since the accident Daniel had let himself go, but this morning he made a little more of an effort and it paid dividends. He put on his clean black jeans rather than the tatty blue ones that he had loafed around in for weeks on end; his trainers, although a little scuffed, were given a quick once-over with a damp rag and he chose to wear the new blue sweatshirt Lisanne had bought him for his birthday, as opposed to the green one with the holes in the elbows. He even brushed his thick, dark hair, so that it was sleek and smart. In all likelihood he would turn a few heads that morning.

The sky was bright, yet despite the sunshine there was a decidedly sharp edge to the day. Daniel turned right out of the gate and headed for Green Lanes. Daniel liked Green Lanes, and had in fact been drawn to the

Daniel's Dream

area because of its particular brand of buoyant activity, which ensured the place was alive day and night. This part of London, known locally as Cyprus City because of its preponderance of Greek and Turkish Cypriots, owed more to the mores and customs of the Mediterranean than to those of England. When, at five-thirty, many other parts of London started closing for the day, Green Lanes was still a thriving, bustling market, subsumed in a welter of activity as the locals thronged the busy pavements in search of the best fruit and veg of the day, or queued noisily in the bakeries, buying loaves of fresh-baked aniseed bread or baklava by the kilo. It was always busy, which was how Daniel liked it. He hated neighbourhoods that became ghost towns after six o'clock, whose only activity centred around the doorway of the local pub. Green Lanes was full of vitality even at ten at night, and with its strong local flavour always made him smile. Indeed, on a bright, sunny Sunday morning, to wander past the grocery stores with their colourful produce bursting out on to the pavements and the Greek music pouring forth from strategically placed ghetto-blasters, was to be put more in mind of Heraklion than of Haringey.

That morning however, all was quiet. Daniel walked along past closed and shuttered shop-fronts, dismayed by the lack of life and activity. Was it a holiday of some kind? Did that make a difference? It was only when he had walked as far as the jeweller's and, nosing casually through the glass, caught sight of the time on a large carriage clock in the window that he realised what was wrong. It was only eight-thirty. In all his days living in Green Lanes he had never been up at that time, never walked along Green Lanes before ten o'clock at the earliest, and consequently had never seen the place asleep. He could not help but find it amusing, a revealing comment on what used to be his unconventional lifestyle.

Rather than return home Daniel decided to continue walking for a while. He made no specific decisions but just wandered where his fancy took him. By nine o'clock he found himself a couple of miles up the road in Wood Green. As he walked he became increasingly aware of a difference in his mood. The cool morning air seemed to hone his senses, and he felt clear-headed and awake; not particularly happy or especially depressed; just clear.

In contrast to Green Lanes, Wood Green High Street was wide awake and ready for business. With nothing better to do, Daniel walked into W. H. Smith and, heading for the magazine racks, began studying the titles. Although nothing in particular caught his eye, he was drawn to the brightly coloured front covers. However, after ten minutes of gazing at the various titles – studiously avoiding anything connected with photography – he became bored and made his way upstairs to the book department, where he found himself altogether more interested in what was on offer.

It was a long time since Daniel had browsed in a bookshop, but he found himself suffused with a warm, familiar pleasure as he started to eye the shelves upon shelves of crisp new editions, all lined up neatly one after another, each one a repository of knowledge, information, fantasy or just sheer fun, each volume a gateway to a new – perhaps hitherto unknown – world.

As he worked his way round the department, once again avoiding the few shelves devoted to cameras and photography (lest he start to feel depressed again), he found himself drawn back time and again to two sections. Not surprisingly, the section that interested him most was the travel section. Before the accident it would have been a rare week when Daniel did not purchase a guide book, travel memoir or coffee-table extravaganza detailing some far-flung corner of the world that he had not yet visited.

For Daniel, travel abroad was the greatest gift of all. He had never lost sight of his good fortune in this way; he had made his name as a freelance travel photographer, had deliberately chosen to specialise in this field to enable him to travel the world, and he had never become blasé about it. Although he had visited dozens of countries during the previous ten years or so, there were still hundreds of places to see, countries whose names evoked mysteries and pleasures unknown, cities that tantalised the imagination with promises of adventure and excitement. Travel, be it with a specific purpose in mind or just for the sheer hell of being in a different place, was for Daniel the essence of what a good life was about. Travel abroad was life distilled to its most potent pleasures; it was nigh impossible to get bored when you were in a strange place, as there was always something new to see, hear, taste, touch, something new to experience, to capture – perhaps with lens and celluloid, or just with a word or flash of memory. Travel abroad was life without the dull bits; it was the edited highlights.

So it was that, even though his interest had been dormant for months, now that he was confronted with the array of tantalising titles – the survival manuals, the adventure narratives, the weighty, large-format tomes with their gleaming colour plates and footnotes – he could not resist them. He stood before the shelves, selecting titles at random and leafing through them excitedly, like a man who has been told that a number of ten-pound notes have been hidden between the pages.

Having sated his appetite for travel books, he meandered over to the fiction section to see if there was anything there that tempted him. Since the accident Daniel had had plenty of time on his hands but curiously, even though he was an avid reader, he had not so much as picked up a novel in all that time. Not even ones recommended by Lisanne who, after all, should know about such things.

He searched row upon row of paperbacks, hoping his interest would be altered by a familiar name or an alluring title, but nothing appealed to him. It was only as he was about to leave the shop that his attention was drawn to the New Titles section. There, among the new fiction was a book with a curiously appealing cover. It was a slim novel called *Greek Idyll*, by a writer Daniel had never heard of before. The cover showed a water-colour of a deserted beach with golden sand and azure sea; the branches of an olive tree intruded into the scene from the right-hand side, and lying on the sand towards the centre of the picture was an open book, its pages fanned out. The book cast a shadow of what appeared to be a face, but Daniel could not be sure.

Daniel studied the cover for several minutes; it was as if he were being drawn into the picture. The more he gazed at the clear, still sea and the deep blue sky, the more mesmerised he became. At one point he felt sure he could hear the gentle lapping of the waves against the shoreline, and feel the heat pulsing off the dry, shimmering sand. Then suddenly, with an almost subliminal brevity, a snatch of music, played with brilliant clarity on the bouzouki, filtered into his consciousness with such presence and at

Daniel's Dream

such a high volume that he almost dropped the book in surprise. Still shocked, he looked around him, certain that someone was playing a trick on him, that Greek music was being played over the public address system in the shop. But the music had disappeared as swiftly as it had arrived, leaving behind it a strange, deep longing, quite unlike anything Daniel had ever experienced before. He knew that piece of music, knew that tiny sample of melody; it was the music of his dream from the previous night.

Without reflecting further, he took the book to the cashier's desk, handed over five pounds in coins, and watched the sales assistant earnestly as she rang up the price. He felt oddly excited and yet on edge, as if he were in some way stealing the book, or at least procuring it under false pretences, rather than making a perfectly legal purchase.

Consequently, fired up by the small but potent adrenalin rush brought about by this misplaced sense of danger, Daniel found himself slightly agitated that the sales assistant did not respond to his purchase with greater interest, excitement or urgency. Having rung the price up on the till, she simply put the book in a paper bag, tore the receipt from the till and handed it to him together with his penny change. She did not smile once, nor intimate that anything out of the ordinary had occurred. The paper-bagged book lay on the cashier's desk. She did not pass it to him, but went on to serve the next customer.

Disappointed, Daniel lifted the book from the desk and left. He had hoped she might at least say something to him; so far that day a number of curious things had happened, and he badly wanted someone else to acknowledge that it was indeed a day with a difference, that something new, strange, uncertain, was happening. But it was not to be. The entire transaction had been completed without either of them saying a word. Not even a greeting.

Daniel sighed, pretended it didn't matter; what were words, after all? What did it matter if the plain-faced young girl hadn't said 'Good morning' or 'That'll be four pounds ninety-nine pence' or even 'Thanks' when he had handed over the money? It made no difference. Still, he could not help thinking that some sort of intimation would have been appropriate. Something odd was happening, but, without confirmation or acknowledgement from someone else, he feared it might all be down to a sudden overactiveness of his own imagination.

By the time he had walked back to Green Lanes the shops were all open and normal business activities reigned. Although he had lost enthusiasm for the idea, he decided he had better purchase what he needed to cook the meal he had promised Lisanne. He still wasn't sure why he had made such an atypical offer. All he knew was that, ridiculous as it sounded, for some reason he was destined to make moussaka.

In a grocery store he bought a pound of aubergines, a tin of chopped tomatoes, a couple of large onions, several large potatoes, a pound of minced lamb and a huge hunk of feta cheese. He was pretty sure that Lisanne had all the necessary herbs and other bits and pieces back home. What else went into a Greek moussaka? There were dozens of cookbooks at home but Daniel was loth to use them. He cooked – or so he told Lisanne shortly after they first met – by instinct, which was why he never looked at cookbooks. This was, in fact, only partly true. Daniel did cook by instinct, and did so remarkably well. But

Daniel's Dream

the reason he never looked at cookbooks was that he was too lazy to follow recipes. All that measuring and weighing and making sure you had exactly the right ingredients; it was too mechanical and, for Daniel, detracted from the fun of it all.

For Daniel, cooking was akin to painting or drawing or writing; it was an artistic, creative pursuit, motivated by inspiration, and not a chemistry experiment involving so many cubic centimetres of this added to so many grams of that and heated at such-and-such a temperature until it changed colour. As a result, while he was a dab hand at anything that involved rice, pasta, meat or cheese, his occasional forays into baking had resulted in unmitigated disaster.

Daniel spent a short while nosing around the shelves in case anything else took his fancy, but after five minutes of investigation his only additional purchases were a pint of milk and a few bulbs of organically grown garlic. Satisfied that he had everything he needed, he returned home.

Back in the familiar environment of the kitchen, Daniel unpacked the groceries, made space in the refrigerator for the meat, milk and cheese, then, as much by reflex as genuine desire, filled the kettle and switched it on. Since the accident, 'tea-drinking' had become a major pastime, vying with 'watching television' and 'staring into space' for the number-one spot.

Killing time had become a major preoccupation for Daniel since he had been rendered jobless; each day drifted past him slowly, as if it refused to acknowledge his presence, disallowed his participation. He had tried to occupy his time with reading, writing letters, doing crosswords, but after the first three months he had lost enthusiasm. Now he wandered through the days like a zombie, a man without purpose, without direction, often to be found waiting pitifully for Lisanne to return from work to break up the monotony of his otherwise featureless days.

The water boiled vigorously, filling the room with misty clouds of water vapour. Daniel made himself a mug of tea, going through the motions unconsciously, like a programmed automaton. It was only as he was stirring in the sugar that he became aware of his actions and, in that same moment, he was overwhelmed once more by the world-weary sadness that had dominated his life for half a year.

It wasn't the tea, of course; it was the knowledge that for six months most of his life had been played out in this way, going through the motions, barely aware of what was going on. It was as if he wasn't really there at all, but just an observer, unable or perhaps unwilling to participate in his own life.

A sliver of bright light from somewhere behind his head distracted him. He turned to see that the morning sun had risen from behind the trees and was now filtering through the windows of the living room, illuminating it with a bright, optimistic aura. Hope and optimism had been decidedly thin on the ground of late. Daniel grabbed his mug and the paper bag containing the new book, and walked through to the living room.

He put the book and the mug on the coffee table then went across to the record racks beside the hi-fi. He ran his forefinger along the spines of the record covers, and selected 'The Köln Concert' by Keith Jarrett.

Daniel was no reactionary, neither did he suffer from

Daniel's Dream

any especial technophobia, yet despite the onward march of progress that threatened to consign the vinyl record to the dustbin of history, he had yet to make the transition to compact disc, with all its supposed advantages of fidelity and convenience.

Daniel had grown up with the vinyl record, and his teenage years had been dominated by the newest releases from the great rock bands of the seventies. Since his early teens Daniel had always possessed a stereo system of one kind or another, the earliest being a birthday gift from a well-to-do aunt. He had grown up understanding the importance of high-fidelity music reproduction. As soon as he had been able to afford it, he had started to customise his hi-fi, adding, exchanging, replacing, tweaking, all in order to obtain the maximum enjoyment from his treasured record collection.

But it was the records themselves with their black sheen, colourful centre labels and extraordinary covers that Daniel coveted the most. If there was one thing above all others that put him off the current digital medium, it was the way the packaging had shrunk so dramatically that CD covers could simply not compete with the masterpieces of cheap art that had once graced the covers of LPs. And then there was the whole ritual that revolved around the actual playing of a record. There was something deeply satisfying about the procedure, something of the nature of a religious ritual to it. Even now, years later, he still derived a strange pleasure from the process.

Daniel eased the first of the two records out of its paper inner sleeve, removed all traces of electric charge from its surface with an anti-static gun, then placed it carefully on the deck and eased the stylus on to the revolving disc.

He turned on the amplifier, adjusted the volume and, satisfied that he had everything as he wanted, sat down on the sofa and allowed himself to be drawn swiftly into the melodious, extemporised piano playing.

The opening refrain, as familiar to him as his own name or the sight of his face in the mirror, caused a deep, satisfying shiver of pleasure to pulse through him. He loved this music, perhaps more than any other. Like the best travel experience it meandered and shifted, never wholly certain, so it seemed, of which direction it was taking, but every now and then breaking through in a flourish of extravagance to produce the most moving and delightful of phrases, like the perfect views glimpsed from a moving train.

Daniel listened to the music ebb and flow, uninterrupted for several minutes, until, calmed by its gentle rhythms, he found himself in a state of deep relaxation. He reached over, took his new book, *Greek Idyll*, out of the paper bag and allowed his gaze to drift back and forth across the cover, focusing here and there when something took his interest. Daniel knew nothing about the contents of the book, but he was greatly attracted to the cover. It was wonderfully evocative; the use of water-colours, the delicate application of hue and tint, the clever manipulation of light and shade. Once again, Daniel became aware of how well the artist had captured that sense of summer, of heat and stillness; it seemed to radiate from the picture with startling verisimilitude.

Daniel studied the scene carefully. There was no longer any doubt in his mind; the shadow cast by the open book on the sand was certainly a face. The features were not delineated with any particular definition, but he could

Daniel's Dream

make out the hairline, the sunken eyes, the Roman nose and the point of a beard. Daniel examined the line that separated the sand from the sea. It was an inviting (though, now that he looked more closely, slightly disturbing) scene; it asked questions of the viewer. Whereabouts was this beach? Was it on an island? Who does the book belong to, and where is that person now? What is the book about, and why has it been left open on the sand? Why does it cast a shadow of a face?

Daniel searched the opening pages for some information about the author, Robert Jameson, but could find no photographs or biographical notes. Having nothing better to do (or to be more accurate, having nothing at all to do), Daniel embarked upon the first chapter.

He still wasn't really interested in reading fiction, and even if he had been it was unlikely he would put his efforts into a book by a complete unknown. It was unlike him to make an impulsive purchase based on, of all things, a cover, but the front cover of *Greek Idyll* had lured him in, and there now seemed no alternative but to continue.

The first chapter was narrated in the first person, and its initial themes, its setting and to a degree its main character seemed uncomfortably reminiscent of John Fowles's *The Magus*, though lacking the latter's finesse and cleverly crafted intrigue. Daniel read the first chapter with a gnawing sense that he was being taken for a ride. His interest dwindled swiftly and, finding himself unaccountably tired, he put the book to one side and allowed his eyelids, already heavy with sleep, to close.

What a pity, he thought as he tuned out of the world of letters and into the world of sounds. Jarrett's ingenious and delightful improvisation was embracing him once more with delicious wisps of melody and rhythm. He had thought, for just a moment, that something extraordinary and enticing was about to happen to him; the curious coincidence of spotting the book with its Mediterranean setting had caused a frisson of excitement and identification when he saw it in the bookshop that morning, as if he had been meant to find it just then. For a few moments it had reverberated with some sort of sympathetic vibration, a sense that there was more here than met the eye. And yet, within minutes of starting to read the opening chapter, Daniel found himself once more disappointed and distressed. The world, he sensed, was not about to provide him with the meaning or excitement or pleasure that he craved and that had been absent from his life for so long.

The record came to an end, but Daniel remained seated on the sofa, his eyes closed, his heart heavy with longing for something which had no name or recognisable form, but which nevertheless called out to him like a drowning man going down for the third and final time.

2

Daniel found himself walking along an unfamiliar dirt track. The sun beat down from a pale-blue sky, and a heat haze made the air above the track shimmer. Little wisps of dust lifted with each footfall, the dirt puffing and swirling about his sandalled feet in small, almost imperceptible eddies. The aroma of pine needles, quite distinct and tinged – curiously – with the faintest hint of fresh coffee, wafted past him like a gentle breeze. In the distance, barely audible, he could just make out the familiar and haunting sound of the bouzouki.

As he walked, he became increasingly aware that there was something disconcerting about his situation. He tried to remember where he was, but it did not come easily to mind. But he had been here before, hadn't he? Daniel wasn't sure. Still, it didn't seem to matter. There was nothing overtly dangerous or threatening about it; it was just odd.

And hot. So *very* hot. Droplets of perspiration condensed between his shoulder-blades, gathered into little pools of sweat, then separated into dozens of spidery rivulets which trickled down his back.

Daniel slowed his pace and gazed around him inquisitively. He appeared to be completely alone. To his left he could see parched fields that led down to a brightly shimmering sea. From this distance the sea was mirror-like and motionless, more like a photograph or a painting than the real thing. Daniel wiped a dry forearm across his damp forehead; the sea looked immensely inviting; he would go down for a swim, to cool off. Yes, that would be nice.

Directly in front of him, in the middle of the road, was a circular wooden platform, about eight feet in diameter and one foot high. The raised dais formed what could only be a traffic roundabout, but there were no vehicles of any kind to be seen or heard: no cars, trucks or even bicycles.

I wonder where everyone is? thought Daniel, listening carefully for any evidence of human activity, but all he could hear was an increasingly familiar melody, ringing out in distinctive tones, and drawing him ever closer to its source.

Daniel stopped walking for a moment and studied the wooden roundabout. In the centre of the platform stood a rusted old hand-pump that clearly had once raised water from a well. He was tempted to climb up on to the roundabout and work the pump; he was starting to overheat under the relentless, direct sunlight, and thought the gushing water might cool him down.

He was about to clamber on to the dais when his attention was distracted by a rustling from over his shoulder. He looked behind, expecting – or perhaps hoping – to see someone. But all he saw was a crumpled sheet of newspaper, tumbling along the dirt track towards him, nudged along intermittently by the occasional breeze. He watched,

Daniel's Dream

disappointed, as the sheet of newspaper zigzagged down the road, stuttering now and then before again picking up speed, its passage halted periodically by a stone or twig. It came to rest by his feet, its progress impeded by the roundabout. Curious, Daniel picked up the newspaper, and made an attempt to prise its stiffened folds apart, flattening the many creases with the palm of his hand.

It was not in English. Daniel studied the page for a few moments, before identifying the familiar, but incomprehensible script: it was Greek.

He could not remember arriving in Greece, could not recall any specific events leading up to this moment, or indeed *any* events that related to his present circumstances. It was all very strange. And yet, if he examined his feelings, it was also evident that he was neither uncomfortable nor afraid. If anything, he felt pleasantly relaxed. How fine it was to be wandering in such sunshine, even if the heat was making him thirsty. And those wonderful, sun-baked odours; it was undeniably, *quintessentially* Mediterranean, and as such deeply evocative of holidays, travel and freedom. No wonder he felt so at ease. If only there were some other people about; he wanted to know the name of this place, to discover exactly where he was.

Daniel took one last look at the newspaper, then crumpled it up into a tight ball and, placing it on the ground, gave it a gentle push, setting it on its way once more. No sooner had it passed the sheltering influence of the roundabout than a cross-breeze caught it, insinuated its way into the rolled-up ball's cracks and crevices and sent it scampering away across the track towards the dry, thirsty fields that led down to the sea.

* * *

Ahead of him, just past the pump, the road forked; the main road (if one could define a dusty gravel track bereft of markings that way) continued in a straight line, then seemed to dip down out of sight, while to the right a winding path led off into a greener area. Daniel thought he saw a few buildings nestling among the trees, but he could not be sure. He decided he would investigate later.

Directly to his right, looking on to the roundabout with its rusting hand-pump, and of greater immediate interest, there was a small, attractive, one-storey building, recently whitewashed from top to bottom. The building had a flat roof and sported just one open door and a couple of large, shuttered windows. In front of it was a deep, raised patio upon which a number of tables and chairs had been arranged. Each table was covered with a brightly patterned red-and-white checked tablecloth, and set as if for dinner. An intricate trellis above the patio was covered in vines, which stretched the length of the building. The vines, tangled and matted in places, grew in such profusion that they spread in all directions to overhang the trellis at every edge and corner in whimsical curls and strands, giving the whole building an appealing, organic appearance, as if it had grown out of the earth. Baskets of red and white flowers hung from the front edge of the trellis, and big earthenware pots filled to overflowing with similar blooms stood at regular intervals along the front edge of the patio.

A simple picket fence ran along the front of the patio, and this too was interwoven with climbing plants and creepers. Music, *that* music, drifted across from behind one of the shuttered windows. Daniel stood admiring the building for some time, while a dozen or so mosquitoes buzzed around him in an enigmatic aerial ballet.

Daniel was really sweltering now. There was something timeless about his surroundings. There was also the merest hint that it was not, somehow, entirely real, and he could not help but continually test the environment for tell-tale signs. And yet everything seemed normal. He could feel the ground – hard, uneven, solid – beneath his feet. He was sweating heavily, the bright midday sun roasting his uncovered head, the salty beads dripping down his forehead making his eyes sting.

Needing shelter from the harsh sun, and mesmerised by the ever-present sound of the bouzouki, Daniel walked past the hand-pump to the gleaming white taverna, climbed the three steps that led up to the patio, looked around at the empty tables, and chose a seat beneath a large, gnarled olive tree, which afforded him a respite from the intense heat. The bouzouki music played on; a crackly, scratchy sound, the source of which was evidently an old record-player somewhere inside the building.

Daniel examined the red-and-white tablecloth, the sprung-steel clips that secured it to the square, wooden table. He toyed with the salt and pepper shakers, turned the oil and vinegar bottles upside down, and cleaned his fingernails with one of the toothpicks that stood in a small box in the centre of the table. It was lovely in the shade, relaxing. The fact that music was playing persuaded him that people could not be far away.

A gentle breeze wafted across the patio; it was a relief to be out of the sun and to rest his feet. He had walked a long way . . . or had he? His aching calves certainly suggested that he had been on his feet for several hours, but if he had been walking, where had he walked from? And where was he headed? Daniel did not know. He turned in his chair to peer through the doorway of the taverna, but could see very little in the darkened interior except for a few tables and what looked like a bar on the right-hand side. Why was the place empty? Where was everybody?

Suddenly, out of the corner of his eye, Daniel registered a slight movement and a tremendous, inexplicable fear overwhelmed him. In panic he turned swiftly to catch sight of whatever it was that had moved. As he turned he seemed to lose his balance, and before he knew what was happening he had slipped from his chair and was falling rapidly through empty space . . .

Daniel woke with a start. For several seconds he could not figure out where he was; the world was blurred and appeared to have fallen on its side; it was unrecognisable. It was only as his eyes refocused that he realised that he was looking at the far wall of his living room as seen from between the legs of the coffee table at an angle of ninety degrees to the perpendicular: he had slipped from the sofa and the fall had woken him.

Although surprised and a little shocked to find himself in such an unlikely position, he had not hurt himself, or at least he did not feel pain anywhere, save for a slight headache which might well have been attributable to the sudden rush of adrenalin. Taking care not to hit his head, he levered himself on to his knees, shook his head, then, certain he was not about to fall over in a heap, got to his feet. He looked around him as if he were in a strange environment rather than the familiar setting of his own living room; he felt decidedly

Daniel's Dream

disoriented, still caught in limbo between wide-awake and half-asleep.

He glanced at his watch and realised he had been asleep for several hours. Clearly he had dozed off listening to the music, but where exactly had he been? He had been dreaming, certainly, but it was not like his usual dreams at all.

Daniel had had dreams that were both bizarre and surreal. He had experienced meandering, meaningless ones which left him unfazed and disappointed, and he had had the terrifying nightmares with their expanded sense of hyper-reality that induced fear and panic. He had also had dreams in which not a single feature was recognisable from his life: the people he met, the places he visited, even the language he spoke; none of these things was familiar. When he woke from such dreams, Daniel felt sure that he had experienced *someone else's* dream.

But never had he had a dream that was so real, so like waking life, where experiences had the same form and feel as they did in reality, and where events unfolded in linear fashion just as when he was awake.

And that music. He could still hear it, playing quietly in the back of his mind, ebbing and flowing like the tides.

In the kitchen Daniel made himself a cup of strong coffee. What was he to make of it all? It was clear now that he had been dreaming of the same place the previous night and had woken with a less distinct – but still potent – memory of it. What was strangest of all was that, real though it had all seemed, it was not a place that Daniel had ever visited. He had been to many Mediterranean countries and enjoyed each for what it had to offer, but the visions from his dream did not correlate with any of the places he had seen.

Just a dream, thought Daniel, suddenly aware that his thoughts were becoming bizarre. It was just a dream, no more relevant or important than any of a thousand dreams he had had before, marked out from the others only because of a difference of structure or sense or . . . something.

With a few of the sights, smells and sounds still lingering in his thoughts, Daniel decided to get on with preparing the meal he had promised for that night. At least it would take his mind off the matter. He reached for the chopping board, the sharp vegetable knife and a large onion and, without being fully aware of what he was doing, began cutting it into thin slices. In movements that were almost automatic, he lit the gas, put a large frying pan over a low heat, poured in a generous amount of olive oil and began frying the onion with the mince. He crushed a couple of cloves of garlic, added them to the mix and, without thinking, selected the small bottle of dried oregano from Lisanne's spice rack and poured half the contents into the sizzling mass. The powerful odours of garlic and onion lifted into the air, carrying the more subtle scents of olive oil and oregano as they rose. In an instant Daniel found himself whisked back to the edges of his dream, but it lasted only for a brief moment, and he was soon brought back down to earth by the spluttering of fat and flesh as the minced lamb started to brown seductively. The chopped tomatoes were added to the already mouth-watering mix of ingredients and allowed to simmer slowly, releasing little pockets of scented steam that made Daniel's stomach rumble in anticipation.

The following half-hour found Daniel going through the

processes of making moussaka as if he were a practised chef for whom the dish was a commonplace, rather than a gifted amateur who had never attempted it before. If, as he claimed, Daniel cooked by instinct, then that instinct was particularly finely honed that afternoon.

He lined a deep baking dish with seasoned slices of parboiled potatoes, then poured the thick, smouldering concoction into the dish where it bubbled and steamed like a volcanic pool for several minutes. Without recourse to recipe book or readily prepared packets, he produced a wonderful, fluffy béchamel sauce that had suspended within it no less than half a pound of the fresh, crumbled feta he had bought. He poured the smooth, creamy, pungent sauce over the meat mixture and, adding a little grated cheddar to the surface, threw the lot into a pre-heated oven. The preparation had taken him less than an hour, and the time had flown by. Not once had Daniel had to think about what he was doing; it was almost as if some invisible agency guided his hands. The experience was deeply satisfying.

He allowed the dish to bake for an hour or so, then turned off the oven. He could hardly wait for Lisanne to get home. This was the first time he had cooked in six months, and he was anxious to taste the fruits of his labour.

That afternoon, Daniel made a second attempt to read *Greek Idyll*.

In the book, the protagonist, a young man called Johnny, bummed around Europe for a few months one summer, and ended up on a small, virtually uninhabited island in the Cyclades. Daniel read as far as the point where Johnny, the anachronistic hippie, finally set foot on the island, about which there was, he commented, 'something strange, enticing, even magical', and then gave up. The prose was so leaden, the protagonist so irritating that it was a wonder the book had been published at all. And so derivative! If he hadn't known better, Daniel could have sworn he had once read something virtually identical: not *The Magus*, of course, which was an altogether more measured and sophisticated novel, but something lightweight.

The rest of the afternoon passed slowly. As Daniel sat in the armchair waiting for Lisanne to come home, his mind returned once more to the business of dreams.

It struck him that people's ignorance – his own included – of dreams had its roots in the great emphasis placed on materialism in Western culture. Elsewhere in the world, dreams were regarded in an altogether different way. In some countries, particularly in Asia, they were treated with great reverence, as portents. They were an intrinsic and inseparable part of the daily lives of the people. Nowhere was this more true than in India.

Daniel recalled one occasion, several years previously, when he had been travelling in the south. He had been sent by *National Geographic* to photograph the remarkable Sri Minakshi temple in the pilgrimage city of Madurai.

The Sri Minakshi is probably the finest example of Dravidian architecture in all India, and it was one of the most colourful buildings that Daniel had ever encountered. The temple complex covered an area of fifteen acres and was bounded by high walls and a series of *gopurams*: huge, rectangular-based pyramids, typical of the Dravidian style, which were undoubtedly the most exciting feature.

Every evening in the Sri Minakshi the most colourful of

Daniel's Dream

ceremonies took place; part of Daniel's brief was to capture the essence of this event, a task which turned out to be a great deal more problematical than he at first realised.

On his first evening, he arrived early and tried to take some light measurements. The interior of the temple was gloomy, to say the least, and there were so many obstructing pillars that he soon realised taking photographs was going to be a major problem.

Knowing that the ceremony took place every evening, Daniel decided to abandon any idea of photos this time and just watch the event, so that he would be better prepared the following evening.

A number of pilgrims and tourists gathered in the dark, musty interior, and assembled around a central statue of some deity or other, then waited for something to happen. They did not have to wait long.

During the ceremony, an image of the great god Siva was carried in a highly ornate palanquin by four stout bearers, from an unseen inner sanctum to the bedroom of Parvati, his wife. The image remained curtained off, invisible to all but the most devout acolytes, one of whom constantly fanned away the smoking incense that poured out of the curtained box, as if Siva himself were on fire, no doubt anticipating the pleasures of the night that lay ahead.

The procession, which lasted no more than twenty minutes, was marked by a sense-shattering amalgam of noise, action and ritual. Every now and then, the parade would halt for a moment while a dozen devotees marched with great fervour around the palanquin. Throughout, musicians playing drums and reedy, trumpet-like instruments kept up a constant and impressive barrage of sound, until the palanquin disappeared from sight into Parvati's bedroom.

It was all over far too fast for Daniel's liking; he saw nothing but problems in trying to record the event in a series of images suitable for publication in a magazine which, as was well known in the trade, set the highest standards of all.

Ritual was everywhere in Madurai, and, as Daniel soon discovered, one could not negotiate the streets surrounding the temple for long without encountering an opportunity to be blessed by an elephant. The elephant, considered a good-luck symbol in India, was exemplified by the most favoured of all Indian gods, Ganesh, the elephant-headed son of Siva and Parvati. The elephants that cruised the streets of the city were friendly, lumbering beasts, often painted in bright, colourful patterns along their flanks and across their trunks.

Daniel wasted no time in taking some shots of these mighty animals, particularly as they performed the blessings. Men, women and children would gather round for their chance to be blessed. They would place a small coin in the elephant's dextrous trunk; the elephant usually 'shook hands' with the participant, before passing the coin to its mahout. The elephant would then raise its trunk high and bring it down on the participant's head with a gentle tap. Then it was on to the next one.

Both these events – the ritual of the palanquin and the elephant blessing – were perfect examples of that aspect of India that Daniel found so appealing. In India, by and large, religious and spiritual matters were not separated off from the everyday: on the contrary, they were integrated. Spirituality was not ethereal or other-worldly; it was commonplace, down-to-earth, immediate. People spoke of the gods, not as if they were mythical beings, but more as if they were their next-door neighbours. Even the notion of what was and wasn't sacred had a completely different spin on it; when one of the most sacred objects in a culture is the humble, docile cow, one's views on the sacred are bound to come in for a bit of revising.

But it wasn't just religion that had secured its place in the day-to-day routines of existence. Indians were much more comfortable with matters of the mind, the psyche and the subconscious than even the most learned or open-minded people that Daniel met in the West. Without the heavy rationalist, materialist bias, the Indian mind seemed much better equipped to deal with and understand those esoteric areas of everyday existence that, at home, caused such consternation, confusion and controversy. Ghosts, spirits, visions, gods, miracles; all were a daily reality for many if not most Indians, regardless of their caste, status or education. And dreams were never marginalised, never dismissed as irrelevant or meaningless. Every dream meant something. It did not necessarily have to be profound or far-reaching; it could be relatively trivial. But it was never without relevance, and as such had to be treated with as much respect as any sensorial information.

So when Daniel mentioned at breakfast to one of his colleagues that he had dreamt he had returned to his home town and spent the whole night trying unsuccessfully to find his father, it came as no surprise to hear the waiter chip in, 'Oh, your father is missing you,' in a manner which suggested the waiter had personally received a telegram to this effect.

Of course, the waiter had received nothing, save for the accumulated wisdom of generations, which informed him that, when one dreams about a friend or relative who does not actually appear in the dream, then this has one (and only one) meaning: your presence is missed – perhaps actively being sought – by said person.

Needless to say, Daniel phoned his parents that very morning.

Daniel had always felt that in the West – and perhaps most of all in England – people were too blasé about dreaming. The ease with which such a complex area of human existence was dismissed by supposedly sensitive, intelligent individuals was extraordinary. Even in the arts – one of the few areas that at least paid homage to dreams – there was still surprisingly little attention given to the whole process. There was no serious literature in Britain that dealt with dreams (unless one counted horror and the occasional foray by science-fiction practitioners). Otherwise, mention the subject in polite company in anything other than a trivial context and people thought you were half-baked; a New-Age, crystal-toting, mantra-chanting weirdo. Either that or a dope-head.

But dreams *had* to mean something. Why else did they exist?

'My God,' said Lisanne between mouthfuls, 'this is fantastic. I didn't know you could do Greek food? Why haven't you done this before?'

'I don't know,' said Daniel, in complete honesty. 'It just never occurred to me, I guess.'

'You're full of surprises, you.' She smiled then, with genuine pleasure, for the first time in an age. She could

Daniel's Dream

not have been more delighted. To others it might have seemed a small matter and nothing to get excited about, but to Lisanne the fact that Daniel had made the effort to cook was enough to make her think that perhaps, just perhaps, there had been a small shift in their circumstances. Maybe this was the start of the recovery that Dr Fischer had been promising for months. Perhaps Daniel would start to become interested again in all the things he used to enjoy, the things that had given him such pleasure in the past: reading, photography, going to the theatre and concerts. Who knows, she thought, maybe he will rediscover his interest in me. It was so long since they had made love she had almost forgotten what it felt like.

She shovelled another forkful of moussaka into her mouth.

'So what's the secret, champ?'

'Huh?' said Daniel, who found himself starting to tune out of their conversation. He too was enjoying the meal, but something about it made him anxious.

'Your secret; for cooking such a brilliant moussaka.'

'Uh . . . I don't know. Luck I guess.'

Lisanne found this unenlightening response disconcerting, considering how enthusiastic her reaction to the meal had been, but she knew better than to question Daniel closely. Rather than provoke or annoy him with unnecessary questions, she comforted herself with the knowledge that, all being well, this was the first step on the way to recovery. She couldn't wait to tell Dr Fischer about it.

They did not make love that night, as Lisanne had hoped, but they did cuddle for a while, which was a marked improvement over their usual bedtime arrangements.

Lisanne eventually drifted off to sleep secure in the knowledge that tomorrow would be a brighter, more hopeful day.

Daniel, however, was not thinking about the following day at all. His own concerns were much more caught up with the night, and while Lisanne snored peacefully and contentedly in the bed beside him he waited anxiously for sleep to arrive.

3

'You okay?'

Daniel opened his eyes and blinked once or twice. He found he was staring at a concrete floor and a set of wooden table legs. He looked up and was both surprised and relieved to see a young man staring back at him. The man had a dark, swarthy complexion and a thick rug of matt black hair. When he spoke his deep-blue eyes registered genuine concern.

'You okay? You fall off chair!'

Daniel shook his head and tried to lever himself off the floor. His new acquaintance held out a hand and helped pull him to his feet. Daniel steadied himself, brushed himself down, then quickly found a chair to sit on. He felt dizzy, as if he had just jumped off a fast merry-go-round.

'Thank you,' said Daniel, decidedly disoriented. He was still having difficulty focusing. 'I'm fine, really.' He clenched the fingers of his right hand: they felt stiff and a little sore; he wondered if he had used that hand to break his fall.

'You fall off chair. I think you hurt,' said the man. Daniel could see that he was worried, so he smiled to put him at ease. The man was dressed in a white-collared shirt and neatly pressed black trousers. Daniel suddenly realised where he was: he was back at the vine-covered restaurant that overlooked the funny old hand-pump, and the man standing over him with such concern was evidently the waiter.

Daniel smiled. I'm back, he thought with delight; I've come back! He looked down to his feet and saw that, once again, he was wearing sandals. His feet were grey and dusty from the road outside, his forearms, bared to the sun, tinged with the first pink of sunburn.

After a moment or so his vision cleared. There was no doubt that he had returned to the same place. Everything was as he had seen it the first time; the vines, the whitewashed walls, the shuttered windows: exactly the same.

And the music. That glorious melody, the haunting strains of the bouzouki, played gently and slowly rather than in the frenetic style that he had always associated with the instrument. He would have to find out the name of the song – if that was what it was; he had never heard anything so beautiful in his life.

Daniel licked his lips and tasted the salty tang of fresh sweat on the fringe of his moustache. He realised that he was immensely thirsty, and in dire need of a drink. On cue, as if he had read Daniel's mind, the waiter spoke.

'What you want? You want drink maybe?' His accent was thick yet musical.

Daniel nodded. The waiter smiled and pointed to the table. There, lying on the red-chequered tablecloth, was a menu, with bright-red letters printed on shiny white card.

Daniel's Dream

Daniel was surprised to see it there; he did not remember seeing a menu on the table previously.

'Do you have coffee?' asked Daniel, picking up the card but unable to make sense of it; he was still a little groggy from his fall, and although his vision was clearer the words on the menu seemed to dance around continually, and would not settle long enough for him to read them. 'And some water perhaps?'

'Yes, yes,' said the waiter enthusiastically. 'Water yes, coffee yes; I bring you.' He turned and headed towards the doorway of the taverna.

Daniel gazed around at the pretty, flower-bedecked patio. The temperature in the shade was just perfect and a slight, mimosa-scented breeze brushed past now and then to freshen the otherwise still air. His head was full of questions, but curiously none of them seemed urgent. His most pressing question – where was everyone? – had been partly answered; the very fact that there was a waiter, busily rushing around to assist visitors in distress meant that Daniel was not alone. And presumably there were others. Somewhere.

Daniel shifted a little in his seat so that he could see out on to the dirt track and past the pump. He looked out to where the road forked and wondered where the right-hand track led. He thought that on his previous visit he had seen buildings nestling among the foliage, but he could not now see anything of the kind. He looked in the opposite direction, back down the track, but there seemed to be no other houses or buildings of any description. And yet, he surmised, if this was a restaurant, then surely there would be a town or a village nearby. Daniel sighed. He wondered if he would ever find out about this place.

A moment later the waiter returned with a large white cup full of steaming black coffee, and set it down on the table along with a small stainless-steel jug.

'One coffee!' beamed the waiter.

'Thank you,' replied Daniel.

'You welcome. You like maybe baklava?'

'No, no, that's fine.' He wanted to talk to the waiter, to ask him where this place was, where everybody was, but he didn't want to appear foolish. He was also fearful that too many logical intrusions – questions included – might break whatever spell had returned him to the taverna. More than anything he hoped he might be able to stay a little longer this time. It was so relaxing, so easy. Perhaps, he thought, this was what he had needed all along; a holiday in the sun.

While he played with these thoughts, the waiter once again disappeared inside, and Daniel was left to sip his coffee alone.

The warm brew tasted strong and refreshing; it was dark and fragrant. He looked into the steel jug, dipped his finger into the thick white liquid and tasted it. It was sweet and sickly: condensed milk. The last time he had tasted condensed milk was in the same circumstances, pouring it into a cup of black coffee while sitting in a remote taverna somewhere in the Cyclades. It had been many years ago now, but the taste of that coffee had never left him. He took a sip from the cup and savoured it. He took great, rather exaggerated pleasure from the idea that something as simple and down-to-earth as a cup of coffee could bring such rich rewards. But was it real? Was any of it real?

The branches of the large olive tree swayed gently in

Daniel's Dream

the breeze, its roughened boughs contorted into wondrous shapes that held the direct sunlight at bay.

This is a dream, thought Daniel. I've been here before, but only in a dream. If I pinch myself, I shall wake up and find myself back in London. If I pinch myself this wonderful place will disappear.

Daniel toyed with this idea for several minutes, unsure whether to test it out. He knew there was such a thing as a recurring dream; indeed, when he was younger he had suffered from one, a nightmare in which he was chased along an empty street by a big black dog with huge fangs and flashing red eyes. It was a dream he had had every week for the best part of a year. He knew all about recurring dreams.

But not dreams like this. He had never heard of anything quite like this, where you returned to the same place and picked up where you left off. That wasn't a dream, that was a soap opera. Besides, the whole place felt far too 'real' to be a dream; all his senses were intact; he could taste and smell and see everything vividly. The sound of the music was clear, and the table had substance, the coffee was hot and fragrant, and even the breeze could be felt brushing across his skin.

But if he were logical about it he knew it wasn't real, that it couldn't be, and that, as he had already found, one little shove, one abrupt fall, was all it needed to jolt him back to reality, to wakefulness, and – if he was completely honest about it – a world that he cared little for.

With that admission Daniel realised that he wasn't about to test this idea, because if this was a dream, with its strangeness and sunshine and sweet, sweet smells, and reality was a darkened room in a terraced house in a busy, crowded street in north London, then despite the strangeness, despite the mysterious circumstances, despite the lack of answers, he'd rather stay than return. At least for a while.

Daniel looked back towards the doorway. There must be someone other than the waiter working there, he thought; he couldn't be alone. What if someone wanted to eat, or a whole family came along? Perhaps the owner was there, or a cook or someone?

In the darkness, Daniel could see the shadows move. 'Excuse me!' he called, quite loudly. The shadows stopped moving for a moment, and then the waiter appeared at the doorway.

'Yes?' he said cheerfully. 'You like some baklava now?'

'Ah . . . no. I was just wondering who owns this place.'

'Eh?' replied the waiter.

'This place . . . taverna,' continued Daniel undaunted, 'it belongs to you?'

The waiter smiled again and then started to laugh. 'Belong me?' he chortled. 'No no. Taverna belong Berry.'

'Berry?'

'Yes yes, Berry. You not know Berry?'

Daniel shook his head.

'You wait, I bring Berry.'

Daniel nodded. Berry? Well, perhaps this Berry might be able to answer some of his questions. He sipped some more coffee and reached into his pockets to see if he had brought any cigarettes. At the same moment, a rather prosaic, but none the less relevant question arose: how would he pay for the coffee? It had only just occurred to him that he probably hadn't any money with him, and even if he had,

Daniel's Dream

it would certainly not be in the right currency, whatever that might be. He feared an embarrassing situation.

But that's plain daft, he thought. After all, it's just a dream and, what's more, it's *my* dream.

In his pocket, much to his surprise, Daniel discovered a full packet of cigarettes, a box of matches, and a few dirty, crumpled banknotes. He spread them out on the table and examined them carefully. There were three notes, all the same size and colour – a sort of dull pink – and they all had '100' printed on them. The rest of the script looked similar to that he had seen on the sheet of newspaper that had tumbled towards him along the dirt track outside.

Drachmae? Daniel had no idea whether possessing three hundred drachmae made him rich or poor, not that it could possibly matter. After all, was he really expected to concern himself with such mundane matters as conversion rates and paying bills? Surely one did not have to worry about such things in dreams. And yet, this place, the circumstances that surrounded him, seemed to demand that he take it seriously; after all, it had few qualities to distinguish it from waking life, so how was he to know that he was in a dream at all?

Daniel opened the packet of cigarettes, tore out the carefully folded rectangle of gold paper that covered the filter tips, and eased a cigarette out. He placed it carefully between his lips, ensuring that his actions were not sudden or dramatic. His last fast move had knocked him from his seat and sent him hurtling back to his home in Cyprus City.

He held the matchbox in his left hand between his thumb and forefinger and, with a match resting against the edge, closed his eyes and struck. This, he thought, is when I wake up; the intensity of this action, the release of this energy, will be sufficient to hurl me back to reality.

He felt the resistance of the match-head rasping against the roughness of the striking surface, the tiny, intermittent hesitations as it caught, the friction activating the chemicals into combustion. The match spluttered and sparked. Daniel opened his eyes, stared at the compact, concentrated focus of silver and gold explosions as they spat and crackled, then settled into a familiar, silent, yellow and blue flame, a wavering teardrop of hot gas and fire.

And then he lit his cigarette.

Daniel drew deeply on the nicotine. The powerful drug coursed through his system instantaneously. He looked at his hand holding the cigarette, at the red-and-white tablecloth beyond, and smiled. Nothing had changed; he was still sitting on the patio at the open-air taverna, and all was right with the world.

There was still no sign of the mysterious Berry, but now that Daniel had satisfied himself he was not about to be shot back to his other life, whatever and wherever that was, he was content to sit there and enjoy his surroundings. With his vision restored he was able to study the menu more carefully. He was attempting to decipher the prices when his concentration was interrupted by a noise from the taverna. He looked up to see a now familiar figure.

'Hello, Mister,' came the voice of the waiter from the doorway. 'This Berry, man who belong taverna.'

Daniel looked up to see a tall, slender, handsome man with deep-blue eyes and light-brown hair. The man reached out his hand towards Daniel and smiled.

'Hi,' said the man, in an unmistakably American accent. 'I'm Barry.'

Daniel's Dream

Ever the Englishman abroad, Daniel stood abruptly and held out his hand. Whether or not his swift movement was to blame Daniel did not know, but for a second, just before the two hands came into contact, Daniel experienced a brief dizzy spell. Everything around him started to soften at the edges, to become blurred. He had a strong sense that time was slowing down, as if he were caught in a slow-motion playback of a real-time event, and as he looked around for some sort of confirmation of this, he noticed that everything – the tables, chairs, vines – looked pale and translucent, as if they might disappear at any moment.

In a moment of insight Daniel knew that if he touched this man's hand everything would fade away, that he would lose his dream, that he would be thrown back to reality. But it was too late to do anything about it.

As they clasped hands, everything in the taverna dissolved into a misty haze. Daniel fixed his eyes on Barry's face, and had just enough time to call out, 'I'll be back . . .' before blackness descended.

Daniel awoke in a panic. He opened his eyes but found only darkness. He fumbled anxiously for the light-switch, his heart beating furiously. The white taverna had disappeared, as had Barry and the waiter. He was in his bed, in his room, in London. His breathing was deep and rapid.

'Dan? What is it? What's wrong?' Lisanne was sitting up, squinting uncomfortably.

'Uh . . . nothing,' said Daniel. He was thoroughly disoriented and confused, but sensed that it was important not to alarm Lisanne. 'It's okay, love, nothing at all. Bad dream. Sorry I woke you.' He leant across and kissed her lightly on the cheek, then turned the light off immediately, to assure her that there really was no need to worry.

But Lisanne was not so easily mollified. On many occasions in the past few months she had been woken in the night to find her once calm and contented husband in distress. In fact, his torment was often so advanced that for several minutes after waking, despite her greatest efforts, he remained inconsolable. Admittedly, it was a couple of weeks since he had had a truly bad attack, but other occasions were still too fresh in her mind to allow her to dismiss his claims so easily.

She also knew that to show any indication of panic was to court trouble. Timing her moves carefully, she paused, then reached out and gently ruffled his hair. She then waited a further few moments before speaking so that it would not sound as if she were panicked or being pushy.

'Are you sure you're okay, Dan?' she whispered, her tone even and calm. 'We can talk if you like.'

'I'm fine, really. It's just the same old nightmare,' said Daniel, hoping to reassure her. 'Go back to sleep.'

Lisanne hesitated. She did not want to pry; she had learnt that, since the accident, if Daniel was in one of his uncommunicative moods, pushing him to talk would only aggravate him.

'Well, if you're sure . . .'

'Just a silly old dream, Lisanne. Please don't worry.' Daniel leant over once more and gave her a kiss. 'Now go to sleep or else you'll be a wreck in the morning.'

Lisanne bit down gently on her lower lip to stop herself from prying further. She turned on her side and repeated a now familiar mantra to herself several times in order to stay calm: 'He's safe and fine and all is well, he's safe and fine and all is well, he's safe and fine and all is well . . .' Over and over she repeated the words, silently in her head, an exercise in hope, a prayer for the living. She could not now remember when she had first started using the repetitions, but she knew that at times like these it was the only way she could stop herself fretting. 'He's safe and fine and all is well,' she said again, hoping that whatever magic was contained within these few simple words was working at full power. In the morning she would have forgotten all about this; in the mad rush to get up, get dressed and go to work, the disturbance of the night would fade into insignificance. But in the meantime, Daniel, his fears, worries and concerns preoccupied her. Even his dreams, it seemed, had become her responsibility.

Certain that she would get nothing more in the way of explanation that night, Lisanne stroked Daniel's cheek once more. Then, with a whispered 'Goodnight', she turned over, sighed silently, and prayed that sleep would come quickly, so that she would not have to spend the night fretting and worrying like an old fool.

Daniel did not know why he had lied to Lisanne. He had long ago told her the contents of his regular, nightly roller-coaster ride, had explained what it felt like being forced to turn somersaults in an endless procession, about the forces which slammed him up against the walls, only to peel him off, roll him up and send him spinning over and over yet again to meet the same fate against another immovable object. He had not shied from describing in detail the experiences of his terrifying nightmare, despite the fact that it could only unsettle her. So why did he now keep secret from her the extraordinary contents of these new dreams? Twice running he had travelled somewhere new in his dreams, but he was loth so much as to suggest that anything had changed in his nightly excursions. And it was not because he did not want to bother her. His decision was much more deliberate, much more active than that. This new dream was something different, something special, and he did not want to share it with her.

Daniel waited quietly until he heard the reassuring sound of Lisanne's deep breathing, indicating that she had fallen asleep, and, satisfied that she was not about to wake, settled down once more. He waited patiently to be drawn back into sleep, trying to keep his mind clear of his troubles and confusions so that his descent would be swift and easy, but the sound of the bouzouki in his head kept him awake for hours, and it was not until the first glimmer of dawn crept through the gap between the curtains that Daniel slipped peacefully into unconsciousness.

4

At ten, Daniel awoke for the second time. He vaguely recalled having woken in the night, but could not remember why. He knew he had woken Lisanne, but could not recall anything else about the disturbance. Had it been his usual nightmare? He thought not. Once again he had woken with his head clear, his body cool and dry, free of the black thirst that usually plagued him after a night's sleep.

He looked at the ceiling, searching for clues, his concentration distracted momentarily by half-remembered visions of Mediterranean vistas.

Just a dream, he said to himself, just a dream.

On the kitchen table was a note from Lisanne, reminding him of his appointment with Dr Fischer. Great, thought Daniel, just what I need. He considered the possibility of telephoning Fischer and making some excuse, but he knew that Lisanne would be upset if he missed his appointment. Fischer was, after all, a great family friend, a pillar of the community and a rock of ages in these troubled times. Such a pity, then, that he doled out the sort of healthcare treatment that Noah (or, indeed, any one of his animals) might have expected on emerging from the ark.

Daniel had to steel himself for the visit in the only way he knew how. But at ten in the morning, not surprisingly, the scotch went straight to his head, and he arrived at the surgery half an hour late having taken several wrong turnings along the way.

Daniel entered the surgery and sat down in the black, cracked-leather chair facing the doctor. He looked around him at the familiar, dowdy room, with its antiseptic smell and ageing wallpaper, and then at Dr Fischer, who, Daniel noted with some concern, appeared, like the wallpaper, to be yellowing and peeling at the edges.

'So, how are you feeling, Daniel?' croaked Dr Fischer, peering over the antique pince-nez balanced precariously on his bulbous nose, its intricate web of capillaries spreading out across its surface like a road map of the home counties.

'Okay,' said Daniel, who had learnt of late to be as non-committal as possible; every admission, he had realised, seemed to land him with another prescription for yet more drugs to throw down his throat, this being Fischer's first line of attack: redemption through chemistry.

'I see,' said the doctor, who had grown familiar with Daniel's unhelpful attitude. 'And how are you sleeping?'

'The same as ever,' replied Daniel. 'I have yet to enjoy a complete, restful night's sleep.'

'I see,' repeated the doctor, with a nod. 'And are you still taking the sleeping tablets?'

Daniel's Dream

'Yes,' lied Daniel. Any attempt to thwart Fischer's regimen would only end in tears.

'And, in view of their qualified success, do you suppose you could manage without them? Barbiturates are addictive you know; we don't want to turn you into a junkie, do we?' Dr Fischer gave a little, stifled laugh, as if he had made a joke.

Daniel forced a smile. 'I could manage without the sleeping tablets, yes.'

'Good. We'll keep you on those anti-depressants for a bit longer so that you don't suffer from complete withdrawal, eh?' Daniel thought he saw the doctor smirk, but did not respond. 'Now then, are you still having problems with the fainting?'

Daniel bristled. 'It only happened that one time, Doctor; I'm sure it was an isolated incident.' Why did Fischer always have to bring that up? It was a one-off, a feeble swoon across the counter of his local newsagent's. Nothing to make a fuss about.

'Quite possibly. As I think I explained, some of the medication tends to lower the blood pressure a little. Now then, up on your feet. Right, now walk towards me swiftly and then about-turn a hundred and eighty degrees.'

Daniel sighed noisily; he hated these absurd tests, and the way Fischer treated him like a six-year-old.

'Come along, Daniel,' said Fischer, standing slowly. 'It's just to check your balance.'

Daniel did as the doctor requested. He could not help but resent all these investigations into his state of health and mind. He knew the doctor was there to help him, but it all seemed somehow invidious, prying where it was not welcome.

And what good did it do? What good did any of it do? Had Fischer cured him of his depression? No. Had he given him hope? Instilled some sort of optimism? No again. What did he honestly hope to achieve? Daniel was no New-Age mystic, but he knew one thing for sure: if you wanted to heal someone, the first thing you had to do was get them on your side, gain their trust, their respect. A patient has to believe the healer is capable of healing. If not, the whole process is a waste of time.

Daniel rose slowly, marched five paces towards the doctor, and turned on the spot.

'How was that?'

'No problem,' lied Daniel, his head spinning a little. He knew the anti-depressants made him prone to dizziness if he stood up too quickly, but he didn't want to be taken off them. They could take away the blasted barbiturates that gave him the dreadful hangovers, but the anti-depressants were a godsend on the occasional days when things got tough.

The doctor scribbled erratically on a pad of prescriptions, folded the piece of paper in two and placed it deliberately to one side of the desk. He clasped his elephant-hide hands together, and leant forward.

'Daniel, I have to tell you that I'm a bit unhappy about your progress.'

Oh shit, thought Daniel. The pep talk. Must be that time of the month.

'I know you've had a nasty experience . . .'

'Nasty?' Daniel bit his tongue. There were all manner of things he would like to say to the good doctor, but he knew that for the sake of good relations, it was better that he kept quiet. Besides, any misbehaviour would only

Daniel's Dream

upset Lisanne, and he had done quite enough of that already.

Fischer paused, seeing the distress on Daniel's face, and tried a different approach. 'Well . . . perhaps that's not quite right. But tragedy is an integral part of living, Daniel, and you can't allow one incident to defeat you this way.'

Daniel shook his head in disbelief. 'I can't believe what you just said. Do you have *any* idea what I went through?'

'Well, of course I can't know exactly—'

'That's right,' interrupted Daniel sharply, then, with a small sigh, apologised. 'Sorry,' he murmured, 'but you *can't* know, Doctor. You just can't.'

Dr Fischer drew a deep breath and nodded slowly. 'Yes, well, even if that is the case, I do have some experience in these matters, and despite what you say, you can't go on like this indefinitely. It's been . . . let me see—'

'Six months,' interjected Daniel dryly, and gave a heavy sigh. The doctor fixed him with a glare.

'Let me tell you something, Daniel. I've dealt with cases like this before, and others far worse . . .'

Oh God, thought Daniel, he's going to say it again! Please don't say it; please, please, please.

'. . . and I can tell you that time heals all.'

Daniel closed his eyes and bit down on his lower lip. For Lisanne's sake, for the sake of maintaining peace at the expense of his own feelings, he would not say what was uppermost in his mind; namely, that Fischer was a meddling old fool who should probably have been struck off years ago. 'Thanks, Doc,' he said, cringing. 'You're a brick.'

'You'll see, Daniel. You have so much to live for, so much to look forward to. You're young, talented, you have a beautiful wife . . .'

'Yes, thank you, Doctor; I've already counted my blessings once today.'

Fischer sighed. 'Yes, well then, you presumably do not need an old fool like me to remind you.'

Daniel felt stung by this. Fischer *was* a meddlesome buffoon, but it was not his intention to insult the old man.

'I'm sorry, Doctor. I didn't mean—'

Fischer held up his hand. 'No, no, no need. I like you Daniel, and as you know I'm very fond of Lisanne. I just don't want to see you get bogged down in all this. And neither does Lisanne. I spoke to her just the other day—'

'Wait a minute,' said Daniel, leaning forward. 'I appreciate that you've known Lisanne since she was in nappies, but I don't think it's right to bother her like that. She has a lot on her plate just now.'

'Look, Daniel, I don't want to be harsh, but you're a bright man, and I'm distressed that you can't pull yourself out of this hole. You can't go on this way for ever. There's only so much sympathy your friends and family are able to feel for you. The world keeps revolving, Daniel, and if you want a future, you'd better consider rejoining it as soon as possible. I'm sorry I have to be so direct . . .'

'Don't be,' snapped Daniel. How he hated being patronised. So he was depressed. So he was making everyone's life miserable. So what? It was no reason to be treated like a child.

'Don't be,' he repeated, less aggressively.

Daniel's Dream

The doctor sighed and nodded very slowly. He handed Daniel the prescription.

Daniel stood up and walked to the door. As he opened it, he turned to face his examiner.

'Look, I'm sorry for snapping at you, Doctor. I know you're just doing your job, and I appreciate the help you've given me, only . . .' He didn't finish the sentence. He just shrugged, forced a smile, and closed the door behind him.

As he left the surgery, Daniel felt a drop of rain strike his face. He looked up into the grey skies and a feeling of great relief passed over him. He wouldn't have to see the doctor again for two weeks; perhaps, he thought, as he sauntered along in the light rain, I may never have to see him again.

Back home, and all alone, Daniel sulked. Without doubt, one of the greatest impediments to his recovery had been his complete lack of interest in other people. Lisanne had attempted to bring him back to some nominal socialising by holding a couple of dinner parties for their closest friends, but these had been unmitigated disasters, during which Daniel had remained uncommunicative and bad-tempered. Everyone had been very understanding about it, but it was clear that they were not going to force themselves on Daniel. As both Janice and Vince (their closest friends) had said to Lisanne, he'd come round when he was ready.

But Daniel was not ready, not really. What did he have to say to these people? He could not speak about the accident to anyone. He could no longer talk about his work, as he didn't have any, or his travels, as he hadn't been anywhere, and besides, he was so depressed most of the time he did not want to inflict himself on the few people who might still care about him. Consequently, for six months he had had little or no contact with the people to whom he was closest.

But perhaps that could now change. After all, now there was something he could talk about. Something he felt he *had* to talk about.

He decided he would telephone Vince and arrange to meet him, but no sooner had he made the decision than he fell into a sudden, debilitating depression, brought on by the realisation that it had been so long since he had called his closest friend that he could no longer remember his phone number. It was a petty matter, but it was indicative of his present state, and he could not help but be upset by it.

Daniel tracked down the address book, nestling discreetly on the shelf below the telephone and dialled Vince's work number. Perhaps unsurprisingly, Vince was not available to come to the phone. Daniel, who saw this as a further taunt, left a message saying he had called and then, sick to death of the inside of the house, dressed swiftly and, with no plans in mind, grabbed his jacket, wallet and keys and headed out.

Without any particular purpose to his movements, Daniel found himself walking towards Wood Green again. He did not stop to peruse the magazines in W. H. Smith but continued to the Underground station.

It was dark and grimy in the station; the early-afternoon sun never penetrated the station's dank interior. Daniel knew he was not alone in believing that there was something disturbing, even threatening, about the Tube, with its miles of black, labyrinthine tunnels with their stale

Daniel's Dream

air and ominous electric hum. Five months previously, just a few weeks after the accident, caught up in the dark twists and turns of one of his blacker moods and consumed by despair, Daniel had stood on the platform at Holborn during the rush hour, and contemplated, with all due seriousness, throwing himself into the path of an oncoming train. He had located himself towards one end of the platform and perilously near the edge while twenty-two trains – he counted them – came and went, disgorging one set of impatient, sardined passengers on to the concrete ledge before vacuuming up the waiting throng who shuffled, shoved and elbowed their way into the crowded compartments. He had studied the commuters with great curiosity as they brushed past him, leaving their day jobs behind, to return to husbands, wives, lovers, children, pets, televisions, soft beds and comfy chairs, each one striding with such urgency, such intention, that Daniel could only look on with envy and despair. All these people, rushing, running, pushing, shoving, as if life were too short, too important to fritter away on something as trivial as a journey on the Underground.

Oh to be in such a rush, he had thought as the multitudes hastened past him. To want anything that much – if only a wish to get home as soon as possible – had seemed something much to be desired.

But even when the crowds had died out and Daniel had the platform all to himself, he knew he could not throw himself on to the live rails. Such a premeditated act demanded an expression of intent, and, for all his distress and desperation, he simply did not possess the will to carry it out.

Finally, exhausted by the spectacle and embarrassed by

his own lack of courage, Daniel had turned his back on the trains and left the station. On his way home he had found himself curiously light-headed.

Thoughts of suicide no longer plagued him, it was true, but as he purchased a travel card and walked through the barrier towards the escalator, he was aware that a deep malaise still clouded his every waking hour. Fatalism had become his religion, and as if to prove its omnipresence, no sooner was he through the barrier than he was confronted by a small blackboard with a child-like scrawl chalked across it, which read: 'Services on the Piccadilly Line will be delayed due to a body under the tracks at Leicester Square.' Great, thought Daniel, recalling his previous journey on the Underground. Just what I need.

He stepped on to the escalator and held tight to the rail; he was still not entirely steady on his feet, and he worried about falling and further damaging his neck.

As he descended into the bowels of the system, he stared at the advertisements that lined the stairs. Daniel had always believed that these particular ads had to be especially effective, as they flashed past one's eyes with almost subliminal rapidity. He suspected that there was a special department of hot-shot copywriters and graphic designers locked away in the depths of each advertising agency, their sole task to design these specialised, high-intensity commercials.

He also reflected that by and large, hot-shots or not, they usually missed the mark. Only rarely did an image or phrase reach out and grab his attention. Most of the time they were inane, banal or just nasty. And

Daniel's Dream

sometimes they had effects that, Daniel was sure, were not intended at all.

'Do you need help?' asked one advertisement for a pregnancy advisory service. Daniel briefly studied the photograph of the pretty girl with the sad expression. Yes, I need help, he said solemnly to himself, I need an advisory service.

Another headline caught his eye: 'If you miss out this time, you'll kill yourself!' sang the bold type for a hi-fi store having its annual clearance sale. Daniel shuddered; just the sort of nasty, cheap trick he despised. He reread the copy as it disappeared behind him. 'Bargains galore at Lapdogs! If you miss out this time you'll kick yourself! Don't miss our annual sale of hi-fi and video!'

Daniel stood on the southbound platform and waited for the train. The long corridor was empty save for an old man sitting on a bench at the far end. The man was evidently just one of the growing number of the homeless and dispossessed, an itinerant army growing greater by the day. Where do they all come from? wondered Daniel as he peered at the unkempt, unshaven tramp, who was drinking from a large brown bottle and muttering to himself between swigs.

Or was he? Although Daniel could not see anyone else, he supposed it was unfair to assume that the tramp was necessarily carrying on a wholly one-sided conversation. One man's reality, thought Daniel, momentarily recalling his strange, Mediterranean dream world, is another man's fantasy. Or vice versa, perhaps.

Out of the corner of his eye Daniel watched the old tramp nattering away and could not help but wonder what had brought the old man to this state of affairs. What miserable conspiracy of events could be responsible for such a sad decline? What had brought him to this, drinking cheap booze on a lonely station platform?

Daniel looked on in increasing distress, his assumptions and conclusions veering dangerously towards the naive and sentimental. This poor man, thought Daniel, with his filthy clothes and drunken rant had once been an innocent child, loved, presumably, by caring parents, siblings, aunts, uncles and friends. He had probably had a promising future once; perhaps he had been top of his English class, or top scorer for the school football team? Perhaps he had been handsome, prematurely good-looking, a string of pretty teenage girls following in his wake. And maybe he graduated from a fine red-brick university and ended up a wealthy man. Perhaps he had once been a bank manager or company director. And perhaps, thought Daniel, watching the tramp slide from his seat and collapse in a heap on the platform, perhaps he had once been happy.

That the man might have been an axe-murderer or paedophile did not occur to him. In those few moments Daniel, who had created his own reality for the pathetic victim at the end of the platform, was plunged into morbidity. Was this how he, Daniel, would end his days; alone, unloved, desperate . . . reduced to a bag of grey skin held together by rags and bits of string?

It was not such a great leap from where he currently stood. If Lisanne left him, then how long would it be before he found himself on the same platform, bottle in hand, talking to people no one else could see? Lisanne already thought he dressed like a tramp – it was true, he had let himself go – and without a job he was wholly dependent on her income. If something should happen to

Daniel's Dream

her, then Daniel knew he would not survive. He was frail enough as it was. Another blow – another death – would send him over the edge for sure.

Poor Alex. If only . . .

But there was no point in wishing; there was no 'if only'. Alex had died, victim of an unforeseen accident in a foreign country where the death of one more person meant next to nothing. Poor Alex. So young, so promising, so beautiful, her whole life ahead of her . . .

Daniel could not bear to think about it, and yet the knowledge haunted him day and night. Was it any wonder he felt so morose, so hopeless?

He sat down on the nearest bench and, rather than look at the tramp, buried his face in his hands and waited anxiously for the train that would spirit him off to an alternative, albeit temporary, future.

But the train did not come. Daniel waited impatiently for twenty minutes, then remembered the chalk-scrawled message on the blackboard. Death, it seemed, would be his undoing one way or another. A body under the train at Leicester Square. An accident? Or something more active, something with greater intent, like murder.

Or suicide.

He returned to the escalator, rode it silently to the top. He exited into bright, glaring sunlight and walked home through the empty streets, carefully avoiding Green Lanes with its bustle, activity and life. For reasons that he hoped he would never have to explain, there were times, such as now, when the sight of another human being was more than he could bear.

5

'Pleased to know you, Daniel. You here on vacation?' Barry shook Daniel's hand firmly.

'Ah, just passing through,' said Daniel, looking around him swiftly. There was no doubt about it. He had returned.

'Oh you should stay a while. You'd like it here. It's a little quiet in the afternoon, but it livens up in the evenings.' Daniel placed the accent as unmistakably East Coast rather than the softer, less characterful Californian drawl that he usually associated with American television sitcoms. He was grateful for the distinction.

They unclasped hands and Barry turned momentarily and looked over towards the taverna as if someone had called out to him.

'Well, I gotta get back to work. Why don't you call in later tonight? Come and see me at the bar and let me buy you a drink to welcome you to Atheenaton. Okay?'

'Atheenaton?'

Barry frowned at him and Daniel realised that he must

have made some unpardonable *faux pas*. 'I mean,' he said, covering as best he could, 'I didn't know that was how it was pronounced.'

Barry nodded and smiled. Daniel could not help thinking there was something knowing in that smile, something a bit theatrical. But, if so, there was certainly nothing threatening in such playfulness.

A noise like someone shifting a large, heavy piece of furniture emanated from inside the darkened building. Once again Barry turned and this time he called out in a language Daniel did not recognise.

'I'd better get back or else there'll be tears. So, about that drink. We'll see you later?'

'Yes, of course. That'd be great. Thank you.'

'Sure.' Barry turned and strode back into the darkness of the taverna.

Atheenaton. That must be the name of the village. It certainly sounded Greek, but if so, it was not a name that Daniel had ever come across before.

But then, why should he recognise the name of a fantasy town? At least, he had to assume it was a fantasy, even if it did seem as real as his own life. Still, wherever he was and whatever it was called, Daniel was now sure of only one thing: the only way of visiting was in his dreams.

So what do I do now? wondered Daniel, finding himself alone once again. What had Barry said? That the place was livelier in the evenings? Then where was everyone? Where were they hiding? Daniel peered out on to the dirt track outside the taverna; there was no more sign of life than the last time he had looked. It was a little disconcerting.

He looked down to the table, to the empty coffee cup and remembered that on the previous occasion he had had

Daniel's Dream

some sort of money in his pocket. He checked again and sure enough there was a small bundle of well-thumbed notes. He picked up the menu and tried to figure out the price of the coffee. He found the drinks section, and a little '60' next to the 'Nescoffee'. That must be it.

He picked up his cigarettes, left one of the crumpled pink banknotes on the table, and descended the three concrete steps which led back to the road. As there was nothing to be seen along the main road, Daniel chose to investigate the narrower track that led off to the right; if there was a village anywhere around, it had to be in that direction.

It was still extremely hot, but although this caused Daniel to sweat profusely it was a comforting heat, which seemed to penetrate down through his light clothing to warm his muscles and bones. He wandered slowly, keenly alert to all possible movements; if there were other people about – and there surely had to be – he wanted to meet them. He had no idea who Barry was or what an American should be doing in such a place, running a taverna of all things, but he sensed that the more people he met and spoke to, the more likely he was to be able to put together some explanation.

The track twisted, snake-like among the olive trees and Daniel was grateful for the shade they provided. To his left the foliage was fairly sparse and if he peered between the trunks and branches he could just make out the main road and, beyond, faint and distant, the shimmering water. To the right, however, the trees were dense and terraced, rising up a steep hill.

He had walked only a few hundred metres when his suspicions were confirmed; ahead of him, spanning both sides of the narrow lane, was a small village. It was, from a distance, both quaint and picturesque, an impression that strengthened as he approached it.

The first building Daniel came to on the left-hand side was a small grocery store. It was a two-storey building, whitewashed like the taverna, with a narrow balcony jutting out half-way up the front façade. The building was covered in trailing plants, and a neat open staircase wound its way up the outside of the left-hand wall. A few chairs and tables were set out on the shop's large concrete forecourt. The windows were grey and dusty, and beneath them were stacked several wooden boxes full of brightly coloured fruits and vegetables; Daniel recognised apples, lemons, grapefruits, eggplants, watermelon and small, squat cucumbers that he guessed were zucchini. Once again, the place looked deserted.

He wandered across the forecourt and peered in through the opalescent windows. Inside he could make out a wooden counter, several ramshackle shelves full of unidentifiable boxes and packets, and an antiquated cash register that would not have looked out of place in a museum. Behind the counter were stacks of cigarette packets, but none of the designs was familiar. An old-fashioned set of scales rested on the counter next to the cash register. But there was no sign of life.

Perhaps it's siesta time? thought Daniel. Certainly the place was suffused with a sleepy, dreamy air. Daniel remembered at once that this place wasn't real, that it was all probably a figment, a construct of his unconscious. For a moment, a familiar panic seemed to overcome him, but this diffused swiftly to make way for a much more pleasant sensation, that of warmth and comfort.

He proceeded along the track at a slow pace, taking

account of all the new sights and sounds. On his right he came across a single-storey green building, which looked very run-down. Paint peeled in large untidy swathes from around the doors and windows, and on the ground there were little piles of what looked like green and white pebbles, where the plaster had cracked and fallen from the walls. It was pitch black inside, and again there was no sign of activity. Outside, leaning against the building was a small wooden telephone kiosk. The telephone, supported on a small, rickety wooden shelf, was an ancient Bakelite model, maybe forty years old, with a heavy, chunky handset.

Three or four more buildings bordered the track, among them another grocery store, a bakery, and something that looked like a small butcher's shop. There was no meat displayed in this last, but the red-streaked wooden benches looked as if they had only recently been wiped down. The town was asleep, certainly, but it was not dead.

After the buildings, the track forked again; to the right, it led up and into the hills. Daniel wandered along the left-hand track and found himself back on the main road. He stood in the centre of the road and looked back towards the pump; he could see it quite clearly in the centre of the road, and could just make out the Pumphouse under the trees on the left. Behind him, the main road disappeared beneath the brow of a hill.

As Daniel walked back along the road towards the pump, he noticed several tracks leading off to the right and down to the sea. At one of the intersections he saw a hand-painted sign which read: 'Neraida Taverna: Fresh fish, Greek Specialities.' Daniel followed the path down to the sea, wandering between half-built shacks and unkempt gardens. Just before he reached the beach he saw the taverna off to the left, with its open, canopied patio. Like everywhere else, it appeared deserted. He continued to the beach, and soon found himself walking along a wide, clean and uninterrupted stretch of white and gold sand that swept around in a huge, shallow bay that seemed to go on for miles. It was, without doubt, the loveliest beach he had ever seen. It was also completely empty.

Daniel took off his sandals and allowed the warm, white grains of sand to slip between his toes. The sand felt soft and comforting, and the simple pleasures of walking on such a surface, with all its associations of holidays and foreign affairs, brought a smile to his face.

The beach stretched about fifty metres down to where the sea lapped against the shoreline, and seemed to continue for miles in both directions. The sun was still blisteringly hot, although it had fallen from its zenith and could now be viewed above the horizon, a part of the general aspect.

The sea was still sparkling, an ocean of white diamonds and silver glitter. With the sweat still heavy on his brow and the sand now starting to burn the soles of his feet, the water could not have looked more inviting. He walked swiftly to the shoreline and, fearing for a moment that the sudden contrast of hot skin and cool sea might trigger some unwanted response and send him hurling back to his other, waking life, he stood by the edge of the water, hesitating.

But his will abandoned him, and, more in faith than certainty, he took off his shirt, shorts and – ascertaining that he was still quite alone – slipped off his underpants and took a few tentative steps into the shallows. The luxurious blue waters were refreshingly cool. Tiny fish swam around

Daniel's Dream

his ankles as he stepped out into deeper waters, and the gentle sea breeze blew his hair around.

He ventured a little further, wading in up to his thighs. The water was crystal-clear and quite motionless, like liquid glass, and when he stood still he could see his feet quite clearly and without distortion, gleaming white against the warmer tones of the yellow sands.

He wandered in further still, until the water lapped gently around his waist. He turned slowly so that his back was towards the sea and looked towards the beach. From this position he could see the wide expanse of gleaming sand, the taverna directly in front of him, a few more similar buildings scattered at intervals along the beach, and, behind all this, the surprisingly verdant hills with their groves of olive trees and rocky precipices: an impressive backdrop.

This must be paradise, thought Daniel, scooping up handfuls of shimmering sea-water and allowing it to pour in crystalline rivulets down his forearms. Paradise, or something close.

And then, just as he was beginning to lose himself in wistful day-dreaming, a movement on the sand distracted him. Way off to the right, a figure, dressed in white, was walking slowly along the beach. Daniel couldn't tell whether it was a man or woman from so far away, although as the figure came closer the small, swaying motions of the walk suggested not just femaleness, but femininity.

Daniel made his way back to dry land, never taking his eyes off the apparition in white. He dried himself brusquely with his shirt and quickly pulled on his underwear and shorts.

By the time he had finished making himself presentable

the mysterious figure was close enough to be seen clearly. She was perhaps twenty-five years old, her most prominent feature a mane of dark-blond hair, thick and full-bodied, that hung down her back in a cascade of waves and curls. As she came closer, Daniel noted other things about her. She was not particularly tall, neither was she slim, although it was difficult to be certain, as she was wearing a white wrap which covered her from her breasts to her knees, leaving her bronzed shoulders and calves bare.

He was struck by her appearance, not least because she was the first person he had seen since leaving the Pumphouse. He hoped that she spoke English, that she was friendly, that she wanted to talk; he had so many questions, so many things that he wanted to ask, that he needed to know.

Daniel walked up the beach to meet her; he noticed the way she regarded him, slowing her pace as he neared her. Good, he thought, she wants to talk. He walked up to her slowly and waited for her to speak.

'Hi,' said the girl, and smiled. She nodded towards the sea. 'Warm, was it?'

'Yes, very,' said Daniel haltingly.

'Usually is this time of day. You're new here, aren't you?'

'Yes I . . . I arrived today . . . sort of.'

'Then welcome,' said the girl, and smiled. 'I'm Kate,' she said, holding out her hand. Daniel took her tanned hand in his, and, just as he had done when clasping Barry's hand for the first time, suddenly felt strangely out of phase with everything around him.

'Pleased to . . .' he began, his head starting to spin. Oh God, no, thought Daniel as the skies above him started to

Daniel's Dream

darken and the horizon began to shift and skew as if he were drunk. 'My name's . . .'

'Daniel,' said the girl, just before she vanished into nothingness.

6

Daniel reached for the pen and notepad, found a clean sheet of paper and started scribbling furiously: *Greece, waiter, coffee, baklava, taverna* . . .

Even as he wrote, the pictures began to fade. He concentrated harder; more words came to him:

. . . *Berry, Barry, beach, blonde* . . .

The final images faded, leaving him frustrated once again, with just an aftertaste of the experience, the merest hint that something extraordinary – the nature of which was still indeterminate – had happened during the night.

Lisanne was not beside him. Daniel looked at the clock. Half past eight; she had already left for work. Daniel got up, showered, dressed, made himself a strong cup of instant coffee, smoked his first cigarette of the day, then fell, as usual, into depression.

One thing was clear; he had to talk to someone about his dream, or else he felt sure he would go mad.

Daniel reached for the phone and tried Vince's number

again. Vince was probably not the most empathetic person in Daniel's world, neither was he, intellectually, the best equipped for a discussion of esoterica, but he would at least be prepared to listen to what Daniel had to say without automatically dismissing it all as the rantings of a lunatic.

The telephone rang twice before it was answered: a familiar voice. Daniel smiled.

'Vince? It's Daniel.'

There was a pause, which although only momentary was rather longer than Daniel felt comfortable with. Had his best friend forgotten who he was?

'Danny? Shit . . . sorry Danny boy, only you were just about the last person I expected to . . . hold on a sec, will you?' There was a noise like someone smothering the telephone, accompanied by the distant, muffled hubbub of voices followed swiftly by the sound of a door being slammed shut. 'Sorry 'bout that old son; just had to shift a few bodies.'

'Is this a bad time?'

'Not at all, not at all. I was looking for an excuse to get them out the office. You couldn't have timed it better. Now then, is this a social call or are you looking to order half a hundredweight of animal feedstuff?'

Daniel smiled. Just hearing Vince's north-London wide-boy intonation again lifted his spirits. 'You guessed it; Lisanne says I'm eating like a pig these days so why not eat *as* a pig? What sort of discount can you do me?'

He heard Vince laugh, more out of politeness than genuine amusement, but still it put him at his ease.

'I always look after my friends, Danny, you know that,' said Vince.

Daniel's Dream

'I know,' said Daniel. 'How's tricks?'

'Can't complain Danny, can't complain.'

'And Janice?'

'She's well . . . busy as ever, no time for yours truly since she snagged that promotion. Between you and me I think she's letting that greasy boss of hers give her a length now and then. What do you reckon?'

'Well she always was a tart, Vince.'

Vince laughed loudly. 'I'll tell her you said that.'

Daniel grinned. Janice was one of the most refined women Daniel had ever known, which made her marriage to Vince all the more extraordinary. In truth, Vince *should* probably have ended up with some fellow East Ender, but the lovely and elegant Janice had fallen for his rough and rather dubious charms when they met at a wedding. They hit it off in a big way and within six months were on their own honeymoon, somewhere in the Caribbean, where Vince had enjoyed the rum cocktails but had not thought much of the food. Six years on they were, to all appearances, a happy and loving couple. Vince had lost little of the rough edge that had attracted her in the first instance, and Janice had – despite the new culture and morality that Vince had brought to the marriage – survived with scruples, ethics and charm intact. Which was why, of course, they could both talk about her in this way.

'So,' said Vince, sensing Daniel's need to get down to the matter in hand, 'if you've quite finished insulting my wife, what can I do for you?'

Daniel took a deep breath. 'I'd really like to see you, Vince. Perhaps over a drink or something?'

'We can do better than that. Why don't you and Lisanne come over for dinner one night? I'll give Jan a call and—'

'Actually,' said Daniel, cutting Vince off as swiftly as he could, 'I was thinking that . . . well, perhaps just the two of us could meet. I kind of need to talk.'

'Of course, old son. Say no more.'

'It's not about Lisanne,' said Daniel hurriedly, fearful that Vince might get the wrong idea and say something to Janice who, being close to Lisanne, would be on the phone quick as a flash to find out what the trouble was. 'I mean, everything with Lisanne is fine. I just need to talk to a mate without the distractions of having the women around.'

'Message received and understood. Now then, when and where did you have in mind?'

They arranged to meet at the White Horse near Covent Garden the following evening; it was close to where Vince worked and was relatively quiet for a central London pub; they'd be able to talk in peace. Vince asked no more questions, for which Daniel was thankful. Neither did he ask about Lisanne, perhaps sensing that, despite what Daniel had said, there was grief on the home front.

Daniel replaced the handset, lit another cigarette and inhaled deeply, drawing the volatile nicotine, the vaporised tars, the noxious gases and myriad pollutants deep into his lungs. The drug made his head spin; he did not want to think about the other, unseen effects that the smoke was having on his body. He had stopped smoking years ago, had reformed and become one of those virulent, holier-than-thou ex-smokers that he had once despised. But after the accident he found some sort of solace in cigarettes, and was soon back to his pre-reformation pack-a-day consumption.

He stared mindlessly at the cigarette smoke as it

Daniel's Dream

ascended into the still air in a continuous, barely wavering plume before breaking up chaotically at about head height into countless streamers and spirals of cloudy grey. If he did not find some sort of motivation soon, he knew, he risked descending into a static, meaningless limbo in which his existence, previously active and adventure-filled, would come to resemble the life-cycle of the average houseplant.

Fortunately, his recent exposure – real or imagined – to the clean, fragrant air and bright, hot sun of his dream world had induced a kind of temporary claustrophobia, so that whereas he had previously been prepared to spend the whole day indoors doing nothing, he now found the four walls around him oppressive, the atmosphere inside the house stifling. Despite the self-generated inertia that frequently kept him pinned to the spot, sitting in the same armchair hour after hour watching daytime television, his discomfort at being indoors now pushed him to his feet and out into the street.

Daniel decided to make another attempt to head for the West End. He would have a hunt around the record stores, search out some new music; something, *anything*, to get him out of the house.

Determined this time to complete his journey, Daniel set off with false confidence. He bought his ticket and clutched it tightly in his hand. He kept his eyes from straying to the advertisements as he descended the escalator, and when he reached the platform and sat down he closed his eyes until the train arrived. No tramps, no strange messages shouting at him from the posters on the wall, no fear.

A couple of minutes later a nearly empty train pulled up and Daniel got on board. As it pulled away, he considered that he was perhaps being unnecessarily cautious. All the omens and portents that had risen up before him yesterday were – could only be – figments of his imagination, over-active and over-zealous as a result of being kept dormant for so long. Words and symbols were just that, and could be interpreted any way the observer wished. If he wanted to see doom, despair and warnings, then that was what he would see. It was all down to mood and there was, in truth, nothing to fear.

Daniel took a deep breath, relaxed into his seat and allowed himself to look around. After all, what was there to be afraid of?

He did not have to wait long to find out. As he gazed around the carriage he saw, in quick succession: a poster above the window opposite advertising holidays in Greece; another wretch in filthy clothes drinking noisily from a brown bottle; and a piece of graffiti on the carriage door which read, 'What do you suppose you did to deserve all this?'

Daniel looked away and flinched. Was he losing his mind? These were all just coincidences, surely? The world did not work that way, slipping arcane messages to you through public media. It was ridiculous to think that every sight, every sound, every vision was directed towards one person, a cosmic conspiracy in which every message was loaded with meanings or warnings or worse. It was absurd: the world did *not* revolve around him.

The train lurched suddenly and came to an abrupt halt in the middle of the tunnel. The interior lights dimmed and, despite his attempts to remain calm, Daniel's heart began to beat faster, and he felt the tell-tale dampness in the palms of his hands. Oh great, this is just what I need,

Daniel's Dream

he thought, hoping that an attempt at ironic commentary, albeit strictly internalised, would help keep panic at bay.

From the other end of the compartment the drunk leered at him and starting making loud, unpleasant noises like a cross between a dog barking and a machine-gun being fired. Daniel shuffled around uncomfortably. This wasn't what was supposed to happen, this wasn't how it was supposed to be. It wasn't as if he was asking for much; just a chance to head into town, to get out of the house, to reacquaint himself with the once familiar metropolis . . . for Chrissake, it wasn't as if he was asking for the moon and the sun and the stars. So why all these difficulties, all these obstacles? It was truly as if someone or something didn't want him to make the journey.

The lights dimmed further. The drunk was still staring in his direction, making him feel more uncomfortable by the moment. What was wrong with the blasted train? Why wasn't it moving? The drunk's peculiar rant became louder and now seemed to be directed at him. Daniel looked away and, out of nervous habit, started whistling noisily and rather tunelessly, oblivious of the other passengers, who studiously avoided looking at him. Not that Daniel could have cared less; he just wanted to drown out the tramp's awful, insane racket.

A minute passed slowly. The tramp stopped making his gut-churning noises and collapsed into insensibility, but Daniel was unable to calm down. He was no longer sure what he was whistling, and began repeating over and over the eight-note melody that preceeded the chimes of Big Ben. He sensed that this was starting to irritate the other passengers even more than the tramp had done, but he could not stop himself. A tall, thickset young man dressed in dirty jeans and a leather jacket started eyeing him up, and Daniel sensed he had better quieten down or else he might have to deal with more than just imaginary messages and harmless, noisy drunks.

Just then the carriage vibrated into life, the lights flickered and then burst into full brightness, and the train pulled off, picked up speed for about thirty seconds and then decelerated swiftly as it approached the next station.

With an intense feeling of both relief and gratitude, directed at no one in particular, Daniel rose quickly to his feet and, as soon as the carriage doors had opened, leapt from the train and on to the platform, almost flooring two elderly ladies in the process. He pushed his way through the crowds waiting to embark, putting as much distance as possible between himself and the train, then stood with his back to the wall, waiting impatiently for the carriage doors to close and for the train, with all its intimations of foreboding, to move on. It seemed to take for ever, and all the time Daniel feared that the drunken vagrant might suddenly take it into his head to leap out of the carriage and attack him.

Eventually the doors slammed shut and the train began to gather momentum, but Daniel did not feel safe until it had attained full speed and had disappeared into the black hole at the far end.

He looked up and down the platform. Other passengers had disembarked and were now heading for the escalators, and within seconds Daniel found himself alone.

Although he was feeling calmer, he could still feel his heart beating frantically in his chest, and his palms were soaked with perspiration. Jesus, he thought, I can't carry

Daniel's Dream

on like this: one short train journey and I break into a nervous panic.

When the next train came, he boarded swiftly, found an empty corner and, avoiding all advertisements and shunning eye-contact with the carriage's other occupants, sat still and silent until he arrived safely at his destination. He disembarked and, keeping his eyes firmly on the passengers in front of him, followed the crowd out along the corridors, up the stairs and through the ticket barrier, then on to the bustling, noisy street.

He wandered along the road, past the recently refurbished statue of Eros, carelessly bumping into oncoming pedestrians. He still felt ill at ease, and wanted nothing more than to find a patch of grass – away from the throb of the crowds – to sit down and gather his thoughts. He felt the first pulsing waves of an oncoming migraine, and knew he had to find a seat somewhere out in the open and unwind. He took a deep breath and tried to concentrate. The closest seats, he recalled, were the benches around the statue of Shakespeare in the centre of Leicester Square Gardens. Not exactly peaceful, but it would do.

En route he was accosted briefly by two leathered and chained punks, their colourful, anachronistic plumage wavering in the wind, who pestered him for money. Daniel side-stepped them and pushed his way through the assembled masses at the half-price theatre ticket booth, at last finding solace on a bench beneath the cacophonous twitterings of a huge family of starlings, perched high in the branches above his head.

He sat quietly and watched the milling masses as they paraded before him: the elderly tourists trundling along, talking noisily, behaving badly; loud-mouthed youths with matted hair and enormous, aggressive-looking dogs, inadvertently terrorising elderly, grey-haired ladies with shopping bags and furled umbrellas; contented lovers wandering hand in hand, pausing briefly amid the bellowing chaos to embrace, fondle, kiss.

Why is this all so sad? wondered Daniel as he watched the parade pass by.

Eventually he rose to his feet and, in need of cigarettes, set off to find a tobacconist. He walked back to Piccadilly Circus and, reminded of his original intentions, followed a crowd of youths through the heavy brass swing doors into Tower Records.

The shop was as crowded as ever. Daniel scanned the New Release racks, but found nothing of any particular interest. Daniel's taste in music had, if anything, become more eclectic with each passing year. He still listened to rock, of course, and every so often would pick up on a new band that could cause the familiar ripple of excitement that he had first felt as a teenager. He also enjoyed the native sounds of many of the countries he had visited on his travels: he was particularly drawn to the cross-cutting rhythms and vocal delights of West African music, and the strange, oriental musings of Vietnam.

However, his tastes were slowly shifting. He had started to tune in to Classic FM at home, and was surprised to discover how often he found himself humming along to familiar tunes or tapping out the complex rhythms of the better-known pieces. Grieg, with his glorious, uplifting melodies, was a particular favourite, as was Vaughan Williams with his dense and deeply evocative pastoral works that somehow conjured up images of the rural idyll that had once been England.

Daniel's Dream

Still, classical music remained something of a closed book to him, and so rather than lose himself in the innumerable titles in the classical section, he headed for the jazz and world-music department.

A sensual saxophone and piano duet oozed out of the PA system as he thumbed through the jazz racks for piano music, but nothing he saw attracted him. His fingers wandered aimlessly over the racks, his attention dissipating among the crowds of music-lovers. He knew what he was looking for, but as he had no idea what the music was called or who it was by, he did not know how to start searching for it. The World Music section was huge. It was many months since he had spent any time in such an immense record store, and he was overwhelmed by the huge selection of CDs on display. There seemed to be music from every corner of the world, and he was mildly amused to discover such oddities as 'Mongolian Throat Music' and 'Folk Songs Played on the Eskimo Nose Flute' among the collections of Ukrainian love songs and Indian *raga*s. Unfortunately, intrigued as he was by these titles, it was music of an altogether different cast that interested him.

In the European section Daniel looked through a selection of Romanian folk music, a collection of Bavarian drinking songs, some popular Italian music, and came eventually to a few records in the rack headed 'Greece – *Syrtaki*'. Although he didn't recognise anything on any of the albums, he was intrigued by the sleeve notes and titles, most of which were written in Greek. He studied each cover with considerable care, hoping – with rather greater optimism than was warranted under the circumstances – for a clue or a hint. He examined every inch of every disc, believing that some sign, word, symbol or picture would spring out from one of the covers and point the way.

But there was nothing. No signs, symbols or suggestions. Graffiti on the Underground and poster advertisements with their cryptic threats and intimations of menace zeroed in on him with the pinpoint accuracy of a computer-controlled smart missile, but the signs and symbols that he actively sought, the icons that might lead him back to his dream world, remained invisible.

Deeply disappointed, he gave a deep, rather theatrical sigh, and began to make his way towards the exit. What, he wondered, had he expected to find? A disc with a little sticker on it saying, 'Dear Daniel, this is the music of your dream'? It was hopeless. It was pathetic. What was the point of fixing on it like this? What did he honestly think he could do about it? He was becoming obsessive, and there was something reprehensible, even vaguely criminal, about it. It was like loitering with intent; here he was, hanging around the edges of his dream, waiting for an opportunity to break in again.

Daniel fought his way through the crowds of enthusiasts, a lone searcher in the midst of strangers. The discomfort and underlying fears that had kept him house-bound for much of the previous six months were starting to reassert themselves, and he found himself feeling more and more nervous. His palms were sweating again, and his breath was starting to break up, coming in short, sharp intakes that somehow failed to fulfil their intended function. An old and unpleasantly familiar sensation of suffocation started to overwhelm him and he began to panic. He had to get out of the store. He started to push and struggle. All these damn people, what did they all want? Why were there so

Daniel's Dream

many of them? Where did they all come from? His heart was beating fast now, his breathing had become staccato and irregular, and he feared he might pass out.

He made it to the swing doors just in time. With the relief of a drowning man breaking the surface, he gulped in the rejuvenating draughts of cold London air, each breath loaded with the poisons and pollutants of a giant industrial city pounding away at full tilt. For a minute or more he stood on the pavement, near the main entrance, doing deep-breathing exercises like a man who has been starved of fresh air for a fortnight, until the combination of excess oxygen and petrol fumes made his head swim.

It was then, his head still reeling, that he saw her. She emerged from the throng of bodies exiting Piccadilly Underground station and Daniel felt his heart leap in his chest as if it had been wired with explosives and detonated by some emotional terrorist, skilled at creating maximum distress and disturbance.

Her hair was a little longer, her complexion a little darker, but there was no doubt in his mind. It was Alex.

'Alex!' he yelled as he made a dash towards her. It was a miracle, a miracle he hadn't dared pray for: she was alive, alive and well, alive and well and . . .

He was only two or three yards away from her when he realised his mistake. He stopped dead in his tracks and stared at the stranger as she walked past, oblivious of the gawking man who had almost bumped into her.

Daniel could feel the tears accumulating in the corners of his eyes, and even though he understood that Piccadilly Circus on a busy summer's afternoon was no place to break down, he could not stem the flow of tears nor prevent a howl of despair issuing from his tormented soul.

A few people stared at him, some with sympathy others merely out of curiosity. Not wanting to embarrass himself further Daniel went down the stairs into the Underground, boarded the first northbound train and headed for home.

The train trundled along the darkened passageways that bored through the London subsoil, turning the capital's foundation into a hole-ridden hollow, like a giant slab of Gruyère.

The incident at Piccadilly Circus had unsettled Daniel. It was precisely because of the possibility of such events that he had sought solace, safety and solitude in the confines of his own home, hiding from the Big Wide World and all that it threatened. Because if there was one thing clear in the morass of confusing signs and signals that obsessed him, it was that the world did not forgive, did not forget, and would take any and every opportunity to remind him of his past misdeeds and misdemeanours. Why else was he now haunted by ghosts and chimerical apparitions? Not that he had done anything really bad, really evil; certainly nothing that required this level of punishment. Hadn't he suffered enough? Weren't his physical injuries, the disabilities that still prevented him from returning to work, the mental torment that he had to endure . . . weren't they enough? Hadn't he done his penance?

Poor Alex, thought Daniel as he emerged from the Underground station at Manor House, and started to walk home.

Poor me.

He had been walking for only a few minutes when a peculiar sensation came over him; a discontinuity of some kind, like *déjà vu* only not as clear or well-defined. He had, of course, walked that road before – the section of Green Lanes that ran alongside Finsbury Park – a hundred times or more, so a sense of familiarity would not have been strange or alarming. It was not the sights of the street that disturbed him, but an altogether less prosaic vision. For a split second as he looked down the road, all the shops and cars and buses and people, all the noise and tumult and smog and stench disappeared, and he was once more walking along the sandy beach of his dream. So realistic was the vision, so complete in detail, that had he not known better he would have sworn that, for a split second, he had been transported to another place, another time.

The vision, which was enchanting and disruptive in equal measure, stopped him in his tracks. This can't be happening, he thought to himself: it just can't be. It was one thing to see visions of paradise in one's dreams, but to conjure up such Arcadian scenarios while wandering down a busy north London thoroughfare was beyond a joke.

And then he heard it, playing faintly in the background, almost drowned by the noise of the passing traffic: the music of his dream. Only the source of the music was neither ethereal nor other-worldly; it was emanating from the open doorway of Aphroditi, a music shop, just a few yards ahead of him.

A sign in the shop's window proclaimed it to be the biggest Greek music store outside Athens. Daniel had passed it on endless occasions and not once had it ever occurred to him to go inside. Even though he had lived in this overwhelmingly Cypriot community for years, and even though he knew his local greengrocer, off-licence, dry-cleaners and newsagent well, there were certain establishments that he still felt were off-limits to him. Green

Lanes was littered with Greek or Turkish men's clubs that were as foreign to him here in his own neighbourhood as they would have been in Cyprus. And while Aphroditi was nothing more exotic than a music and record store, like many of the clubs, with their indecipherable signs and air of exclusivity, he had never felt bold enough to enter.

He took a few steps towards the door and was both surprised and thrilled to hear the strains of the bouzouki become louder; for a moment he had thought it might be some sort of musical hallucination, the aural equivalent of his disturbing encounter with Alex's *doppelgänger* earlier that day. But as he entered through the half-opened door, there could be no doubting that this time the experience was real, for the music spluttered and crackled from the ageing loudspeakers on the counter, and echoed all around.

Daniel felt transported. He wanted to close his eyes and allow himself to be whisked back to Atheenaton, to the village of his dream, but feared he might faint or collapse or do something equally embarrassing. Instead he took a few moments to look around and, once he had assured himself that there was nothing either dangerous or threatening about the environment, wandered over to the racks of records that stood in great banks along the walls and beneath the windows, and started to thumb through them.

This was more like it, he thought, recalling the frustrating experience of earlier that day when he had had to flick through hundreds of those nasty plastic CD cases, squinting at their tiny covers to try and make sense of the titles and names. Here it was a different matter altogether. Clearly Greece was still a few years behind in its embracing

Daniel's Dream

of the digital format, and to Daniel's great delight the majority of the music in the shop came in the form of the now outmoded vinyl LP.

Even though he had no idea what he was looking at, Daniel derived a warm, comforting sensation from flicking through the racks of twelve-inch covers with their big, bright photographs and strong, clear typography. It reminded him of his youth and of the days spent with his friends rummaging through the racks of the second-hand record stores in Notting Hill Gate and Ladbroke Grove, searching for that elusive Yes album or Genesis single.

It was an odd sort of shop, part record store, part newsagent and grocery store, and though it had an extensive selection of Greek-looking album covers stacked in the racks, it did not, in truth, look as if it could possibly stock the biggest collection of Greek records in the country. Still, Daniel did not dwell long on this. Neither did he prolong his search of the record sleeves. He knew exactly what he wanted.

The gentle, lilting bouzouki was still playing, joined now by the deep, mellifluous tones of a baritone, singing in what could only be Greek. It was a wonderful combination, and even though Daniel had no idea what the man was singing about, he felt a delightful tingling at the back of his neck – the same sensation he used to have as a teenager when he listened to his favourite bands. Daniel stood quietly and listened, allowing the music to flow over him as if he were standing beneath a waterfall of sound. That the music was beautiful was beyond dispute, but there was also something sad, heart-achingly mournful about that voice.

When the song came to an end Daniel could barely stand

the silence, which entered him like a vast, empty hunger, and he was greatly relieved when the resonant sounds of a bouzouki playing the opening refrain of the next track swelled from the speakers and filled the air around him.

The store was deserted. There was no one behind the counter, and Daniel could not hear anyone moving around in the back of the shop. He walked to the counter and peered into the gloom. Nothing. The area behind the counter was filled with shelves, stacked floor to ceiling with records. To one side was the antiquated stereo system; the record was still playing, but it was too far away for Daniel to be able to see the label. On top of the counter, however, lay an empty record sleeve. Daniel picked it up and examined it.

The front cover was a collage of old photographs and postcards. The photographs were mostly the sort of ancient family snapshots that one could find in the bottom drawers and attics of a million homes the world over, many of them in sepia, others cracked and faded with no attempt to disguise or retouch them. The postcards were, if anything, more interesting: turn-of-the-century views of the Acropolis and period impressions of other famous Greek sites. Together they made a pleasing composition.

There was nothing written in English on either the front or the back cover, and Daniel could not decipher any of the strange Greek letters that made up the titles. But as his eyes scanned the foreign symbols he felt again the momentary faintness that had caught him off-balance outside, and experienced the strange but unmistakable sensation that he was standing on a beach in the bright sunshine with the sweat dripping from his forehead. He could even, for a split second, feel the sand between his toes.

Daniel's Dream

The sensation disappeared as swiftly as it had arrived, leaving Daniel a little dazed. He reached out to the counter and steadied himself, then took several deep breaths. As he was recovering his balance, he saw someone move in the back of the shop. A moment later a young man with black hair and several days' worth of stubble emerged from the darkness, clutching a stack of records which he placed carefully on the counter. He smiled at Daniel and then nodded towards the cover.

'Mitropanos. Can't beat him, eh?'

'Huh?'

'Dmitri Mitropanos; *the boss.*'

Daniel smiled and nodded swiftly. 'Right,' he said, still not fully understanding what the assistant was saying, then handed the cover to him. 'I'll take it.'

Once home, Daniel slipped the album carefully out of its cover and placed it on the turntable. He turned on the amplifier, cranked up the volume, and waited for music.

Music arrived.

Daniel could hardly believe the clarity of sound that emanated from the loudspeakers on either side of the bay window. In the record store – and in his dreams – each time he heard the music it was being played on an old record-player, the sort that could not possibly do justice to music of such finesse and delicacy. But here, on his own hi-fi, the music came into its own. The sound of the bouzouki, full and resonant, seemed to spring from the loudspeakers with an almost hyper-real intensity, each note ringing with the clarity of a struck wineglass; it was, quite simply, sublime. And when the vocalist began to sing in his deep, melancholy voice, he imbued words that remained mysterious with a quiet, unmistakable force that made their translation – for the time being, at least – unnecessary.

But it was neither the resonance of the bouzouki nor the power of the voice that sent Daniel into paroxysms of pleasure; it was the melody, the harmonies, the nuances of timing and timbre that most deeply affected him and confirmed beyond a reasonable doubt that *this* was the music of his dream.

Daniel closed his eyes and allowed the music to conjure up visions of Atheenaton. Perhaps, he thought, if he concentrated hard he might find himself back there, wandering along the sand or swimming in those crystal-clear waters. What, he wondered, had become of the girl with the mane of blond hair who had greeted him, who knew his name? Where was she now? And where were Barry and the waiter? Did they still exist, locked into a world to which he had only occasional access? And what did he have to do to gain access again?

But no matter how hard he tried, when Daniel opened his eyes he was still in his living room in north London, and his dream world was an eternity away.

In desperation he sought ways to trigger his return. He ran up to the bedroom and grabbed his notebook, thumbing anxiously through the pages, rereading his tired scrawl, the notes he had written on waking from his dreams, in the hope that the strange melange of vaguely connected words might precipitate the return he longed for. But it was to no avail.

He retrieved the paperback that he had bought the other day, Robert Jameson's *Greek Idyll*, and spent ten minutes gazing at the cover believing that it might be a gateway to his lost world. But nothing happened. He even read a

Daniel's Dream

few more pages, but the prose was so turgid that it only annoyed him.

'I want to go back,' he mumbled aloud, too ashamed to cry out loud but desperate to give vent to his frustrations, but the songs, shifting from one mood to another, like his random words, echoed each other and would only hint at sights unseen. Frustrated at his inability to bring back something as simple as a dream, Daniel sulked miserably.

The first side of the record came to an end. Exhausted by his exertions, Daniel decided he would lie down on the sofa for a while. He kicked off his shoes, padded over to the hi-fi, lifted the disc from the turntable and replaced it carefully in its sleeve. He examined the cover again; somewhere among the pictures and words, there had to be a key, a password; something which would show him the way to Atheenaton. If there were clues they remained undetected, but in some way, he felt sure, the music would provide his ticket to paradise.

Daniel returned to the sofa, plumped up the cushions, then stretched out upon it. He snuggled into the soft comfort, closed his eyes, and within moments felt that pleasing sense of discontinuity as the web of logical notions, recollections and ideas began to unravel and fragment, and snatches of surreal nonsense eased their way into a train of thought already careering off the rails. Even though the hif-fi was switched off, the music continued to play. How wonderful, thought Daniel as the first, flickering intimations of sleep beckoned; how absolutely wonderful.

7

'How do you know my name?'

The girl smiled; there was something provocative, perhaps even cheeky about her grin; Daniel thought it rather fetching.

'Let's just say that we don't get many unexpected visitors to Atheenaton.' She raised her eyebrows as if to invite comment, but Daniel thought it best to say nothing. 'So, how about a drink? We can go to the Neraida,' she said, nodding her head at the taverna on the beach.

'Sure . . . but I don't think it's open,' said Daniel, still puzzling over how the girl had known his name. He decided that she must have been at the Pumphouse and spoken to Barry.

'Oh, I should imagine we'll find someone to serve us. Come on, my treat.'

Without waiting for Daniel, Kate started to walk in the direction of the taverna, her long fair hair swaying in the breeze. Daniel followed, a couple of paces behind. His heart was beating fast, and his mouth was dry; thirst seemed to be a recurring feature of his visits, but he didn't care. All he could think as he followed his escort was: I'm back; I've come back to Atheenaton.

Kate chose a shaded table, the one nearest the sand, eased herself into one of the straight-backed wooden chairs and placed her feet casually on another. Daniel sat opposite her and arranged his chair so that he could look out on to the sea.

'I really do think this place is empty,' he said, looking around.

'Nonsense,' laughed Kate. Her eyes flashed; a look of supreme confidence. 'These places never close, especially when we have guests.'

'Guests?'

'But of course, my dear: you.' Kate turned her head towards the doorway of the taverna and called out, 'Vangeli!'

A moment later, a slim, dark-haired young man appeared in the doorway. He was dressed like the waiter at the Pumphouse: black trousers, black shoes, and a plain, white, collared shirt with the sleeves rolled up to just below the elbow. When he saw Kate, Vangeli smiled broadly and strode across swiftly to greet her.

'*Yassu*, Katy. How are you?'

'I'm well Vangeli, very well. Vangeli, allow me to introduce you to our new friend; this is Daniel.'

Vangeli nodded. 'Yes, I heard. Please, you are most welcome.' He shook Daniel firmly by the hand. 'How long you stay?'

Daniel, who was baffled but not displeased by this curious charade in which everyone treated him as if he was an honoured guest, found himself hesitating before replying. What was he supposed to say?

'Well, I'm not sure—' he began, only to be interrupted.

'Is not long enough!' boomed the waiter, and laughed. 'You talk with Katy; once you come Atheenaton, you never want to leave. Now, my friends, what you like to drink?'

Kate ordered (in what Daniel presumed must be Greek) and Vangeli dashed off towards the kitchen.

'They make their own wine here; it's quite unusual, quite unique . . . you do drink wine, don't you?'

'Yes, absolutely,' replied Daniel. He felt a little uneasy at this ebullient, overdone hospitality, the rather forced manner in which he was being made to feel at home, but he considered it would be both churlish and ungrateful to comment upon it. Besides, there were more pertinent matters uppermost in his mind. Most particularly, who was this woman who had suggested that he, Daniel, had been expected? And if she knew his name, and knew to expect him, then what else did she know about him?

He felt a familiar, nagging sensation gnawing away at him and realised that he was in need of a cigarette. Kate had shifted her position a little and was now looking out to sea, so while fishing around in his pockets for his cigarettes he took the opportunity to look at her more closely.

The first, and most striking, thing about her was not, in fact, her mane of golden hair; it was her face, which, with her rounded, chubby cheeks and deep-blue eyes, gave her the look of a particularly pretty cherub. It was clear now, both from the curves of her face and from the soft, well-padded fingers and forearms that Kate possessed what Daniel's father might have referred to as a fuller figure. To his surprise, Daniel found this appealing. He had always been drawn to slim, petite women – Lisanne was a case in point – but there was something about Kate that he found undeniably attractive. In part it might have had something to do with the way she carried herself; Daniel had noticed the graceful way in which she had sashayed across the sand, the noticeable but not pronounced way she swung her hips, how she held her head high. And then there were her looks; she was disarmingly pretty, her beautiful blue eyes set off by a charming, slightly snub nose and full, red lips.

He fished the packet of cigarettes out of his pocket along with another handful of crumpled banknotes, which he spread out on the table. He examined them perfunctorily while fiddling with the cellophane wrap on the cigarettes, and sighed. This small, magical occurrence alerted him once more to the truth of his current situation: only in dreams could one's pockets fill with cash, mysteriously, without effort.

He lifted one of the pink notes and stared hard at it. It looked vaguely familiar, but was still not identifiable. He waved it towards Kate.

'Kate?'

Kate turned her head slightly and looked at him. 'Uh-huh?' she said, her voice warm and soft and comforting. She appeared to be smiling contentedly, like a woman who hadn't a care in the world. What, wondered Daniel, did one have to do to achieve such a state of grace? How did you live a dream life? For a moment he felt envious.

Daniel waved the note again. 'What's this? I mean, what's it worth? I, uh . . . I'm not familiar with the currency.'

'That's a one-hundred-drachma note.'

Daniel's Dream

'Right. And what's that in sterling?'

Kate shook her head. 'No idea. But it'll buy you two carafes of wine, a piece of roast chicken or a big *souvlaki*,' she said, and laughed. 'Or moussaka and salad . . . just. And that's all it's worth; this much food, that much drink. Don't worry, you'll soon get the hang of it.'

Daniel frowned. That last remark had been delivered as if he was new to the whole concept of money. Where does she think I've come from? thought Daniel, and was just about to broach the matter when Vangeli returned from the kitchen with two small, dirty glasses and a rough-cast ceramic carafe which he placed on the table with a gesture which, in different circumstances, might have suggested triumph. Vangeli looked in turn at Kate and Daniel and then nodded.

'Drink to your health,' he said, rather obliquely, and left.

Daniel reached out to touch the carafe and was pleased to find that, despite its rough appearance, it felt smooth and well-worn. He was going to offer to pour but thought it best to wait until asked; for all he knew there might be some strange or unfamiliar ritual regarding the drinking of wine in Atheenaton; there frequently was in other countries. And wasn't that where he was? Another country?

Kate poured the wine then lifted her glass.

'This is a red retsina,' she said. 'You don't see much of it around, and it's definitely an acquired taste. The first glass usually takes the skin off the back of the throat; after that, it's like nectar.' She clinked her glass against Daniel's. 'We're very pleased to have you with us.'

Daniel looked at her askance. 'We?'

'Yes, all of us,' she said, as if that was all the explanation that was necessary, and then threw back her head and swallowed the wine in one gulp. Daniel looked on in amazement. Kate caught his look with its hint of disapproval and burst out laughing. 'It's the only way to drink it! Go on, try it.'

Daniel did as he was told. The wine, if that was what it was, tasted strong and acidic, almost sour. He flinched as he swallowed, and felt tears come to his eyes.

Kate shrieked in delight. 'There! Wasn't that wonderful? Here, have another; you'll find this one tastes even better.'

Daniel took a deep breath as Kate refilled the glasses. What was she playing at? Surely she wasn't trying to get him drunk? Daniel found himself amused by the idea and – as he considered its possible objective – even a little flattered.

'You're going to love it here, Daniel; I do hope you can stay.'

Daniel gazed around him at the tables and chairs, the rush mats that covered the patio floor, and the track he had walked down. He registered the soft yellow sand, the calm azure sea, the glass of ruby liquid on the table, the colours echoing correspondingly in Kate's golden hair, dark-blue eyes, and full, red lips.

'So do I,' he said softly, and lifted the wine to examine its rich hue and heady bouquet. He stopped short of drinking and put the glass down. 'Shouldn't we make a toast? Or isn't that customary?'

'Yes, of course. What would you like to drink to?'

Daniel shrugged. 'Well, to be honest, I'm not sure. Perhaps we should drink to this wonderful place.'

'Do you mean the taverna or Atheenaton?'

Daniel's Dream

Daniel paused. He had not yet spoken the name, and knew that to do so would, in some obscure way, be giving it still greater credence. He took a deep breath and, bracing himself in case of any sudden transformation, let the word issue from his wine-wet lips.

'Atheenaton.'

There were no rumbles of thunder or flashes of lightning; no intimations of disaster.

Kate smiled, then nodded a touch solemnly. 'I think that's a very wise choice. To Atheenaton.'

She clinked her glass, filled to the brim, against Daniel's, then sank what remained in one easy move before filling it for the third time. Daniel, who had yet to loosen up but none the less found Kate's uninhibited embrace of the rough and ready retsina infectious, followed suit.

This time the wine tasted sweet and full-bodied and Daniel could not control the expression of surprised delight that lit up his face.

'Told you,' said Kate, reaching across and placing her hand on Daniel's wrist. 'And this is just the beginning; there's so much more . . . *so* much more.'

Daniel didn't understand what Kate meant, not that it really mattered. He watched the seagulls circling overhead, his head muzzy and his tongue singing with the acid of the retsina. He swooned slightly as the exotic aromas of pine and sea-air filled his nostrils, felt the breeze, now warm and salty, blowing around his head. From the doorway and windows of the taverna came the sweet, familiar sounds of the bouzouki, and the deep resonant tones of the baritone. Daniel twisted in his chair, his whole body trembling with pleasure.

'My music,' he murmured.

Kate looked at him and smiled. 'You like this music?'

'Oh God, yes. It's very special . . . very. Don't you think so?'

'Of course. Mitropanos is very popular here.'

'He's the singer?'

'Uh-huh. This is one of his older recordings. It's called "Synaxaria".'

Daniel nodded. 'Does it mean anything? The name, I mean.'

Kate shrugged. 'I suppose so.' She turned towards the taverna. 'Vangeli!' she cried out. 'More retsina.'

Daniel balked at this. 'Wait a minute, Kate . . .' he started, feeling decidedly light-headed.

Kate looked at him blankly. 'Is there a problem?'

'Well, not really . . . it's just I'm not used to drinking so much at this time.' Daniel lifted his left wrist reflexively, as he had done thousands of times before but this time as he glanced down casually to check the time he discovered that his watch was missing. 'Oh shit,' he said, as habitual a reaction as checking the time. 'I've lost my watch.'

'I doubt that,' said Kate, pouring the last drops from the carafe into Daniel's glass.

Daniel was already searching the table top for it. 'But I had it . . .'

'It doesn't matter,' said Kate softly, once again placing her hand gently on his arm. Daniel stopped his search and looked up at her. 'Really, Daniel, it just doesn't matter. Not here, anyway.'

'But I . . .'

'You really are going to have to learn to relax. Now take it from me: you don't need a watch. No one in Atheenaton has a watch.'

Daniel's Dream

'Don't you have a watch?'
'No; and neither do you. Now.'
'How will I know what time it is?'
'You have an appointment?'

Daniel shrugged, then smiled reluctantly; he did not think he was being obsessive about his watch, it was just that he was used to knowing what time it was. Even when he was on holiday.

'Okay, point taken; but what happens if you do have to know the time?'

'You ask someone. Look, here's Vangeli; ask him.'

'But I . . .'

'It's okay; he won't bite, and he understands English really well. Go ahead.'

As Vangeli approached the table, a full carafe of wine in hand, Daniel took a cigarette from out of the packet and lit up. He offered one to Vangeli.

'English cigarette? Thank you, yes, I will take one.'

Daniel struck a match and held it out for the waiter. 'Vangeli, do you know what time it is?'

'Time?' said Vangeli. He looked out to sea, squinting at the bright reflections and then sighed. 'It is afternoon; maybe three hours before sunset.' He paused a moment and drew deep on his cigarette. 'A good time for smoking, I think. And for drinking retsina.'

'See?' said Kate, unable to conceal her amusement. 'You just have to ask.' It was clear to Daniel that Kate believed she had just won a small victory. 'Vangeli, Daniel wants to know what "Synaxaria" means.'

' "Synaxaria"? It is like "meeting place" . . . something like that.'

Kate looked at Daniel and raised her eyebrows. 'How

appropriate,' she said, not able to rid her voice of its inflection of knowingness.

Daniel smiled. He had just witnessed a charming, one-act play, a performance put on just for his pleasure. He could not imagine why Kate had gone to such lengths, when it was evident that she had known the meaning of the word all along. Perhaps she just enjoyed the dramatic?

Vangeli replaced the empty carafe with the full one and then disappeared.

'One for the road?' said Kate, grabbing the carafe and filling the glasses again.

'The road? Are we going somewhere?'

'Well, perhaps not just yet. It's going to be such a beautiful sunset. Perhaps we should just sit here and wait for the sun to go down.'

She raised her glass and waited expectantly for Daniel to follow suit.

Oh well, thought Daniel, in for a penny in for a pound. Or a drachma, perhaps. After all, if you couldn't be reckless in your dreams, when could you be? Besides, it was a very long time since he had tied one on; it would probably do him good.

Daniel sipped some more wine and was surprised to find that the taste had changed again; this time it tasted mellow and fruity.

'Is this the same retsina?'

'Uh-huh,' said Kate. 'Same same but different.'

'What was that?'

'Same same but different . . . sorry, it's just one of those local things. You know, sayings that catch on.'

'Right,' said Daniel, who didn't really understand at all. He took another sip of wine and wondered how long he was going to be allowed to stay this time. He felt pleasantly relaxed, even a little tipsy. It was a warm, lovely sensation, something he hadn't experienced for a long time, and he wanted to find a way to make it last. He felt comfortable here, even though he was among strangers. He decided he had been unfairly judgemental; there was nothing forced about the hand of friendship that had been offered here; it was just that such casual, easy hospitality was so rare these days that he hadn't recognised it.

How wonderful it would be to stay for a while, thought Daniel, as a hint of pine wafted through the taverna. How nice to live in the sun for a while, to make friends of these charming people: Kate, Vangeli, Barry.

But would it ever happen? At the back of his mind, while he had been drinking and talking and smiling, he could not ignore the fact that he was inside a dream, something that, by its very nature, was illusory and unreal, even if it felt like a real, flesh-and-blood experience. How could he get so excited about a dream? If, of course, it *was* just a dream, something which even now he was not sure of. Daniel was scared to think about it too much in case scepticism precipitated his return to reality. And he was in no mood to leave.

The wine was starting to take effect. The pleasant buzz inside him had now fizzled out leaving him warm, contented but decidedly dozy. Probably the sea-air, he thought, as he downed another glass of the heady, potent retsina. There were so many questions he wanted to ask, so much he wanted to know, but he was nervous of breaking whatever spell held him in Atheenaton. Still, there was one thing that he needed to know for sure, or else he suspected he might carry on fooling himself indefinitely. He decided to ask Kate straight out and get the matter cleared up once and for all.

'Kate?'

'Don't, Daniel; don't say it.'

'But . . .'

'In fact, you'd do better to put the thought from your mind; it won't help you. Not here.'

'Help me?' said Daniel, baffled. 'But you don't even know what I was going to ask?' He realised then that he was starting to slur his words. The retsina was more powerful than he had thought.

Kate nodded slowly, then looked out to sea. She held out her hand and pointed to the horizon, then swept it in a long arc from one end of the sea shore to the other. 'All this,' she said, quietly but with a certain reverence. 'You're wondering if all this could possibly be real.' She paused and gazed deeply into his eyes. 'We know; we've all been there, been through that stage. All visitors to Atheenaton arrive in much the same way. So, you see, we understand.' She reached out, took hold of Daniel's forearm and gripped it firmly, then offered her free hand, too. 'Here,' she said, offering him her hand. 'Hold my hand. There, now tell me *that* isn't real. Tell me that this wonderful retsina, with its complex of flavours and colours and aromas is just an illusion. Tell me that the sun isn't bright, that the sea isn't warm, that the music – *your* music – doesn't resound in the air around you. It's all here, it's all real, and it all exists for you.'

But it was too late. As the last of Kate's words echoed around the patio, Daniel felt his eyelids grow heavy and knew he was about to fall asleep. The air became hazy, Kate's outline became fuzzy and indistinct, and

Daniel's Dream

the sound of the bouzouki, until then so prominent, faded away.

'Too much retsina I expect,' he laughed, as the sky darkened and extinguished the sun. 'Just too much retsina . . .'

8

Lisanne opened the morning's mail absentmindedly; three requests to read manuscripts, one savage reply from an author she had declined to handle, and a thick, heavy manuscript entitled *Another Chance* that she had been expecting.

As she fumbled with the manuscript she knew her usual enthusiasm for the day's work was sadly absent; her mind was full of Daniel, past events, present transactions. What was wrong with him? More to the point, what was happening to her? The other day's commotion over the sleeping tablets was just one more fiasco in an ever-lengthening list of muddles and misunderstandings that threatened to bury them both. Lisanne did not know if she could cope with it any more. For how much longer was she expected to play the dutiful, understanding wife who never complained and took everything in her stride, met every crisis head-on without demur and triumphed over adversity? Who did people think she was? Wonderwoman? Lisanne was strong; she was capable and she was tough. But she wasn't Atlas, and she was no longer able to shoulder the burden of Daniel's world alone.

Not that she had stopped loving or caring for him. Despite the way he behaved towards her these days, and notwithstanding the almost complete absence of any real love or affection on his part, Lisanne still cared deeply. That was partly her problem. There were times when she wished she *didn't* care: that way she could just walk out on him, leave him to sort out his own mess.

But that was not an option. Even now, even in their much-reduced state, she was still all too conscious of the fact that Daniel was the most important factor in her life. Meeting Daniel was the best thing that had happened to her, and even though she suspected his current behaviour was intimately linked, not to guilt over Alex's death, but to shame of an altogether less dramatic and more prosaic nature, she could not simply leave him in his hour of need. Even if that hour had swollen and expanded to fill half a year.

Besides, she had no proof that Daniel had ever been anything but completely faithful to her. The fact that he had lost interest in her physically *could* be just a reaction to the accident. There had never been any suspicious tell-tale signs; no strange perfumes or inexplicable female odours, no lipstick traces or other foolish things. Neither were there rumours, chit-chat, tittle-tattle, hearsay . . . none of the little snippets of scandal that, she believed, would disseminate around the sort of small circles that she and Daniel inhabited. In fact, there had been nothing to suggest to her that her once-loving, now-broken husband had ever strayed from the straight and narrow.

Nothing, that is, save for a disturbing, intuitive frisson

that reverberated like a struck tuning fork every time she heard the name 'Alex'. Of course, there was every likelihood that her reaction was nothing more than a sort of ghoulish jealousy: Daniel was mourning *her*, a woman Lisanne had never met, had never even heard of prior to the accident. And even if there had been nothing between Daniel and Alex beforehand, there certainly was now: a bond, a link, an unspoken, unacknowledged covenant between them. He had survived: she had perished, and the manner in which that association now impinged upon Daniel's conscience clearly acted as a wedge between him and Lisanne. Daniel and Alex were connected in a way that she, Lisanne, would never know or fully understand. And all she could do was look on with mounting unease.

She had thought of confronting him, had played through in her head all the possible scenarios, but as most of these contained tears, screaming or – in one particularly unsavoury version – blood, she had decided against it. Besides, what good would it do? What would it accomplish? Would a confession of infidelity spur her into action, make her throw him out, cause *her* to walk out, perhaps? Lisanne had thought about all these variants and more, and had come to the conclusion that knowing the truth would, in the long run, probably cause more harm than good. Alex was dead, her existence obliterated, and when confronted with that irrevocable fact, matters such as faithfulness and infidelity paled, if not into insignificance, then at least into something less grave. Daniel was such an integral part of her life these days, that life without him was all but inconceivable.

Lisanne warmed her hands on the half-empty coffee mug. She flicked through the neatly typewritten pages of

Another Chance, aware that the manuscript would receive scant attention until she solved the mystery of Daniel's ever-worsening behaviour. She should, perhaps, call the author and let him know. He would be anxious to hear her response. However, the thought of speaking to Robert Jameson did not appeal in the least. Since his success with *Greek Idyll* he had become unbearably conceited, and she was in no mood to pander to him just now. She would leave it for a day or two.

Daniel woke up to find himself still stretched out on the sofa, his mouth dry, his head pounding with what could only be the vestiges of a hangover.

Confused and befuddled, he made his way to the kitchen sink and turned the cold tap on full. He splashed the water on his face, then drank a pint and a half of the cold, chlorine-tainted fluid. Vaguely refreshed, he made his way back to the living room, sat down on the sofa and stared at the telephone.

Should he call her? Whimsical dreams notwithstanding, Daniel knew he had been behaving increasingly badly towards Lisanne and that he had to find some way to make amends. If he continued to lash out at her, take her for granted, keep her at arm's length, then it was just a matter of time before she walked out on him. And yet, whenever he tried to find ways to make it up to her, he always failed miserably.

Perhaps if he just told her everything? About everything that had happened in India? Would she understand? Or was it too late for such a confession?

With guilt hovering round him like a sickly aura, he reached for the telephone and called the office.

Daniel's Dream

'Hi,' he said as she answered the phone. 'It's me.'

'Daniel?' said Lisanne, surprised to hear his voice. Why was he phoning her at work? What was wrong? 'Are you okay?'

'Yes, yes, I . . .' Daniel paused for a moment, heard bouzouki music playing in the distance. 'Is that the radio I can hear?'

'Radio?' Lisanne could hear nothing. 'Not here, no. Is everything okay Daniel? You sound upset.'

'Everything's fine,' said Daniel. The music had stopped, leaving him confused. 'I . . . I just phoned to say . . . I'm sorry, Lisanne. I've been acting like a complete shit lately. I don't know what's got into me. But I'll make it up to you. Somehow.'

Lisanne was taken aback by this unexpected confession. 'Daniel, this isn't really the time . . .'

'I know, I know. I just had to let you know. You're too good for me, you know? I don't know why you put up with me.'

'Daniel . . . look, can we talk later? I'll come home early.'

'No, no . . . I just . . . I just want you to know. I *do* love you.'

Lisanne, nonplussed, gave an embarrassed laugh. 'I love you too,' she whispered.

Through the receiver, Daniel could hear voices in the background, and the sound of doors slamming.

'Listen, darling, a client's just walked in. I'll have to go,' she said, a touch sadly. It had been a long time since she had heard those words. 'Will you be okay?'

'Yes, I . . . oh, by the way, I'm seeing Vince this evening for a drink.'

There was a moment's silence before Lisanne spoke again. 'Oh, that's . . . that's nice. Send my love, won't you.'

'Of course.'

'Bye, then.'

'Bye.'

He replaced the receiver and sat looking at the phone. Why should a matter as simple as phoning Lisanne leave him so drained? He felt as if he had just run a marathon.

Outside, the wind was starting to howl, and the beginnings of a summer storm threatened to erupt. Exhausted beyond reason, Daniel lay down on the sofa and gazed half-heartedly through the window as the rain started to fall. But he could not get comfortable. He yawned a couple of times and shifted around uneasily. From beyond sleep, familiar sounds beckoned him. Barely able to keep his eyes open, Daniel trudged upstairs, stripped swiftly and slipped into bed. He still had a few hours before he had to meet Vince; a little nap would do no harm.

It was warm and cosy between the sheets, and as his eyes shut fast Daniel felt himself being drawn inexorably out of this world and into another. Within moments he was fast asleep.

9

'Where have you been?' asked Kate, passing Daniel a tall glass filled to the brim with a colourful and exotic concoction. Slices of fruit and chunks of ice bobbed around in the glass, and a thick white straw protruded from the top. Daniel took hold of the drink and tried to pretend that everything was normal, even though he felt totally disoriented.

He took a small sip as he looked around him, like a detective looking for clues. It was night-time, and they were seated on the patio of the Pumphouse. A string of lights which hung from the vines above their heads cast a warm glow over the taverna, and the place buzzed with noise and excitement. It was this hustle and bustle of activity that had taken him by surprise. The tables were filled by dozens of people, all engaged in conversation and all around him men and women were smiling and occasionally breaking into peals of laughter. It was such a contrast to the first time he had sat in the Pumphouse that he hardly recognised the place.

He returned his attention to Kate, to find her looking at him expectantly, clearly awaiting an answer to her question. He tried to frame a suitable response, but with all the noise and activity going on around him he was too distracted and could not think what to say.

'Been?' he gulped, playing for time. What sort of answer was she looking for? Surely she knew where he had been? He took a sip of the garish concoction that Kate had thrust into his hands and found himself breaking involuntarily into a smile. It was a piña colada. Daniel hated piña coladas. He had never developed a taste for sweet cocktails or any of those ridiculous drinks adorned with fruit salad and miniature garden furniture. But still he could not help smiling; despite himself, it tasted delicious.

Kate continued to stare at Daniel expectantly. 'Yes; we've missed you.'

There's that 'we' again, mused Daniel. Was she serious? Had he really been missed? Had anyone even noticed that he had not been around? It seemed unlikely.

Daniel decided that it was probably in his best interests to play along with the game; it seemed harmless enough. Dreams, like day-dreams, were intrinsically fragile things, easily blown away by cynicism and disbelief.

He shrugged and smiled. 'Sorry,' he said. 'I was, um . . . sort of busy, I suppose.'

Kate leant across, took hold of his left hand and smiled. 'Well, I'm pleased you're back,' she said, with what seemed genuine warmth. 'It's always good to have new blood in Atheenaton; I hope you'll stay a little longer this time.'

Daniel nodded and risked a wry smile, as if to alert Kate to the fact that he was on to the charade and yet happy to play along with it. But he did not receive the

Daniel's Dream

equally knowing response that he expected; it was as if Kate's inquiry were genuine.

Daniel could hear music playing in the background, but to his surprise it was not the sound of the bouzouki but something altogether more contemporary and energetic, suggesting that somewhere inside the taverna was a dance floor. Exactly the sort of thing, mused Daniel, one would expect if one were staying at a holiday resort. Daniel frowned. Was that what Atheenaton was? Certainly the warm air, exotic scents and lively atmosphere all suggested a holiday atmosphere.

'Is it this busy every night?' Daniel took another sip of his drink. It really did taste exceptional.

'More or less,' said Kate, waving to a young couple sitting at a nearby table.

'Where do they all come from?' asked Daniel, dispensing with the straw and drinking the cool, delicious liquid straight from the glass.

'Oh, around,' said Kate enigmatically, then swiftly changed the subject. 'Barry makes a great cocktail, doesn't he? Have you met him?'

'Barry? Yes, I met him earlier.'

'You must go and say hello to him; he'll be so pleased to see you again. I expect you'll find him inside.'

Daniel hesitated for a moment. He still felt a little uneasy, and had not yet adapted to being back in Atheenaton.

Kate picked up on this immediately and gave his arm a reassuring squeeze. 'It's okay,' she said softly. 'I won't disappear.'

Daniel nodded and smiled, a touch reluctantly. 'No,' he said, 'but I might.'

Kate laughed. 'Trust me,' she said, then made a little

shooing gesture with her hand. Daniel grinned, placed his glass carefully on the table and, making sure he didn't trip up on anything or bump into anyone, walked into the taverna.

In contrast to its appearance when Daniel had last seen it, the inside of the taverna was now bright and cheerful; small wall-lights complemented candles in the centre of each of the dozen or so tables that filled the place. On the right-hand side of the spacious interior was the well-stocked bar with its long, polished wooden counter and a few tall bar-stools. Behind the bar stood Barry, busily mixing a drink in a stainless-steel cocktail shaker.

'Hey, Daniel! Good to see you,' he boomed across the bar as soon as Daniel appeared. 'Here, let me get you a drink. What are you having?'

Daniel approached the bar and perched on one of the stools. 'Whatever you're making, I guess,' he said. 'Are you this busy every night?'

'Hey, didn't I tell you it livens up at night? Stick around; it only gets better.' Barry emptied the contents of the steel shaker into a tall glass and topped it up with ice. 'There you go. Good health, Daniel. Here's to you.'

'Cheers,' said Daniel, and raised his glass to Barry.

Around him, the seated people ate and drank and talked above the background music. Daniel wondered how much 'time' had elapsed since his last visit; he was surprised that, unlike his previous visits, he had not entered the dream at the same point where he had left it, and felt slightly cheated. He hoped he hadn't missed anything important.

Once again Daniel wondered where all the people had come from. Where did they live? Why hadn't he seen them during the day? He hadn't seen anything like enough

Daniel's Dream

accommodation in the village to account for all of them. Was there another village nearby? Did they only come out at night? There were so many questions.

'Have you lived here long?' asked Daniel, reaching into his pocket and finding a pack of cigarettes. He offered Barry a cigarette, took one for himself, and only then noticed that the packet had been full; he also found a couple of five-hundred-drachma notes in his pocket.

'About four years,' said Barry. 'I came, I saw, and I stayed. You know, once you find a place like this, it makes it tough to go back.'

'Back?'

'Yeah, back home.' Barry did not elaborate, but looked towards the doorway and nodded. 'You seen Kate yet? She was looking for you.'

'She's outside,' replied Daniel. He wondered what it was that he had said that had caused Barry to change the subject so swiftly. Clearly there were rules in Atheenaton that you transgressed at your peril. 'Will you join us for a drink?'

Barry smiled, relief evident in his expression. 'Thanks, Daniel. I'd love to but I'm kind of busy right now. Maybe later, okay?'

'Sure.' Daniel tried to cover his disappointment. He wanted to continue talking to Barry, wanted to know what he was doing in Atheenaton, what had brought him here.

Daniel realised how bizarre these thoughts were. Was it possible that he wanted to interrogate the characters who populated his very own dream? Already he was starting to see these people as real, independent individuals. It was impossible to think of them as figments of his own imagination. They seemed so . . . *complete*.

'I'd better get back to Kate before she starts wondering where I am,' said Daniel, downing the contents of the glass and getting up from the bar. 'Thanks for the drink.'

'My pleasure,' said Barry, filling the shaker with another assortment of liqueurs and fruit juices. 'I'll catch you later.'

Daniel stopped by the door, resisting the impulse to wake himself out of his present environment by pinching himself hard. It was all too strange.

Back on the patio, Daniel found Kate circulating among the tables, her unmistakable laughter – a rather dirty guffaw – penetrating the night air at regular intervals. She seemed very popular, and Daniel wondered what it was she actually *did* in Atheenaton. For that matter, what did any of the people seated around the patio on this warm evening do?

He saw Kate beckon him over to a table in the far corner, where a young couple appeared to be busily engaged in conversation. Daniel wandered across and joined them. A few fireflies glowed in the dark beyond the patio.

'Did you see Barry?'

'Yes. I tried to persuade him to join us but he was rather busy.'

'Works like a slave,' muttered Kate, then quietly, so that the others would not hear, added: 'But he loves it. Couldn't survive without the Pumphouse you know; his life's desire.' She patted the seat beside her and motioned for Daniel to sit down.

Only then did he really notice the young couple. Having done so, he found it impossible to take his eyes off them. They were both, quite simply, beautiful.

'Daniel,' said Kate, and gestured towards the young

Daniel's Dream

man, 'this is Kostas. He lives up in the hills behind the village.'

Daniel reached forward and offered his hand. Kostas, who looked as if he might once have been one of those deeply chiselled stone statues of a young Greek god, brought to life by a sorcerer's spell, rose to his feet and returned Daniel's formal handshake. His movements were sure and elegant, as were his clothes: dark navy slacks and a plain white silk shirt open at the neck to reveal a neat triangle of tight, glossy black curls. So thick were these tufts of chest hair that they suggested a body covered almost entirely in black fur. For a moment Daniel felt oddly threatened by this stranger, whose bestial, overtly sexual physique put him in mind of the Priapus of Greek mythology, with his satyr's horns and huge, erect phallus rising from a thicket of goat hair.

'I am pleased to meet you,' said Kostas, his voice deep and resonant.

'Likewise,' said Daniel, who could not help glancing discreetly at the man's groin. He wasn't sure what he expected to see; a suggestion, perhaps, of something larger than life lurking behind the folds and creases. Daniel chided himself for his prurience; this place, he thought, is playing havoc with my imagination.

But greater flights of fancy lay ahead. Sitting beside Kostas was one of the most beautiful women Daniel had ever laid eyes on. She was dressed in a short, pretty cotton dress that revealed long, shapely, deeply tanned legs. She had glossy, shoulder-length hair, jet-black and gleaming beneath the fairy lights. Her dark-brown eyes were almond-shaped, giving her a slightly oriental look, and her full red lips were shaped in a perfect cupid's bow.

She could easily have been a fashion model, and indeed Daniel thought he had seen her before on the cover of a magazine or plastered across a billboard somewhere.

'This is Marianne,' said Kate. The woman nodded and smiled. It was all Daniel could do to avoid staring at her; she was stunning, and Daniel did not doubt that she and Kostas were a couple; they looked perfect together.

At that moment another figure stepped out of the shadows from beyond the patio and walked to the table. When Daniel caught sight of the woman's face he felt his heart shift into overdrive. She was the spitting image of the girl seated opposite him.

'And this is Véronique,' said Kate.

'Pleased to meet you,' said Daniel, rising to his feet swiftly. He wasn't sure why he had stood so abruptly; it just seemed an appropriate response. However, now that he was standing he felt a trifle embarrassed, so he tried turning the move into a chivalrous gesture by pulling a chair out from the table so that the young woman might sit down more easily. Véronique smiled graciously and accepted his offer.

'Sisters?' he asked, looking from one to the other as he took his seat again, then flinched at the stupidity of the question.

'How can you tell?' said Marianne, making no attempt to disguise the sarcasm in her voice.

Daniel burst out laughing. My dream's a cliché! he thought to himself. Beautiful sisters! No doubt before long there would be a mysterious Prospero-like figure inviting him to participate in a bizarre series of games . . .

No one seemed bothered by his outburst, and neither of the sisters had taken offence. Daniel was convinced that

Daniel's Dream

nobody in Atheenaton ever took offence at anything. It was all so easy here; no one sought to explain themselves or their actions, no one seemed hassled or bothered or angry or upset. It wasn't like real life at all. Daniel resisted the impulse to endorse it as preferable, although that was exactly how he felt.

He looked from one sister to the other and nodded slowly. Now that he could study them both it was clear that, although strikingly similar, they were not identical. They were both, however, quite beautiful, and if Daniel had had to choose between them he would have been hard pressed to say which of the two was more attractive, although even after such short acquaintance he found something harsh, even aggressive, about Marianne, which was a little intimidating.

'You are from England?' The young Greek man leant forward in his chair and rested his forearms on the table. Daniel nodded.

'Good, that is good. Perhaps you can help me to improve my English?'

'Sure,' said Daniel, with difficulty shifting his attention to Kostas. 'But I don't know how much use I could be; your English sounds pretty good already,' he added politely, although the man's accent was, in truth, almost impenetrable.

'You are kind, but there is always room for improvement I think, yes?'

Daniel looked across at Kate, who seemed to be enjoying the exchange with unnatural enthusiasm.

'Kostas dances at one of the other tavernas,' she said, seeing Daniel's eyes upon her. 'You'll have to go along one evening to watch him.' She took a long swig from her glass, then sat back, a warm, satisfied smile illuminating her face.

'Dance?' said Daniel.

'Greek dance,' said Kostas. 'You have seen this I am sure.'

Daniel nodded. He remembered the dancing from his first trip to Greece, had delighted in the men's synchronous movements as they linked arms and, wedded to the wonderful bouzouki music, eased their way through the complex series of steps. It was appealing to eye and ear, and Daniel – who liked to dance – had always wished he might learn the steps one day. It looked so fluid, so joyful.

The warmth of the night and the effect of the drinks had made him very relaxed. He watched attentively as Kostas leant back in his seat. Marianne leant towards him and, interlacing her fingers with his, whispered something to him. Daniel wondered if she were talking about him, but thought it unlikely; there was something intimate about the act, even though it had been performed in full view of everyone. He turned to Véronique to gauge her response, but she did not seem to have noticed.

'Have you been staying long in Atheenaton?' he asked, leaning back in his chair. He wanted to appear calm, casual, but even talking to her made him nervous. He hoped she wouldn't notice.

Véronique turned to face him. 'Well, to be honest, I have no idea. One tends to lose track of the days in this place. You'll discover that for yourself, after a while.'

Daniel found Véronique's rich, melodic voice engaging. It lacked the overt sexuality of her sister's but was lifted above the ordinary by the inflexions of accent and the warm, seductive timbre that was somehow soothing.

Daniel's Dream

Daniel wanted to hear her talk more; he didn't care what she said. He tried to prompt her into conversation.

'And are you far from home?'

This time it was Marianne who replied. 'A million miles, maybe more,' she said softly, and gave Daniel a small, knowing smile.

The music played on; more drinks arrived, seemingly without anyone actually ordering them, and once these were consumed, the empty glasses were swiftly replaced with full ones. A stream of people – individuals, couples and occasionally groups of three or four – came and went during the evening in a continuous ebb and flow of new faces, but at the corner table Daniel and his new acquaintances were left undisturbed.

There did not seem to be any particular or obvious traits that connected these visitors; nothing to suggest where they came from. They were of all shapes, sizes and colour, and of differing ages, although curiously there were no children.

Could he really be responsible for all these people? wondered Daniel. Had he really created the four characters who sat around the table, chatting like authentic, discrete individuals, with their own personalities, histories and – apparently – independent thoughts? Daniel didn't like thinking about it; the idea that this was all a phantom world of his own creation made him uncomfortable. So, instead, he sat back and treated the whole affair as if it *were* real, and he was one of a number of holiday visitors enjoying a drink or two among new friends. It was easy enough to do so.

The evening passed slowly, languidly and with an ease and simplicity that Daniel had felt lost for ever from his life.

The drinks continued to materialise before them as if by an invisible hand, and as the company loosened up they took turns telling stories and amusing anecdotes – the sort of traveller's tales told in thousands of late-night bars and cafés the world over. And for the first time in half a year, Daniel laughed freely, unselfconsciously, as if it were the most natural thing in the world.

In particular, Véronique's presence entranced Daniel, and he could not keep his eyes off her. Her mellifluous laughter lulled him into a relaxed mood. In contrast, Kate's percussive giggles provided the necessary energy to keep everybody from falling into an alcoholic stupor, while Kostas's attempts to relate stories of his childhood kept everyone in hysterics. Even Daniel contributed a few stories of his own, something he had not done for a very long time.

Eventually the crowds thinned out and Barry, released from his duties as barman, joined them for the remainder of the night. He brought food from the kitchen: juicy black olives, piquant feta cheese, sweet, ripe tomatoes, warm, crusty bread, slices of refreshing watermelon. He brought bottles of young, fragrant retsina and thick, oily ouzo, and the company of six drank and ate their way through the night. Daniel had never known food and wine to taste so good.

Barry also brought his own unique brand of story-telling, full of sly wit and a carefully crafted cynicism that marked out East Coast Americans from their counterparts in other parts of the country. Every now and then he would nip back inside the taverna and return with another bottle of retsina or a tray filled with hunks of bread and bowls of delicious dips.

Daniel's Dream

The combination of drink and the casual ease of his companions made Daniel unusually garrulous, and he entertained them all with stories concerning his photo assignments in Asia. He did not, however, mention India, Alex or the accident.

Even though he told his stories for everyone to enjoy, it was clear – at least in his own head – that what he most wanted to do was impress Véronique. It was a long time since he had flirted so effortlessly, without fear of reprisals or compromise; after all, it was all just a dream, wasn't it? And if so, then whom was he trying to impress? Himself? A bit of himself? If he stopped to think about it all became confused. So rather than deal with complex philosophical issues, he ignored the occasional stab of conscience, dismissing it as an inappropriate reflex, and just enjoyed himself. That Véronique responded to his tales with pleasure and amusement delighted him.

The inky black night eventually gave way to the amber and crimson dawn. Kostas carried Barry – who had fallen asleep – into the taverna and laid him down gently on the bed in the back room. Marianne and Véronique took their leave and disappeared to wherever they slept, and Kate kissed Daniel on the cheek and led him to her villa on the beach.

As the sun rose over the mountains, she guided Daniel up the pathway, through the doorway, and showed him into a small, white-walled bedroom, with a desk, two beds, and slatted wooden shutters.

'This is your room,' she said. 'You may use it whenever you like; you may stay as long as you wish.'

Daniel looked round the room, but took none of it in; he was too tired. His gaze rested on the inviting bed set beneath the window, and he fell on to it, exhausted.

'Thank you, Kate,' he murmured, as tiredness overtook him. 'I had a wonderful evening.'

Kate smiled. 'Sleep well, Daniel,' she said softly. 'I'll see you in the morning.'

Daniel nodded sleepily. 'I hope so, Kate,' he said, his eyes shut fast. 'I really, really hope so.'

10

Daniel awoke not to brilliant blue skies and the sounds of the sea, but to a dull, cloudy monochromatic afternoon filled with the noise of heavy traffic thundering past the window. He sat up in bed, shocked and disoriented. He did not reach for the pen and notepad, neither did he grab the glass of water on the bedside table. Instead he cursed out loud and collapsed back on to the bed, nearly hitting the back of his head on the wall in the process.

What the fuck is going on? he wondered, the odours of ouzo still redolent in his nostrils. What am I doing back here?

Daniel glanced at the clock. He had been asleep for just two hours, and yet it seemed that a whole night had passed. Frustrated and confused, he got out of bed and wandered downstairs. He switched on the kettle and sat at the kitchen table, waiting impatiently for the water to boil.

Daniel knew, with absolute certainty, that at some point earlier that day he had fallen asleep in a strange bed in a simple villa on a Greek beach that may or may not exist anywhere other than in his head, but that he had woken to the familiar and increasingly soul-destroying surroundings of a bedroom in grimy north London. He also knew that the boundaries between this reality and the other reality, as he now thought of it, were becoming steadily more blurred, and that the definitions by which one distinguished reality from illusion, waking from sleeping, and true from false, had begun to lose their meaning.

Daniel peered into the clouds of water vapour which, erupting from the kettle spout, formed shifting, nebulous shapes in which one could, momentarily, divine other, more solid objects. He had done this dozens of times before, conjuring up all manner of things from the most mundane (flowers, faces) to the surreal (mutilated moonscapes, melting animals) but today he saw only demons and devils, omens of bad luck and portents of evil.

Whenever he returned from Atheenaton to his waking world Daniel felt wretched and dejected. Far from being delighted by his new world, Daniel was more exasperated than ever. There was no telling when – or even if – he would return, at what point in time he would turn up, or for how long he would stay. He also knew that his 'waking' hours were plagued with misery, composed of endless hours of inactivity and depression and filled – for the most part – with people who didn't understand him. Whereas during his 'sleeping' hours, he was a man without a past, without worry, and, perhaps most significantly, without fear.

Yet he seemed to have no control over his access to this other, preferable world. If only I could stay there for a while, he thought as he poured himself a cup of tea. If only I could stay for good.

Daniel's Dream

This last thought both surprised and shamed him. What was he thinking? That a dream world, an ersatz, make-believe world peopled with products of his own imagination was a suitable alternative to the real world? Perhaps he was going crazy after all.

Daniel decided it was in his best interests not to ask too many questions about his present state of mind, as there was every likelihood he would not much care for the answers.

The clock on the kitchen wall reminded him that he should make a move if he was to meet Vince on time. He hoped his best friend might be able to make sense out of a situation that was becoming more and more strange with each passing day. If Vince couldn't help him, then who could?

Vince was already half-way through his second pint by the time Daniel arrived. This was not because he was a heavy drinker; Vince, despite his past reputation as a hard man, practised moderation in most areas of his life these days. Neither was he, by nature, a nervous type. However, the thought of meeting Daniel again had unsettled him.

Daniel's phone call had served only to remind Vince of his shortcomings and how, to a certain degree, he had failed Daniel in the months following the accident. He wasn't the only one, of course; no one had found Daniel's behaviour easy to deal with, but such excuses did not absolve him of his responsibilities. Vince was – had been – was supposed to be – Daniel's closest friend. But he had been unable to cope with Daniel's morbidness, and the pathological fixation on death that possessed him.

Vince felt he had forsaken Daniel in his hour of need, and

while he was, in part, relieved that Daniel now wanted to see him, he was also decidedly apprehensive. Hence the pint and a half of Best Bitter that Vince had poured down his throat in just under thirty minutes. He hoped that, whatever the circumstances, whatever it was that Daniel wanted, he would respond more appropriately this time. If Daniel needed help, of whatever kind, Vince prayed that there was some way in which he could give it.

Daniel strolled up to the bar. There was a moment's pause as the two men appraised one another: it was four months since they had met, but immediately Vince could tell that it was a very different man who stood before him. Although Daniel still displayed the anguish of a man carrying a great weight upon his shoulders, he at least looked like a man alive, rather than the defeated, almost ghoulish apparition that had greeted him last time. On that occasion, still reeling from the consequences of the accident, Daniel had worn his hopelessness and desperation like a shroud. This time there was, at the very least, an air of vitality about him.

'Hello, Vince.'

'Watcha cock. Pint?'

Daniel nodded. He too had felt oddly discomfited about this meeting, but Vince's charming (if anachronistic) greeting put him at his ease.

'I have to say it, Danny boy; you're looking on top form.' Vince paid for the drinks and handed Daniel his beer.

Daniel took a sip of beer and swallowed noisily. 'It's good of you to say so, Vince,' he said a touch mournfully, 'but it's not true, is it?'

Vince looked puzzled. 'I mean it, Danny. Compared to . . .' Vince broke off. Was it a good idea to rake up the past, even the recent past? Probably not. 'Well, let's just say you look like you're on top of things. How's the old shoulder-bone?'

'Still tricky, but at least I can sleep at nights. What about you?'

Without having to make too many concessions, and without a trace of embarrassment on either side, they somehow negotiated the potential pitfalls of small-talk with relative ease. Vince was relieved when Daniel mentioned Lisanne casually. For Vince, this would have been the one area of difficulty. He was very fond of Lisanne, and if there were problems with the marriage he was probably the last person who would be able to help out.

Eventually Daniel managed to steer the conversation round to his dreams. He began by detailing the nightmares he had been having. Vince listened attentively, nodding now and then, not just in assent but to reassure Daniel that he was not alone in this matter and that he, Vince, had undergone much the same experience.

When Daniel shifted tack, however, Vince started to feel uncomfortable. In his haste and anxiety, Daniel had not prefaced his revelation concerning Atheenaton with the light-hearted, dismissive comments he had intended. Consequently Vince found himself on the end of a lengthy, intense account of everything that had happened so far in Daniel's dream. He listened without interruption, trying hard to concentrate on the content of Daniel's monologue, wondering how the hell he was supposed to respond.

It seemed to Vince that, even in the retelling of the story, Daniel was off in some exclusive little world of his own: he had rarely seen anyone deliver a tale with such conviction.

It unnerved him. At times, it sounded not just strange but positively barmy.

Only when Daniel had finished did Vince speak. He had already decided that he was not going to humour his best friend. Daniel had come to him out of great need, and although Vince was at a loss as to what Daniel wanted from him, he figured that, if nothing else, Daniel deserved an honest response.

'What can I tell you, Dan? It sounds . . . well, look, this isn't really my field . . .'

'You think I'm making it up.'

'Not a bit of it. Why shouldn't I believe you? I mean, it sounds amazing.'

'You mean it sounds crazy.'

'I didn't say that.'

'But you thought it.'

'Nah. If I discovered paradise I'd also want it to be like Club 18–30 . . .'

'Vince . . .'

'Sorry. Sorry. I'm not making fun, honest. It's just, well, I mean . . . *dreams*.'

Daniel nodded. 'I know. They're not exactly what you'd call relevant, right?'

Vince cleared his throat noisily. He could see that Daniel was in a real state over this, and desperately wanted to be of some comfort to him. But besides wanting to ease his friend's evident anxiety, he felt he owed it to him to be honest, although he shied away from actually accusing Daniel of being mad.

'Listen to me, Dan. In my world dreams don't exactly hold centre stage. My life's too mundane for dreams to be anything other than a distraction, something that *happens*.

Daniel's Dream

My dreams don't carry over into my real life. Maybe that's wrong. Maybe I'm missing out on something important. All I know is, I've never had a dream like the one you've described, so I can't imagine what effect it might have on me. Common sense suggests I'd probably treat it in the same way as I did everything else. I'd laugh it off. But you *know* me. You know what I'm like.'

Daniel smiled. 'Yeah, I suppose so.'

'I don't mean to dismiss what you've been through. For all I know, you've tapped into something important. All I know is, I'd be careful about who I discussed it with.'

'You *do* think I'm mad.'

'All I'm saying is that you ought to be careful. I'm not the sort to jump to conclusions, but I'm sure . . . Here, you haven't spoken to any doctors about this, have you?'

'No, Vince,' said Daniel wearily. 'Don't worry; no men in white coats are going to come chasing after me with a strait-jacket.'

Vince frowned. He realised too late that he had done the wrong thing, and that any intimation that Daniel was off his rocker was likely to cause harm.

'Actually, you should talk to Janice: she's into that sort of stuff.'

'What sort of stuff?'

'You know . . . aromatherapy, crystals . . .'

' ". . . all that bollocks . . ." '

Vince laughed. 'Yeah, well, she's always rabbiting on about her dreams and how real they are and that. Personally, I don't know what she's on about half the time. Like I said, you're not talking to the right man.'

'But you see the problem. I had to talk to someone who knew me, who at least didn't think I was a nutter.'

Vince twitched uncomfortably at the reference; the thought was now revolving steadily in the back of his mind, flashing on and off like the blue light of a speeding police car.

'Or Lisanne,' he said, hoping to change the subject. 'Why don't you talk to Lisanne? She'd be much better qualified than me in these matters.'

Daniel nodded reluctantly, then sighed. 'I can't. I can't talk to Lisanne about it. And I can't explain why.'

Vince could see that the thought of discussing it with Lisanne made Daniel especially uncomfortable. He could not think what there was in the dream that could not be mentioned to your wife: after all, there was nothing sick or dirty or even shocking in it. Now *that* was something that Vince could have discussed with Daniel, albeit not in such public surroundings. Vince was still crazy about Janice, but there were certain events in his dreams that he would never tell her about.

They had one more drink before Vince made his excuses. He reiterated his offer that Daniel and Lisanne must come to dinner one evening. Before saying their farewells, Vince took hold of Daniel's elbow (the closest he had ever come to showing physical affection to his best friend).

'Listen, Danny, I know I've not been much use to you this time . . .'

'That's not true . . .'

'No, no, let me have my say. I feel like I've let you down in the past, and I haven't exactly made myself useful this time either. But I want you to know . . . I mean, it's important for me that you know I care, and that you can phone any time, day or night. It's something I should have said ages ago, when you came back, only—'

Daniel's Dream

'Vince,' interrupted Daniel, 'you have nothing to feel bad about. You and Janice were marvellous. All this stuff, this business . . . it was *my* responsibility, *my* pain, *my* anger, and I had no right to expect anyone to take any of it away. I didn't deal with it well. In fact, I acted very badly – I know that now. Perhaps I still am. But whatever, it's up to me. You *were* there for me. I just wasn't very gracious about accepting help at the time.'

'Well I don't know . . .'

Daniel grabbed Vince's right hand in his and held it firmly.

'Trust me. You have nothing to reproach yourself for.'

Vince shook Daniel's hand and nodded. 'It's good to have you back, Dan.'

'Thanks. It's good to be back,' said Daniel, and he spent the rest of the evening wishing that sentiment was even partially true.

That evening, after dinner, Daniel and Lisanne sat together in the living room, not talking. There was nothing unusual about that. If Lisanne wasn't working late, the evenings were often spent not talking. Even before the accident, 'not talking' was the steady-state of their relationship. Not because they had nothing to say to each other. On the contrary, before the accident had driven a wedge between them, they had more often than not been perfectly content just to sit with each other, particularly in the evenings.

Often Lisanne would sit and read one of the interminable manuscripts that measured out her days and weeks like milestones, while Daniel sorted photographs, watched television, listened to music or read a book. In this manner they would pass several evenings each week, and there was never any sense that they were being deliberately uncommunicative or antisocial. It was comfortable. In fact, Daniel had once thought this a true test of compatibility – to be able to sit together in the same space for hours without feeling the need to talk.

However, since the accident this habit of not talking had become a convenient way of avoiding the problems that now circumscribed their relationship. Lisanne still read her manuscripts and Daniel still read a novel or watched the television, but instead of comfortable quietude an uneasy silence now hung in the air like a bad smell.

Consequently, when the two of them sat together in the evenings these days, they found themselves trying to involve each other in occasional conversation, to make small-talk, in an attempt to alleviate the strained atmosphere and bridge the cavernous space between them. As if a few choice, well-intentional comments could heal the gaping wounds.

That evening Lisanne sat on the sofa, leafing distractedly through a manuscript. Daniel sat in an armchair, staring fixedly at the television screen, wishing he could be somewhere else. Anywhere else.

An unfunny sitcom gave way to a hysterical consumer programme exposing the dangers of mouthwash. This was followed by half an hour of Bad News – that was how Daniel thought of it these days – and a depressing five minutes in the company of a weatherman who delighted in informing his audience that more rain and cold winds were sweeping down from the north.

Daniel flipped absentmindedly through the channels. He settled eventually on a Channel Four documentary. It was already half over, and as soon as Daniel realised the

Daniel's Dream

subject matter he cursed silently his lack of discipline in the matter of reading television schedules. The documentary was about dreams.

Daniel tuned in intently to what remained of the programme. He was surprised and delighted to discover that the subject was being treated seriously: all too often, programmes about dreams were just an excuse to flood the screen with clichéd special effects (dissolves, soft-focus shots, anachronistic psychedelia and outrageous make-up) before wheeling in a bunch of spaced-out mystics and hippies (usually Californian) who spouted nonsense about ecstatic visions, expanded consciousness and alternative realities. This particular documentary eschewed such trite techniques and focused, in particular, on the work of a German professor who had spent years investigating the phenomenon of lucid dreaming.

Daniel had never come across the term before, but as soon as it was defined, he understood it completely. Apparently, there existed a small percentage of individuals who regularly became self-aware while dreaming and, having established for themselves that they were within a dream, could then *direct* the dream more or less according to their whim. Daniel had never experienced quite this degree of control, but even before discovering Atheenaton he had known what it was to become aware that you were in a dream.

It had happened on a few occasions, all of which followed the same pattern. The dreams were always nightmares, he was always being threatened with torture by individuals whom he did not know or recognise. Often, as the terror reached its zenith, he would realise he was dreaming and knew that he had only to commit some act of self-injury (of a fairly radical nature) to wake himself up and thus escape. Hence, rather than face the punishment threatened by his dream-villains, he would choose to throw himself through a window or leap off the top of a tall building or use whatever was to hand in the dream to shock himself back to wakefulness. It was not an ideal way in which to emerge from sleep, as when he succeeded in escaping from whatever imperilled him in his nightmare he would wake in a panic, a cold, clammy sweat slithering from his face, neck, chest and groin, his heart racing, his throat dry and sore. But, as he usually appreciated once his heartbeat had returned to normal, anything was preferable to the grisly, surreal horrors that his nightmares could conjure up.

So, though lucid dreaming *per se* was not one of Daniel's talents, he recognised the principle. More to the point, the fact that some learned professor had dedicated herself to studying the phenomenon meant he was not a complete fool for wanting to take his dreams seriously.

Daniel watched with increasing interest, as various experiments were detailed, results compiled and theories expounded. The professor – a down-to-earth, no-nonsense woman – clearly believed that there was a good deal more to dreaming than the standard scientific explanation that dreams were just a way of reprocessing information or playing out possible alternative scenarios. Neither was she an advocate of Freud, whose emphasis on children's sexuality failed to explain so much that went on in dreams. If anything, her views tended towards those of Jung, although in many ways she went beyond Jungian analysis to suggest, albeit in passing, that when dreamers dream, they may be inventing domains which, in some obscure way, actually exist. To demonstrate this notion,

Daniel's Dream

the documentary team filmed an experiment which, for Daniel, had mind-numbing consequences.

The professor enlisted the participation of three lucid dreamers. The three men – A, B and C – were unknown to each other before the experiment, but all had a history of being able to control their dreams. The professor introduced them to one another, then separated them and kept them in isolation in three individual bedrooms. She then gave the same task to each man. That night, while they slept, they were to meet up with one another. That was it. No further information was given, and the men were not allowed to have any further contact.

That night while they slept their brain activities were monitored and the periods of rapid eye movement (indicative of dreaming) recorded. In the morning, the professor interviewed each man individually and asked each to recall his dream.

Man A had dreamt that he was walking through a huge, lush forest that seemed to go on without end. He wandered along aimlessly for some time before he remembered that he had to meet the two other men. Eventually he came to a large oak tree in a clearing and thought it a good meeting place, so he stopped walking and waited beneath the tree. After a while, man B appeared and came to stand beside him. They chatted and waited for man C to arrive, but man C did not appear. That was all.

Man B too had dreamt he was walking through a huge forest. He walked for a long time without meeting either of the other two men, and was just about to give up when he spied a large oak tree in a clearing in the distance. He walked towards it and there he found man A waiting peacefully. He joined man A and they talked for a while.

They waited, he said, for man C to appear, but man C never came.

Man C's story was much simpler. He had found himself walking in a huge forest. He walked for hours and hours, but never saw another soul.

By this time the hair on the back of Daniel's neck was prickling as if an electric charge had been passed through it. But the most interesting part was yet to come.

The final few minutes of the programme were devoted to interviewing a pleasant middle-aged Englishman who, it transpired, had dropped out on the hippie trail in the late sixties and eventually wound up in Tibet, where he spent the next twenty years living with an arcane Buddhist sect. These particular Buddhists – some esoteric offshoot of Lamaism, a branch of the Mahayana stream of Buddhist thought – placed great emphasis on the importance of dreams. In fact, long periods were given over to teaching initiates how to dream properly, that is, how to take control of one's dreams and fashion them. This particular novice had spent half his life to date in a world where dreams were accorded equal status with waking experiences. In particular, the Lamas taught initiates how to return to a dream, how to re-enter it and, it transpired, how to pick up where they had left off. After fifteen years of training, most members of the sect had mastered this procedure and consequently experienced and enjoyed serial dreams which were internally consistent and in which they participated not as puppets, guided and moved by external forces, but as individuals, fully in charge of their thoughts, actions and movements.

By the time the disciple left Tibet, he no longer knew which of his two worlds – his dream world or his

Daniel's Dream

waking world – was the 'real' world: they were equally authentic.

When Daniel heard this his flesh went cold. Lisanne, although involved in her manuscript, saw the change in him. She looked over towards the television but saw nothing particularly disconcerting, and returned to her reading. When the programme came to an end, and without drawing undue attention to the matter, she asked Daniel what the documentary had been about.

'Lucid dreamers,' said Daniel flatly. He was disturbed by the Buddhist's confession, but also excited. Someone else *knew*; someone else had experienced the same sensation, had lived in a dream every bit as real as waking life. He wasn't mad, he wasn't hallucinating; it happened. And if it had happened to him, who could say how many other people had experienced similar circumstances?

'Ah,' said Lisanne, her suspicions aroused. 'Like Janice.'

'Janice?'

'Yes. She's often talked about how she controls her dreams.'

'Janice? Our Janice? I mean, Vince's Janice?'

'Yes, of course. Who else?'

'And she's talked about her dreams, lucid dreams, to you?'

'Yes. What is it, Daniel? What's the problem?'

'No, nothing. When did she talk about it? I mean, how come I've never heard her talk about it?'

Lisanne frowned. 'I don't know. Presumably you weren't around when she told me . . . hardly surprising when you think how often you used to be away . . .'

Even before the final word had left her lips Lisanne realised she had made a terrible *faux pas*. She looked away, not daring to meet Daniel's eyes. He was so sensitive these days, so touchy, that anything could set him off. But drawing attention to Daniel's peripatetic past was the sort of thing that was guaranteed to upset him – as if he wasn't already rattled enough. Jesus, me and my big mouth, thought Lisanne.

She looked up and was surprised to see Daniel staring blankly into space, as if he hadn't heard her. Perhaps he hadn't been listening? Lisanne examined his expression for a few moments. There was no doubt about it: Daniel was miles away.

'Daniel?'

'Huh? Oh, yes . . . sorry. You were saying. About Janice.'

'Oh, nothing. Daniel, is this about the nightmares?'

Daniel shook his head lackadaisically. 'No, not really.' He gave a long sigh that turned into an even longer yawn. 'I'm off to bed,' he said, rising from the armchair, his voice tired, his whole body drooping, as if his skeleton had suddenly turned from rigid bone to pliable rubber. Lisanne could hardly believe what she was seeing.

He slouched out of the living room like an old man, leaving Lisanne more disconsolate than ever.

11

'Sleep well?'

Daniel opened his eyes to see Kate standing over him with a cup in her hand.

'Here; I brought you some coffee.'

'Uh, thanks,' mumbled Daniel drowsily. He sat up and reached out his hand. 'Good morning, by the way,' he said as Kate handed him the steaming black coffee.

'Afternoon, actually,' said Kate, 'but I thought I'd let you sleep . . . you looked so tired last night, and there was nothing much to get up for. Anyway, take your time; when you're ready to get up you'll find me on the veranda.'

As Kate drifted out of the bedroom, Daniel pushed open the wooden shutters and allowed the day to flood into the room. He sipped the strong, aromatic coffee, and gazed out at the range of mountains that stretched from one edge of the window to the other, and reached almost to the top of the frame. He tried to focus on the foreground, but it was still too early for him, and he had difficulty fixing his gaze on anything. All he registered was a wash of pale, bleached hues and random, unidentifiable shapes.

Daniel swung his legs out of bed and set his feet on the cool, tiled floor. He threw a towel around himself and went in search of a shower. The villa was not large – just two bedrooms, a combined kitchen and dining room, and the small bathroom – but it was comfortably furnished and had a light, spacious feel to it.

Clean and refreshed, he put on a pair of shorts and wandered outside to join Kate. The sun was high, and Kate was lying on a blanket on the stone veranda, luxuriating in the heat of the afternoon. Daniel walked up to her and sat down on the edge of the stone patio, allowing his feet to dangle over the edge into the long, unkempt grass that led from the villa to the dirt track a few metres away. A few flies buzzed around in the otherwise still, humid air, and a solitary goat lunched on the long grass beside the track.

'What a beautiful day,' said Daniel, not to start a conversation but because it was the dominant thought in his head.

'It's never less than glorious,' replied Kate, opening one eye to look at her newly acquired house-guest. 'If you want some breakfast, there's heaps of food in the kitchen; just help yourself.'

'Thanks, but I don't feel the least bit hungry; probably all that food we ate last night.'

'Oh God yes,' said Kate, propping herself up on one elbow. 'We made pigs of ourselves, but it was a lovely night.'

'Mmm,' agreed Daniel as his mind flicked through these most recent of memories. 'Did everyone get home okay?'

Daniel's Dream

'I suspect so. I saw Barry briefly this morning. He was nursing a fabulous hangover.'

'And what about the girls?'

'Marianne and Véronique? No idea. But they didn't have far to go.'

'Ah,' said Daniel, attempting nonchalance, not altogether successfully. 'Where are they staying?'

'They have a room above a taverna down the beach: "Kyma" – the Waves. That's where Kostas dances.'

'Right,' said Daniel, not wanting to appear too interested, even though he could not erase from his thoughts the vision of Véronique laughing.

Daniel pivoted around and stretched out next to Kate on the patio. They lapsed into a comfortable, easy silence for a while. It was blisteringly hot, and Daniel invited the sun's rays to penetrate through his tender flesh to his tired bones, dissolving his aches and pains away. The contrast between the atmosphere in Atheenaton and that in the cold, wet, grey London of his other life was so extreme as to render any comparison pointless.

As he lay there peacefully amid the sounds of cicadas and the faint tumbling of the waves on the beach less than a hundred metres away, Daniel imagined that, while he was in Atheenaton, he was awake and conscious, and that London and all its problems were just a dream. If he could stay awake indefinitely, perhaps he might never have to return there; perhaps he could stay in this Greek Wonderland for ever.

It was Kate who eventually broke the silence and brought Daniel back from his reverie.

'Daniel?' she said softly, so as not to surprise him or jolt him unnecessarily.

'Uh-huh,' murmured Daniel, turning on to his side to look at her.

Kate drew a long, deep breath, and then paused for a moment before speaking. 'What was she like?'

Daniel searched Kate's face for clues. He knew instinctively that she was referring to Alex, and as she already knew various things about him her question was not altogether surprising. None the less, Daniel didn't answer immediately; he wanted to be sure they were thinking about the same person.

'Lisanne?' he said at last.

'No, silly. Alex. You don't mind me asking, do you?'

Daniel paused. Did he? Did he mind someone – even someone in a dream – breaking the taboo and asking him about Alex? He wasn't sure, but he decided to show willing; after all, if one couldn't experiment in one's dreams . . .

'No, no. Of course not,' he said, as lightly as possible, but even as the words left his lips his conscience was darkened by a rush of memories that he was powerless to forestall.

Alex. No one had spoken her name aloud for months; no one had dared to mention her. Even now, six months after her death, none of his friends had any idea of what had really happened between them. No one understood the depths of his despair, the anguish that he suffered. They thought he was mourning the loss of a colleague, a friend perhaps. But that barely touched upon the truth. Alex was dead, and no one had had the slightest notion of what she had meant to him.

After all this time, Daniel still found it difficult to

concede that he had committed a sin. In his attempts at rationalisation, he told himself that it had been just a fling – a short affair with an attractive, delightful and engagingly sexy young woman who had made it evident, almost on first contact, that she was more than a little interested in him. And what man, stranded thousands of miles from home in a city in a foreign country, would have found it easy to resist such a come-on, especially when he was daily entering war zones and battle grounds, dodging flying fists and occasionally speeding bullets, just to get a picture for the front cover of some newspaper or magazine? It was true what they said: danger was an aphrodisiac, and when one introduced that chemistry into the sort of high-tension environments that Daniel inhabited, then it was only a matter of time before the inevitable occurred.

For all his blustering self-justification – his unvoiced pleas of mitigating circumstances and situations beyond his control – it was true that, up until the time he and Alex had been thrown into the Ayodhya crisis in northern India, Daniel had managed to resist such impulses. Not that such abstention in itself absolved one of the sin, but it was still the case that this one commission was something of a lapse, a black mark in an otherwise unspotted copybook.

There *had* been opportunities previously, and there had been a number of propositions over the years – after all, he was not an unattractive man. But he had resisted, albeit with some exercising of willpower, not least because he truly loved Lisanne, was happily married, and had never wanted to do anything that might jeopardise his relationship with her.

But Alex had turned his head. She was different: not just physically attractive, but possessed of a special quality, not easily defined, that placed her apart from all the pretty young female journalists on the circuit. She had a certain zest for life, an enthusiasm that was both appealing and infectious. One could not help but have a good time around Alex, and in a short time she had established quite a reputation for herself, not just as an outstanding writer, but also as the life and soul of the party, *any* party, whenever and wherever there was one to be found.

Alex was good company, something Daniel appreciated from the moment they met. India was not the easiest of places in which to work, and having someone around to share the burdens made life a good deal more tolerable. This became particularly evident during the Ayodhya crisis.

The Babri Masjid mosque in Ayodhya had become the focus of some of the worst sectarian violence since Partition. Hindus claimed that the mosque had been erected on the site of a sacred temple, razed to the ground by the Mughals, who conquered the area in the fifteenth century. The temple was supposedly the site where the god Rama had been born. Hindu fundamentalists had been agitating for the mosque to be demolished and for a new temple of Rama to be built in its place, and indeed a number of Hindu fanatics had attacked the mosque and caused considerable damage. Inevitably, this had resulted in high-octane confrontations and serious, bloody riots.

Alex and Daniel were both sent by one of the Sunday broadsheets to cover the incident. On their first day in the area, having had to duck various airborne missiles, including several rocks, sticks and bottles, they retired to their hotel, shaken and stirred and ready for a little liquid anaesthetic. Although neither of them was what

Daniel's Dream

Daniel referred to as a 'career drinker', the events of the day had really unsettled them, and, rather than stomach the cheap, locally produced whisky served in the dismal bar attached to the hotel, they repaired to Daniel's room and duly polished off the whole of his duty-free allowance, in the shape of a bottle of Johnnie Walker Black Label.

Looking back, Daniel was to recall that although he had never been seduced before, it did not feel strange or unusual and that, in fact, with a bit of practice he could quite get used to it. At the time, however, he had reservations, not the least of which concerned what would happen if Lisanne ever found out. But, under the influence of strong drink and the attractions of Alex's long, lithe legs, pert bottom and firm, round breasts – all of which she flaunted with the vigour and ease of a professional stripper – even these fears dissipated.

Alex made the first move. It was not in Daniel's nature to chase after women, but he was not immune from the sort of seductive techniques that Alex had practised to perfection. Like most men, Daniel was a sucker for flattery, and Alex used her skills in the one arena where all men were vulnerable: their sexuality. Her manner, while subtle, indicated in no uncertain terms that the object of her interest was, in her eyes, one hundred per cent, gold-plated, high-octane *sexy*. Take a slim, beautiful, exciting woman and have her show a man – any man – that the only thing she wants to do is sleep with him, and he becomes putty.

In bed, she was, if not a revelation, then certainly a very pleasant surprise. Alex was not just keen on sex, she revelled in it. The whole arena of physical contact was a source of endless pleasure for her, and she played an active role in exploring new areas of potential gratification. She was young – younger than Daniel, certainly – and had discovered early that, if you approached it properly, the world could be a great big playground. And in general, while women were her friends, men had become her toys.

And Daniel fell for it. He fell for the compliments paid to his form and physique, to his animal magnetism, his sexual prowess, his way with women. He listened and looked and lapped it all up. Alex understood men, understood their strengths and weaknesses (especially their weaknesses), and used that knowledge to manipulate them wholly and entirely. Even if Daniel had suspected this at the time – that he was no more than the most recent participant in a long-running game – he probably wouldn't have cared. In bed Alex brought his many and varied fantasies to life. She was young, willing and skilled, capable of performing feats and actions that Daniel had previously only imagined.

In the morning they both woke with hellish hangovers and fuzzy but unmistakable auras of guilt, which hovered around them for most of the morning until, in an effort to exorcise these spectres, they decided to go to bed again, this time sober, and face any consequences that might arise. The idea uppermost in Daniel's mind when he made the suggestion was not that this was a cunning way of getting laid again, but that without the booze and blinding excitement caused by the dangers of the previous day, the couple would in all likelihood find each other less than passionately arousing, thus putting paid to any notions of guilt that might otherwise hang around them like a bad smell.

Unfortunately – at least for Daniel's conscience if not his

Daniel's Dream

libido – the second coupling was even more intense than the first, and, much as he would have liked to deny it, with this confirmation of their mutual attraction he soon found himself deeply – and destructively – attracted to his companion.

It was not surprising that the rest of their time in India was spent – when not ducking broken bottles and the abuse of religious extremists – attempting to discover which of two as yet untried sexual positions caused the most laughter, pleasure, discomfort and/or pain.

And then, on what was scheduled to be their final day in Ayodhya, tragedy struck.

They were driving out of town, back towards the hotel, when an aggrieved agitator (whose religious and political persuasions were never discovered) hurled a home-made fire-bomb – a sort of oversized Molotov cocktail – at the windscreen of their speeding jeep. Before Daniel had even registered what had happened, the jeep had careered off the road, out of control, hit a bank of earth at high speed, flipped over several times, then crashed with full force into a banyan tree that for five hundred years had been minding its own business, doing no one any harm.

The driver was killed on impact, and had Daniel not been thrown free of the wrecked vehicle he, like Alex, would certainly have died in the inferno that followed. The flames raged on for hours, fed by hot winds and by the tinder-dry wood of the banyan tree, and when they finally died down there was not enough left of Alex even to identify her.

Alex died, and he lived. It was a result without justice, without reason, without decency. He too should have perished. Or else, they should both have survived. It was an outcome that diminished him, degraded the quality of his life, subtracted from his right to live. If such things could happen in the world, it was not a world in which he wanted any part.

Daniel looked up at Kate wistfully. Here was someone whom he could trust, someone, perhaps, to whom he could pour out his heart. The feelings, thoughts, ideas; the guilt. He had never had a chance to finish things with Alex, to break it off, as would have happened inevitably had she lived. He had cheated on Lisanne, and in some bizarre way the affair was caught in limbo, suspended like a fly in amber, there to haunt him all his days. It was unfinished business, and would always remain so.

But at last, after keeping the guilt bottled up inside for so long, he could talk about it, tell another soul how he really felt. The rush of emotion that accompanied these feelings was so intense that, for a moment, as the words formed upon his lips and he gazed into Kate's eyes, he could feel the world around him starting to thicken, darken and dissolve, found his usually acute senses attenuating, as if he had suddenly been plunged into a giant tank of murky water, and before he had a chance to issue so much as a word, everything went black.

12

Daniel awoke in distress. Something had gone wrong with his dream. He had woken without a single thought in his head: no music, no visions, nothing. He felt bereft, hollow; as if someone had sucked the breath of life out of him. He started to panic; what if he had lost it? What if Atheenaton had disappeared? What had Kate said about questioning it too closely, about not fitting? Had he overstepped the mark somehow?

He went to the bathroom and splashed cold water on his face, hoping it might calm him down. As he dried his face he tried to recall what had last happened in Atheenaton, but he was confused and distraught. He tried to relax with some deep-breathing exercises, but this didn't work. He could not get a grip on it; he could not conjure up a single, solid image of Atheenaton. Suddenly the whole place felt like a mirage, insubstantial and illusory.

He ran down to the living room, turned on the stereo and put on his precious record of Greek music, but although the music was pleasing and familiar it failed to bring anything back to him. He searched around for the dreadful *Greek Idyll* in the hope that it might trigger his memory; much as he hated it, he had to admit that there were undeniable, though tenuous, links between the novel and his experiences in Atheenaton. Perhaps it would help to jog his memory.

Daniel turned the room upside down looking for the book; he could not remember what he had done with it. All he knew was that he had kept it out of sight for fear Lisanne would see him reading it: he knew she would question him on it, and he didn't feel up to an inquisition on the matter.

He found the book eventually, stuffed away in a drawer in the bedroom: Lisanne must have tidied up recently and thrown his clothes on top without realising it. He opened the book where he had left off.

Daniel read three more chapters, trying, with some difficulty, to ignore the turgid dialogue and tedious commentary and to concentrate on what there was of plot. If Jameson's ill-conceived novel had any relevance to Daniel's dream, it lay hidden somewhere in the story-line.

He was about to investigate further when the telephone rang. He hesitated, unsure if he should answer it. If it was Lisanne, she would probably be calling to check up on him, and he was in no mood for that. And if it was Vince, it would almost certainly be because he felt obliged to keep in touch, now that they had re-established contact: if so, it could wait. And if it was someone Daniel had not spoken to for months, frankly he couldn't be bothered.

The phone continued to ring, suggesting to Daniel either

that the call was urgent or, more probably, that someone was calling for Lisanne: some neurotic author having a breakdown and needing *desperately* to talk to her. That Lisanne had actually given out their home phone number 'in case of emergencies' was something Daniel had never understood.

The phone kept ringing. Eventually, against his better judgement, he answered it, hoping like hell that it wasn't some jumped-up wordsmith having kittens because he was 'blocked'.

'Hello, Daniel?'

He did not recognise the voice until the caller had identified herself. It was Janice.

Thanks to some poor calculations on Daniel's part, concerning both the distance between his home and Crouch End, and also an overestimation of his average walking speed, he was about twenty minutes late meeting Janice. Fortunately, the Acacia Tea-rooms, with its mix 'n' match pre-war decor (which Daniel always likened to an ageing aunt's living room), was a pleasant place in which to while away an afternoon, and Janice was clearly not the least perturbed by his tardy arrival.

'Hello, Daniel, how lovely to see you,' she said, kissing him lightly on both cheeks. 'You're looking very well.'

'Thanks. You're not too shabby yourself.'

Janice laughed. 'Oh dear, I'm sure that's not the sort of thing you'd have said if you hadn't spent an evening in Vince's company recently. I swear these terrible expressions of his are contagious.'

Daniel sat down opposite Janice and beckoned one of the waiters over. The walk had made him thirsty, and he was looking forward to a pot of one of their speciality teas. Ever since visiting Darjeeling on a photo-shoot some years previous, he had been a tea *aficionado*. Until then, tea – and in particular, *chai* (the commonly available drink served up all over the sub-continent, made from tea dust, powdered milk and copious quantities of sugar, boiled up together and strained through an oily rag) – had been something of a utilitarian beverage, something you drank more out of habit than intention.

But in Darjeeling all that changed. High up in the foothills of the mighty Himalayas, he photographed the cheerful teams of dark-skinned, brightly clothed women as they moved up and down the steep, verdant hills, picking the leaves by hand with all the swiftness and accuracy of automatons. The bright saris with their brilliant slashes of colour set against the deep, luminous emerald green of the tea bushes and the intense sapphire-blue mountain skies provided him with some of his all-time favourite shots.

And in the dilapidated, Victorian-era tea-rooms that could still be found, perched precariously on the edge of the town overlooking the valleys, he tasted the wondrous, fragrant tea – freshly brewed from the young, green leaves – and discovered that tea could be an exotic and refined beverage, with a variety of flavours and aromas that made it truly something special. Although he had never since enjoyed a cup of tea to rival that which he had sampled in Darjeeling, the Acacia Tea-rooms was one of the few places locally that could provide a reasonable approximation to the real thing.

'You know, it was great seeing Vince again,' said Daniel. 'I felt guilty that it had been so long.'

'You know very well that there's no need to feel guilty

where we're concerned.' Janice smiled, reached across the table and placed her hand gently on Daniel's. 'How's Lisanne?'

'She's well . . . busy, as always.'

'I must give her a call. Did you tell her you were meeting me?'

'No, I just came straight here.' Daniel paused, examining Janice's face for clues. He had no idea why she had insisted they meet; why, in fact, she was being so mysterious. It was not, he thought, in character. 'Janice, it is, of course, lovely to see you again but . . . well, what's this all about?'

Janice nodded gravely. 'I hope you won't be angry with Vince: he told me all about the conversation the two of you had the other night. That's why I thought I ought to see you.'

'Ought?'

Janice was silent for a moment; Daniel could see her urgently trying to compose her thoughts. 'I can't begin to understand what you've been through, Daniel . . . the accident, I mean. Even now, all these months later, I'm sure it still hurts like hell, and I don't suppose anyone will ever understand what that feels like. I can, however, appreciate that it must have turned your whole world upside down, thrown everything into confusion.'

'You said it.'

'Well, I've been through some pretty tough times myself. I don't know if Vince ever told you about my sister?'

'No, I didn't even know you had a sister.'

'She died about ten years ago. We were on holiday together and there was a terrible boating accident. I shan't go into details, because they're not important. What is important was that I was in the boat at the time. I escaped pretty much unharmed, but Mary drowned.'

'I'm sorry. I had no idea.'

'I tend not to talk about it; it's a long time ago now.'

One of the waiters finally approached the table and Daniel ordered. He looked at Janice, at her large, soulful eyes, and for a moment felt a true empathy with her. It was an unfamiliar experience, for he had not previously experienced his own sense of loss as something that might be shared. He had held it to himself, clutching on to it with a sort of macabre desperation, the only thing he could salvage from the ghastly event that had nearly swept him out of this world for good, to become just one of other people's sad, fleeting memories.

'Death,' said Janice with a solemnity that caught Daniel off guard, 'affects people in different ways. Ever since Mary's death I've been uncomfortable being around the bereaved, which is perhaps why I wasn't much use to you when you came back from India. I'm really sorry about that now.'

'Janice, you don't need—'

'No, not because I think I failed you. After all, one can only do what one is capable of, and the fact is that there was no way I could have helped you then. Or at least, I didn't believe there was a way. It's only since Vince told me about your conversation the other night that I've realised that I might be able to help you now.'

'How do you mean?'

The tea arrived. Daniel poured for both of them while Janice stared out of the window, seemingly lost in thought.

'Janice?'

Daniel's Dream

'What? Oh, sorry. Listen, Daniel, I've not spoken about this to anyone, for reasons that you will now probably appreciate.' Janice raised her cup to her lips and sipped carefully. She gazed out through the window again, momentarily distracted. The brilliant blue skies that had accompanied Daniel's walk had darkened, prefacing the onset of a summer storm, and the deep, reverberant rumblings of thunder boomed ominously in the distance. Within seconds the first few drops of rain splashed against the window pane, jolting Janice out of her reverie.

'About a month after Mary died,' she began, hesitantly, 'I had this remarkable dream. In the dream I found myself walking along a dry, dusty path. It was hot and sunny, and I seemed to be completely alone.'

Daniel's interest was instantly aroused. Janice was not the sort of person to play games, and these first intimations of something so familiar caused his pulse to quicken. He leant forward and listened intently.

'At first, I didn't realise that it was a dream at all. It felt as if I was on holiday; you know, blue skies, hot sun . . . it was an automatic assumption. Anyway, eventually, having walked for a while, I came to a small, deserted café. It was so hot that I decided to rest for a while in the shade. It was incredibly peaceful; there was a stillness about the place, a particularly comforting quietness that I can remember to this day. Anyway, a waiter appeared and fetched a drink for me. I remember thinking how pleasant it all was, what a relief it was to be away from home and all the problems I had. I reached for the drink – coffee, it was – but as soon as I drank some, I blacked out. The next thing I knew, I was in bed at home. It was the middle of the night. Only then did I realise I'd been dreaming. I didn't think anything of it at first, but then that night I dreamt about the same place. What's more, the dream started where it had left off previously.'

Daniel could hardly believe what he was hearing. 'Was there a pump outside the restaurant?' he asked urgently. 'Like an old fashioned hand-pump? And Greek writing on the menu? And the owner was a tall American called Barry?' A flash of lightning streaked across the rooftops opposite, attended moments later by a deafening report, an explosive crash of thunder that shook the windows.

Janice stared at the rain streaming down the window. 'No, no pump,' she said distractedly, then returned her attention to Daniel. 'No Greek either. And the owner, when I finally met him, was a German guy called Kurt. It was all rather odd.'

Daniel's face fell. For a brief moment he had dared to believe the impossible: that someone else had visited Atheenaton. He sipped his tea unenthusiastically, having forgotten the raging thirst that had accompanied him into the tea-rooms.

'But the thing is,' continued Janice, so caught up in her recollections that she failed to register the disappointment on Daniel's face, 'it didn't stop there. For several nights I returned to the same place. It was a small village set in this glorious, wind-sheltered valley half-way up a mountain. And it was peopled with the most charming, friendly people. And whenever I was there I felt . . . well I felt great. But I didn't understand it. I didn't understand what the place was. I didn't understand how I could possibly be having this ongoing dream in which the same people always appeared. And I started to feel uncomfortable about it. Anyway, to cut a long story short, eventually I stopped dreaming of the village. But the memories of the place haunted me for weeks afterwards. In the end I went to see someone about it.'

Daniel frowned. 'Someone? You mean a shrink?'

Janice smiled. 'A Jungian analyst, actually. I just had to talk to someone about it, and as I didn't want to be treated like a lunatic I thought it best to discuss it with someone who understood dreams.'

'And what did he tell you, this analyst?' Daniel could not disguise the derision in his voice, but hoped Janice would not take offence.

'Well, to be honest, he didn't tell me anything specific about my dreams at all. He didn't try to analyse or interpret them. Instead, he just allowed me to hypothesise about the village's importance and what it might mean; you know the sort of thing: a safe haven where I didn't feel threatened, an escape from reality and all that.'

Daniel nodded. 'You'll excuse me for saying so, but I could have told you that.'

'Oh sure . . . like I said, he didn't tell me anything revelatory. But he did make it seem okay to think about it, to question it.

'After the first few sessions I figured that, nice as it was to chat about these things, since the dream had stopped there wasn't much point in carrying on. But this analyst insisted that we pursue the sessions for a short while.'

'And how much he was charging, this analyst?'

Janice raised one eyebrow. 'Your cynicism is misplaced. He didn't charge me anything for the extra sessions. I think he was genuinely interested in my experience. He said it was rare, though not unique. He would talk about the place, the village, not as if it were imaginary, but as if it really existed. He said something about how he believed people co-created their dreams, that places in dreams are the active product of several dreamers.'

Daniel flinched. '*Co-create*? What, like collaborate?'

'No, not exactly. Look, I can't remember his exact words, Daniel, but the gist of it was that unconsciously or subconsciously – I can't remember which – when you dream, you create a reality that is every bit as authentic and real as this world, only sometimes you dream a world into existence by yourself, but at other times you simply add to a greater entity. I'm not explaining this very well . . .'

'No, go on.'

'Well, it's just that the dreamers are no more aware that they're creating a reality *with* other people than you are when you dream alone. It's only a theory of course, and a pretty wild one at that, but it would at least help to explain how places can seem both familiar and strange simultaneously.'

This certainly rang true; there were some aspects of Atheenaton that were very familiar, even though the place as a whole was unknown to him.

'There's more. This analyst also believed that when you dream of people you don't know, they're not imaginary at all; they're your co-dreamers. Real people who you haven't met in your waking life, who you would probably *never* meet in your waking life.'

Daniel shook his head. 'Wait a minute Janice; surely this must have struck you as all terribly far-fetched?'

Janice smiled. 'Not in the least. I had been there; I had experienced this place, this dream world, with its real people and its seemingly everyday chronology, events unfolding in what felt like "real time". It didn't seem strange or far-fetched at all. On the contrary, it made complete sense. But I knew that to anyone who had not experienced the same, it would all sound like gobbledegook. Oh come on Daniel, you *must* have thought about these things a thousand times. We're so blasé, so unquestioning about sleep and dreams, and yet we know virtually nothing about them. A third of our life is spent unconscious, on a regular basis, the time filled with scenes and visions, and we dismiss it all as nonsense. Well, I don't believe you can dismiss such a huge percentage of your life just because the explanations that start to ring true don't tally with our scientific or logical understanding of how the world works.'

Daniel sighed. 'Yes, but . . .'

'But what? Do you realise there's no accepted understanding of why we sleep? There's no evidence to suggest that the body needs it. A couple of hours relaxing in an armchair is apparently sufficient for all physical requirements. So there must be some other reason, one which is actually staring us in the face yet which we refuse to acknowledge: dreams are not just some sort of meaningless by-product of sleeping. We sleep *in order* to dream.'

'But that still doesn't explain why we need to dream at all.'

Janice sighed. 'I would have thought your recent experiences would have solved that one for good. Just think, Daniel; it's another life, another chance to experience things, things that perhaps aren't available to you in the waking world. And that's what happened to me. And yes, of course, it sounds like complete lunacy.'

'Which is why you've never told anyone.'

'Exactly.'

'Not even Vince?'

'Not even Vince. Oh, I've probably spouted some of the theories at him in moments of weakness, but if so, they would have sounded like the sort of things I'd read about, not experienced. Besides, Vince hasn't got much time for all that.'

Daniel sighed. 'So why . . . I mean, did you ever understand what it was all about?'

'Not really. I expect it was part of the healing process, like mourning; something I had to go through. But – and I think this is critically important – just because I didn't fully understand what it was all about doesn't mean that it wasn't important. Perhaps it was more important than the things I had been through in my waking life.'

Daniel nodded. 'And how did you feel afterwards, when you couldn't go back?'

'Oh, I have to admit, I really missed it for a while. After all, it was so easy. Everything was provided; you didn't have to work or cook or wash dishes. It was just like being a kid again, I guess.'

Janice hefted the antiquated porcelain teapot and refilled their cups. 'I don't know what relevance any of this has for you Daniel. For all I know, it has no connection at all with your dream. I just wanted to let you know that, whatever else you might be thinking, you're not insane. I know it sounds awfully clichéd, but the fact is that we live in a deeply materialistic world that simply doesn't *allow* people to dream any more. Once upon a time, I'm sure, people incorporated periods into each day for musing, day-dreaming, meditating, activities that most people these days would think of as trivial or time-wasting. Everything is time and money and efficiency and unless you're being actively constructive – making money or *doing* something – you're thought of as a malingerer or wastrel. It's insidious, and if I were more politically attuned I'd believe it was a conspiracy, instituted to ensure that no one has enough time to contemplate the truly valuable things in life. Because if they did, then this time-centred, money-oriented, power-crazed society of ours would just fall apart.'

Daniel laughed. 'You sound like an old hippie.'

Janice smiled guiltily. 'Yes, well, there you have it: I *am* an old hippie.'

'Oh come off it . . .'

'What? Oh, I get it. You think I'm far too respectable and middle-class to have ever engaged in anything as anti-establishment as sit-ins or pot-smoking. Well, allow me to enlighten you. I went to university as a mature student. And before that, I spent my late adolescence and early twenties wandering through Asia searching for Nirvana and getting stoned a lot.'

Daniel thought Janice was putting him on. He tried to imagine her – as she so rightly said, thoroughly respectable and utterly middle-class – wearing loon pants, rose-coloured Lennon specs and a tie-dyed T-shirt, blissing out in Kathmandu and reciting lengthy extracts from Kahlil Gibran's *The Prophet*, but, try as he might, the vision refused to materialise.

'What's so funny?'

'Nothing. I just can't visualise you in a kaftan.'

'Oh piss off, Daniel. You're too young to remember, anyway.'

'Wait a minute, I'm thirty-six—'

'Precisely, which puts you right in the heart of that lost

generation, too young to remember the Beatles and too old to have gobbed at the Sex Pistols.'

'Yes, well, I wouldn't have put it quite that way . . .'

'Doesn't matter. The point is, for those of us who came of age during the late sixties life has always meant more than just earning your pile and getting ahead, even if we do tend to lose sight of it with each passing year. All I'm saying, Daniel, is that *whatever* it's about, your dream is precious, deeply precious, and on no account must you allow anyone to take it away from you. Most people's lives are so cram-packed with activities – jobs, babies, bills, social commitments – that they haven't time to catch their breath, let alone enjoy an excursion to a different world. I envy you, Daniel. You've been through the mill, I know, but I suspect that your life has become all the richer for it.'

Daniel shrugged. 'I wish I could be so sure. Sometimes I wish this dream thing had never started. I can't help feeling that all it's going to do is cause confusion or heartbreak.'

Janice frowned. 'Why do you say that?'

'I don't know . . . like I said, just a feeling.'

By the time they had stepped out on to the pavement the rain had stopped.

'Can I give you a lift?'

'Uh, no, thanks. I'd rather walk.'

'Sure?'

'Yeah. I have some things to think about.' Daniel reached out and took Janice's hand. 'Thanks Janice; it was really thoughtful of you to see me like this. I appreciate it. And for confiding in me. It can't have been easy.'

'I hope I haven't made matters worse.'

Daniel's Dream

'Of course not.'

'And if you want the number of that analyst, I'm sure I can track it down. You never know, it might come in handy.'

'I'll let you know.'

Daniel walked Janice to her car and watched her get in. He was about to wave goodbye when she wound the window down and beckoned to him.

'Just one thing Daniel. This bit really isn't my business, and I don't want to put any pressure on you, only I really think you ought to tell Lisanne about all this.'

'You never told Vince about your dream, did you?'

'No, but Vince is . . . well, Vince is Vince. I don't have to remind you that Lisanne is a sympathetic, intelligent woman who not only has an open mind and sensitive, understanding nature but also loves you very dearly. But this isn't a lecture. Just think about it, will you?'

'Okay,' said Daniel. 'I will.'

But as Janice pulled away, it was not his sympathetic, sensitive and understanding wife who occupied his thoughts, but a woman of an altogether different cast.

13

Daniel munched enthusiastically on another stuffed vine leaf.

'These are delicious,' he said, between mouthfuls. 'What's inside them?'

Kate laughed. '*I* don't know; you'll have to ask Stephano.'

'Stephano?'

'The cook.'

'Oh yeah, of course,' replied Daniel, as if he should have known the cook's name in the first place. 'Y'know, I never used to like these. At least, not the last time I was in Greece.'

'When was that?'

'Oh God . . . years ago.'

'And you haven't eaten them since? At home?'

Daniel shook his head. 'Nope. They're available, of course, especially in the area I live in. But Lisanne's none too fond of them either, so . . .'

Daniel broke off for a moment to refill his glass, but only

a few drops trickled out of the carafe. As Kate held up her hand to order some more, Daniel found himself playing an odd game – a sort of thought experiment. If this is a dream, he said to himself, and I'm aware that it's a dream, then surely I should have some control over it, like those lucid dreamers. And if I had control, then I certainly wouldn't allow the wine to run dry like that. I'd organise my dream so that the carafes were bottomless and never needed refilling, and food would never disappear from the plates. But this isn't the case. None of those things is happening, and wonderful as this place is, it isn't my construction.

While waiting for the wine to arrive, Kate scooped up a mound of pink taramasalata on a crusty piece of bread and stuffed it greedily into her mouth. Daniel loved watching Kate eat and drink; she was positively Bacchanalian in her appetites, and Daniel found this unrestrained hedonism refreshing. So unlike Lisanne. So unlike *most* of the people he knew.

Daniel sat back in his chair and gave a deep sigh of unadulterated pleasure. Life should always be this way, he thought. He gazed out across the sand to the horizon. The sun was setting over the sea, and the beach was awash with a golden glow. The wine appeared, the glasses were filled and a toast – to pleasure, to life, to whatever – was proposed and drunk.

Though he now felt comfortable in Atheenaton, Daniel found it impossible to rid himself of the nagging doubts and unresolved queries that surrounded his visits. It was all so good, so perfect, and yet the very question of its authenticity cast something of a pall over what was otherwise nothing short of miraculous. He did not want

Daniel's Dream

to spoil the easy, relaxed mood that he and Kate now enjoyed, but decided that, regardless of the risks, he had to have some questions answered.

He took a hefty swig of wine, drew a deep breath and grabbed Kate's arm.

'This is a dream, isn't it, Kate? I mean, it isn't reality, is it?'

Kate cast her eyes downward, then looked out to sea. 'Does it matter? You're happy, aren't you?'

'But I don't understand,' said Daniel. 'I only come here when I sleep, and yet it's not like any—'

'I know. We all know how you're feeling. But take it from me, Daniel. You don't have to understand anything; you're here, and that's all that counts.'

'But . . .'

'Daniel.' There was a sudden severity to Kate's tone that Daniel had not encountered before, and it took him aback. He abandoned his objections and waited anxiously for Kate to continue. He sensed some sort of explanation or perhaps even revelation in the air.

Kate waited patiently until Daniel was still before continuing. When she spoke, she did so calmly and deliberately.

'Atheenaton, as you realise, is not like other places. It doesn't function like anywhere else, people don't always behave in the ways you're used to, and things happen here that . . . well, that are just different. However, in some ways it's just like home. It can be baffling, surprising and downright incomprehensible. There are not necessarily explanations that can help you. At some level, you just have to trust; to trust the experience, the evidence of your own senses. Think of it like television: you don't have to know how it works to enjoy it . . .'

'You're fobbing me off—'

'Not at all. There's a sort of unwritten agreement among the visitors who come to Atheenaton; we just accept that it exists, and exploit and enjoy all that it has to offer.'

'Exploit?'

'Certainly. Atheenaton is a very special place, and it serves a very important purpose, but – take it from me – you shouldn't try to question it too deeply, or you'll probably find yourself in for a rough ride.'

'Rough? In paradise?'

'Yes, well, even the waters of paradise have undercurrents, you know.'

Daniel shook his head. He wasn't sure he understood exactly what Kate meant by that last remark, but he knew he didn't like the sound of it.

'Is that a threat?'

'Don't be silly.'

Daniel frowned. 'It is, isn't it? It's a threat. What am I being warned off?'

Kate took another swig of wine. Her expression betrayed an impatience that Daniel had not seen before.

'Relax Daniel. There's nothing *to* threaten you here. You can always leave if you don't like it.'

'You know that's not the problem,' said Daniel, irritated. 'Leaving is not the issue. It's staying. I just want to . . .'

Kate sighed, a touch theatrically. 'I hope you won't take this too personally, Daniel, but that's precisely the problem; you want too much. God knows, isn't this place good enough without you having to analyse it?'

Daniel shook his head, gazed out to the beach and

beyond, just in time to see the last remnants of the sun being swallowed up by the dark sea.

'I'm sorry,' he said, not altogether sincerely. 'It's just so frustrating, never knowing when I'm coming back, or how long I can stay.'

'Yes, I know,' said Kate. 'But if you stop making such a big deal out of it, it'll work out fine. You'll see. The more often you come here, the more you'll get to know and feel the place, and your ties to it will grow stronger. But you have to trust it, Daniel; and you have to fit. If you don't, then you won't be welcome.'

Daniel sensed a note of not only caution but also menace in Kate's warning. He didn't think he was being unreasonable, but at the same time he didn't want to put it to the test. It was better to have Atheenaton and not to understand it than to understand it and lose it in the process. He nodded slowly to Kate, sighed gently, and sipped his retsina.

A moment later, they were joined by Marianne, who had descended the stairs that ran along the front of the taverna, her hair dripping wet, as if she had just emerged from the sea. She sat down next to Daniel, leant across and kissed him on the cheek.

'How nice to see you again,' she said, her voice surprisingly harsh and strident. 'But I wish you wouldn't keep taking off all the time. Véronique was saying only this morning that we would never get to know you unless you stayed for more than a few hours. She thinks you're being unsociable, but I know better.' She smiled, reached for the carafe in the centre of the rickety wooden table and poured herself a glass of wine.

Daniel smirked; he felt pleased that the girls had talked about him in his absence, especially Véronique.

'And where is your sister?' he asked as casually as possible, and noticed Kate's conspiratorial grin, only half hidden by her wine glass.

'She'll be down shortly; she's just showering,' replied Marianne, and then added, 'You're rather keen on her, aren't you?' so meaningfully that Daniel choked on his wine. He turned bright scarlet and spluttered nervously.

'No, well, that is . . . I was just . . . you know . . . just friendly concern . . .'

Kate's crude, fruity laughter embarrassed him further.

'Well, don't worry,' said Marianne, throwing Kate a sly glance. 'She'll be here shortly.'

Marianne's long, ink-black hair continued to drip water; several drops landed on her silk blouse to be instantly absorbed and the damp material clung to her like a second, lustrous skin. This sudden, tantalising moment caught Daniel by surprise, and despite himself he could not help gazing appreciatively at Marianne's breasts.

Fortunately, at that moment there was a sound at the top of the stairs, and Véronique appeared in the doorway. She came quietly down the stairs and walked across to the table. As she took her place opposite Daniel, all thoughts of Marianne filtered away into the ether.

'So,' she said huskily, 'the mysterious traveller returns.'

'I was just saying,' chipped in Marianne, 'how you – that is, we – had missed Daniel. I don't think he believes me though, do you?' She eyed Daniel up and down suggestively, making him feel uncomfortable.

'Of course I do,' he said as nonchalantly as possible, then addressed Véronique. 'How are you?'

Daniel's Dream

'She'll say "fine", Daniel, but don't be fooled,' said Marianne. 'Ever since you disappeared she's been wandering around like a puppy that's lost its mother, haven't you, dear?' Marianne turned towards her sister and smiled.

Véronique glared at her sister; a look, thought Daniel, that although not lethal was probably capable of causing a severe flesh wound.

'How about some more wine then?' said Marianne coolly. Daniel smiled uncomfortably and gave a small, nervous nod of assent; clearly Marianne was not a woman to fool around with.

It was Kostas who responded to the call for more wine. He appeared mysteriously from some dark corner of the taverna, large carafe in hand, which he set on the table with a flourish before patting Daniel firmly on the back.

'So, you have come to see me dance?' said Kostas, evidently delighted to see Daniel again.

'Ah, yes,' agreed Daniel, seizing the opportunity provided by Kostas's arrival to deflect attention away from the two petulant sisters. 'But when do we see you? Do you have to wait on tables all night?'

'No, no,' laughed Kostas. 'This is just a . . . how do you say . . . a disguise.' He guffawed at his own joke, which was just as well, as it helped defuse the dark, acidulated atmosphere around the table. 'In a little while you will see me. But first, we drink a little retsina together, yes?'

Daniel poured out a glass for Kostas, and they toasted the evening.

'*Yamas!*' said Kostas, raising his glass to his lips. The others repeated the toast, and downed their glasses in one.

'And again!' said Kostas, grabbing the bottle and

filling the glasses. 'On a night like this, we must get drunk!'

And in the absence of any alternatives, and with no one finding reason to object, it seemed a perfectly sound idea.

Daniel had no idea how many hours had passed by the time he and Véronique found themselves dancing cheek to cheek, the voice of Dmitri Mitropanos and the sound of the bouzouki transforming the taverna into a magical, musical arena. He knew they had consumed a great deal of wine, and had applauded Kostas's demonstration of Greek dances.

Daniel had spent most of the evening talking to Véronique. At some point the group had dissolved, and the two of them had ended up sitting together in a dark corner, watching the events unfold and talking close, intimately. Oddly, although they had been left on their own, and despite the fact that several hours had passed in this manner, Daniel could not now recall the content of any of their conversations. Had they spoken about themselves? About Atheenaton? About love? Daniel did not know.

He remembered seeing Kate, later in the evening, waving to him as she and Kostas left the taverna together, and that Marianne had disappeared on to the beach with Vangeli from the Neraida. But how he had found himself on the patio of the Waves with Véronique in his arms he did not know. Nor did he need to. Not-knowing, like not-questioning and not-understanding, clearly had its place in Atheenaton, and for the meantime, at least, Daniel was happy to go along with this arrangement and remain unenlightened.

Daniel's Dream

One thing was certain; ignorance did little to distract from the general sense of warmth and well-being that he felt, as he and the younger sister moved synchronously to the beautiful melodies of 'Synaxaria' for the second time that night.

The night air was warm and still, and the stars and fireflies glistened in the blue-black darkness. Just a few metres beyond the taverna, the waves broke against the sand, liberating a platinum phosphorescence that effervesced brilliantly for a few seconds amid the silver-tipped plumes before retreating into the sea.

Daniel felt the softness of Véronique's cheek against his own. The weight of her arms around his neck was comforting, and her body felt firm yet relaxed. He breathed in her fragrance and shivered as she ran her hands down his back until they came to rest on his hips.

Even the waters of paradise have undercurrents; that was what Kate had said. But if it was true, Daniel didn't care. He turned his face towards her and kissed her deeply.

And again.

And once again.

'Paradise,' he whispered. 'This *is* paradise.'

Véronique smiled and, without another word, took Daniel by the hand and led him across the floor of the taverna and to the bedroom at the top of the stairs.

She dragged him in through the open door, slammed it shut with her foot and then threw herself into his arms. They kissed passionately for what seemed like hours, and Daniel was so involved, so engrossed in the softness of her lips, the sweet taste of her, that it was only when she pulled away and crossed the room, leaving him standing alone, that he opened his eyes and looked around.

A single, rather dim bedside light – the only illumination – cast its yellow light on to the whitewashed walls and ceiling. The room was small and spartan, dominated by a double bed which was pressed up against one wall to maximise the available space. It was not dissimilar to the room he had used in Kate's villa, only here there were small, personal touches that suggested something proprietorial: a framed photograph of a family group on the bedside table, an Arcadian landscape in delicate water-colours hanging on the wall above the bed, a vase of flowers on the dressing table.

'Come and lie down with me,' said Véronique, who had pulled off the blue-and-white bedspread, kicked off her shoes and was stretching out on the clean, white sheets.

Daniel slipped off his sandals and crossed the room to the bed. Véronique was lying on her side, her back to the wall, her long, jet-black hair splayed out on the pristine pillow. Her arms and legs, deeply tanned, glowed with a bronzed radiance which contrasted dramatically with the cool white sheets. Daniel lowered himself on to the mattress and stretched out beside her. He put his hand to her face and stroked her hair gently.

'You're so beautiful . . .'

'Shhh.'

'No, I have to tell you. You're one of the most beautiful women I've ever met.'

Véronique blushed. 'You're embarrassing me.'

'But you are.'

'Well, if you think so, who am I to disagree?' She

snuggled up closer. 'You're not too bad yourself,' she said, and flashed him a cheeky smile.

Daniel gazed into her eyes, felt her hands reach out to him and felt his heart beat faster at the prospect of what was to come.

'There's just one thing, Daniel,' said Véronique, pulling away slightly. 'You have to understand, there can be nothing . . . nothing permanent about this.'

Daniel looked at her quizzically. 'I don't understand. What are you trying to say?'

Véronique sighed. 'Whatever happens, whatever we choose to do, it can't be taken as sign or signal or . . . I'm not explaining this very well.'

'What are you telling me?' asked Daniel, shocked. 'That this is to be just a one-night stand?' He laughed unconvincingly.

'No, not necessarily. Unless that's all you want, of course.'

'I don't know how you can even think that.'

This time it was Véronique who was shocked. 'Well, for one thing, I know nothing about you. For all I know you may be a very passionate and attractive man who is incapable of holding down a relationship.'

'Wait a minute—'

'No, listen. I'm not saying that's what I believe. All I'm saying is that I don't know you, or anything about you. And more to the point, you don't know me.'

'Well isn't that what relationships are all about, finding out about each other?'

'Yes, of course. But if there are impediments to that relationship – obstacles that limit its progress – then I think it's only fair that they should be declared before anyone gets too involved. All I'm saying is that, regardless of what happens, there can be no future.'

'I don't understand. What sort of impediments?'

Véronique shook her head. 'That's not important. What's important is that it's clear to you that you can make no assumptions.'

'Of course it's important. Why do we have to set limits before anything's even happened?'

'Because we do. You just have to trust me on this one, Daniel.'

'Not unless you tell me what the problem is.'

'I can't.'

'What?' Daniel sat up and pulled away. 'What is this? You lay down these extraordinary ground rules for a relationship that hasn't even started yet, and you can't tell me why?' Daniel's anxiety started to get the better of him. What was she saying? This wasn't part of the plan; this wasn't the way *he* wanted things to go at all.

Véronique sighed. 'Don't get upset . . .'

Daniel stood up and backed away. Suddenly he felt very uneasy, as if he was being threatened in some way, although Véronique had made no threat, either implicit or explicit.

'How can I not get upset?' he said, realising that the ground beneath his feet was becoming progressively less stable. 'What are you keeping from me? What possible impediments could there be? Are you married, is that it? Well so am I. There, does that make it easier? We can be adulterers together.' Daniel almost chocked on the word. Adulterer: it sounded so old-fashioned, so Biblical. Is that what he was? Rather than a normal bloke with an over-active sex-drive who for reasons too complex to fathom didn't fancy his wife any more?

'You're married?'

Daniel felt faint. He leant back against the wall.

'Daniel? Are you okay?'

Daniel nodded. 'I thought you knew.'

Véronique shrugged. 'No, you didn't say.'

'But I thought Kate . . . I mean, Kate knows.'

'Kate is very discreet. She probably knows everything about everybody, but she never breathes a word. There's no way she would betray a confidence.'

Daniel tried to steady himself against the wall, but he still felt very uneasy. 'I'm sorry. I wasn't thinking.'

She shrugged again. 'It's no big deal. I mean, it doesn't worry me that you're married. It may even make things easier.'

'Easier?'

'Like I said, there can be no permanence for us, Daniel. Please don't ask me why, because I can't tell you. All I can say is, that is the situation. With that knowledge, you can make up your mind whether or not you want to . . . get involved. Now, why don't you come back here and lie down and then you can think about it. I promise I won't interfere.' She gave a small, saucy giggle, then bit down on her lower lip. 'Sorry.'

Daniel wandered uneasily to the bed and sat down, keeping his back to her. He leant forward and put his head in his hands. He was still feeling light-headed, and didn't want to look at her.

'This is all very confusing,' he murmured.

'It doesn't have to be. Nothing's changed, not for now, not for tonight.'

'But . . .'

'I know what you're going to say, Daniel. And all I can tell you in reply is that, as I'm sure you know all too well, there are no guarantees of *anything* in life. I know that probably sounds terribly trite. But it also happens to be true. Nothing lasts for ever. Not even dreams.'

Daniel look round. 'Then this is a dream for you too?'

She did not reply.

'Véronique?'

'Come to bed, Daniel.'

'But . . .'

She raised a finger to his lips to silence him, then leant forwards and pulled him down on top of her.

'We have all night to ourselves. Let's not worry about what's in store. You can't live your whole life worrying about the future when the present is so precious. It's all we have, Daniel. It's all any of us has. Let's make the most of it.'

And rather than face further argument or upset, and mindful that he might, at any moment, be thrown back to his other world, Daniel seized the moment and did not stop to think about the consequences.

Daniel did not sleep that night; he did not dare. Making love with Véronique was more than just pleasure; it was the consummation of everything that had happened to him in Atheenaton thus far. In this mystical, paradisaical world, where every moment was filled with a tremulous wonderment, every scent invigorated the senses, every scene delighted the mind's eye . . . in this extraordinary environment, where he felt safe and warm and wanted, he had found peace and fulfilment of a kind he had thought lost. Even the knowledge that Atheenaton was not real – at least, not by the definitions he would usually have accepted – did not seem to matter. Like a child in a fairy-tale, he had discovered an enchanted kingdom. He had stepped through the mirror, fallen down the rabbit hole, walked through the back of the wardrobe: he had found his wonderland. Only it was not a child's playground but an adult's, filled with potential for grown-up pleasure.

There seemed nothing sordid or reprehensible about sleeping with Véronique; there was no guilt, no sin. It was, after all, just a dream, and as far as Daniel was concerned what went on in dreams was not bound by the usual rules, ethics and moralities of everyday life. How could it be? That the experience had been every bit as sensual, as dynamic, as delicious as making love in real life was no surprise. Hadn't he had erotic dreams that were every bit as torrid as his sexual experiences in reality?

Even so, this *was* different. Everything about Atheenaton encouraged good feelings. It *was* like a holiday; not the crass Club 18–30 comparison that Vince had suggested, but something altogether more serene and comforting. There was something . . .

Daniel searched for a word that could encompass exactly how he felt, how Atheenaton affected him, but it was so unlike anything he had ever known that either his imagination or his vocabulary failed him. If pushed, he would have to say that Atheenaton had a *healing* effect. It made him feel whole, feel right; it took away his pain.

Which was why he was determined to stay. Not just for tonight, not just for a few days, but for ever.

14

'Lisanne?'

Lisanne looked up from her manuscript. Across the room, Daniel was sitting on the sofa with a book open on his lap. Daniel usually slouched when he sat on the sofa, and she could tell immediately that something was wrong. His body was tense, angular, and he hunched over the book like a large bird of prey about to devour a dead beast.

'What were you doing with this book?'

'What book?'

'This book, this one on China.' He lifted the book and flashed the cover at her.

Lisanne stared back blankly. 'I wasn't doing anything with it,' she said, trying to camouflage the note of defensiveness that, as a matter of course these days, managed to turn her every response into an incitement to interrogation.

'But it's open at this story about the butterfly,' said Daniel. He too was clearly trying to control the anxiety in his voice, which threatened to spill over into anger.

Lisanne shook her head. 'I've no idea what you're talking about. You took that book off the shelves yesterday evening.'

'Oh come off it, Lisanne. Did Janice put you up to this?'

Lisanne was baffled. 'Did Janice put me up to what? What on earth are you talking about?'

'Searching this out and sticking it under my nose!'

She gazed at him, nonplussed. Not only did she not know what he was talking about, but the clearly discernible agitation in his tone worried her.

'I have absolutely no idea.'

'This! This story about Zhuang-zi and the butterfly!'

'Daniel, calm down.'

'Oh come on, Lisanne. Stop playing games. Tell me why you're doing this.'

'Who's playing games?' Lisanne was nervous now. She *had* seen him leafing through the book the previous evening, had thought nothing of it and so, of course, had made no mention of it. She rather wished now that she had. What was he getting at?

'Oh, I suppose it's just a coincidence then.'

Lisanne took a deep breath, put down the manuscript, rose slowly and walked across to the sofa. She sat down next to Daniel, and was distressed to see that his hands, clutching the open book ferociously, were shaking.

'Let me see,' she said softly, taking hold of the book. Daniel released it reluctantly, and she read the passage on the open page.

> Last night Zhuang-Zhou dreamed he was a butterfly. Fluttering and soaring, he was a butterfly. Likening

> himself in this way, is it not that he is going along with his own devices? He knew nothing of Zhou. Suddenly awakening in surprise, he is Zhou again. He does not know: is it Zhou dreaming he is a butterfly, or a butterfly dreaming it is Zhou?

Lisanne nodded slowly. 'You've told me this story before, I'm sure. About an emperor who dreamt he was a butterfly.'

'Not an emperor. A fourth-century BC Chinese poet,' said Daniel, warily. 'You didn't leave this open for me to find?'

'Of course not. Why should I?'

He peered at the text again. He could not recall taking the book from the shelves, had no memory of opening it at this page. And if he hadn't done it, then it had to be Lisanne. But why should she lie? It didn't make sense.

'Do you want to tell me why it's so important?'

Daniel shrugged. 'It's just . . . I don't remember looking at this before. I don't remember.' He looked up at Lisanne and for the first time she realised that it was neither anger nor frustration in his eyes. It was fear.

Seeing him in such distress, Lisanne thought it best to employ, once more, her skills in damage limitation. She would rather lie to him than have him so upset.

'Oh, hang on a minute. Maybe I did take it out. I was looking for a quote for one of my authors. I must have borrowed it and forgotten to put it back.'

'But why should it be open at this of all things?'

'Why is that relevant? I mean, it's an interesting story but it's hardly . . .' Lisanne paused a moment, allowing her jumble of thoughts to settle down. 'Wait a minute, is this all to do with this lucid dreaming thing?'

Daniel said nothing, but read on down the page.

'Daniel?'

'Huh?'

'Is this to do with the nightmares? Is that it?'

'Not exactly. Look, I'd rather not talk about it.'

'But it's obviously upsetting you. Perhaps if you talked about it . . .'

Daniel sighed. 'It's not that simple.'

Lisanne could see he was getting irritated, but she felt she had some sort of right to know what was going on. Why, for instance, had he mentioned Janice? And why was he being so secretive? Each day, it seemed, on top of all his filthy moods, his behaviour was becoming more and more incomprehensible. Soon she wouldn't understand anything about him. 'Oh Daniel, why won't you let me help you?'

'I don't *need* help. There's nothing wrong with me.'

'Then what's all the fuss about this story? Why this sudden interest in dreams? If it isn't the nightmare, what is it?'

'Just get off my back, will you!'

Lisanne was taken aback, not just by the remark but by the malicious tone in which it was delivered. She felt the urge to cry catch at the back of her throat, but was determined not to let him get to her.

'That's right, shout at me. Blame me for all your problems.'

'Lisanne, I—'

'You can be a real shit sometimes, you know that? All I've wanted is to help you, and all you've done is block me out of your life and try to make my life as miserable as possible. Not once in all this time have I complained, even when your behaviour has been reprehensible, and now, when I'm trying to be understanding, when I'm trying to be helpful, all you can do is attack me. I think you could just show a little consideration now and then.'

Daniel looked away, embarrassed, but said nothing.

Lisanne's upper lip started to tremble, like a frightened schoolgirl who has been reprimanded by her teacher. Aware that tears were moments away, she made her way unsteadily to the bottom of the stairs and braced herself against the banister.

'You think I don't know . . . that's right, isn't it?'

Daniel pretended to ignore her. He returned his attention to the book, but even as he did so he knew he had overstepped the mark this time.

'You think I have no idea what's going on in that sad, sorry little mixed-up mind of yours,' continued Lisanne, her voice starting to break under the tension. 'But I think you'd be surprised – I think you'd be very surprised. I'm not the fool you sometimes take me for. And one thing I can tell you for sure. I won't let you carry on punishing me for being alive.'

Daniel stopped reading. Lisanne's words pierced him like an arrow.

'It's not my fault, Daniel. It's not my fault that I'm still alive and that Alex is dead. You see, I've just about had it. You can go on wishing you were dead, but I won't have you wishing that I was dead too.'

'Lisanne, please—'

'No, don't interrupt me. I have a life – it was once a

good life – and I'm not ready to relinquish it just yet, and certainly not to appease your guilty conscience.'

'But—'

'No, no more. Not tonight. You know, I'm not sure I *can* help you any more, Daniel, not that I was ever any help in the first place. I can't take away your pain, I can't rewrite history, I can't bring her back. And there's a limit to how much longer I can continue to be "understanding". Because the truth is, I don't understand. I don't understand anything.'

She ran up the stairs and slammed the bedroom door. It was not intended to be melodramatic, but she suspected that's how it must have seemed, which only added insult to her injuries: I speak my mind, display my feelings for the first time in half a year and it comes out like a piece of cheap theatre, she thought, as she curled up on the bed and, without fear of interruption, sobbed bitterly.

Daniel sat motionless, paralysed once again by his inability to react in the way that was expected of him. He knew that what he was supposed to do was run after Lisanne and apologise . . . no, more . . . to beg forgiveness for acting like a complete bastard. But he couldn't. It wasn't that he didn't care; of *course* he cared. And he hated upsetting Lisanne, even if it was something at which, it seemed, he was becoming progressively more adept. But for some reason, he seemed unable to draw on whatever resource was responsible for right and proper behaviour. It was as if the links to that part of his personality had been severed.

He thought of those poor souls who, in the aftermath of serious accidents, sometimes suffered brain damage. There were those who looked normal, who appeared to

Daniel's Dream

have nothing wrong with them, but nevertheless had one tragic flaw in their behaviour that gave them away, like the poor sods who could recall their childhoods in perfect detail but were incapable of remembering anything that had happened five minutes ago. Or the sad saps who led normal lives save for the prosaic but devastating fact that they could no longer name the simplest everyday objects. And Daniel sat there thinking about these pitiful creatures and thought: I'm one of them; I'm some sort of mental cripple, a cerebral paralytic with certain bits cut off or cut out or just no longer functioning.

Or worse. Perhaps it's not even as complicated as that, he thought. Perhaps I'm just plain mad. After all, if you added it all up – the extreme depression, the antisocial behaviour, the complete lack of empathy – it all seemed to point to one conclusion.

And then there was the dream, of course, the dream that had taken over his life and turned him into an obsessive. Crazy? It was starting to look like the only diagnosis that fitted. Perhaps he really should be seeing someone – Janice's hippie-dippie analyst perhaps, with his comforting, wacky theories on dreams.

Yeah, he thought, that's just what I need; someone to reinforce my lunatic notions.

Daniel decided to take a walk to clear his head. He was tired – virtually exhausted – and wanted nothing more than to sleep, but he knew he dared not go anywhere near Lisanne unless he was prepared to make a full and sincere apology, and he didn't believe he could put the right words together, let alone make them sound convincing.

He was about to close the book when his eyes were

drawn to the bottom of the page, where an additional portion of the story had been translated.

> While we dream we do not know that we are dreaming, and in the middle of a dream interpret a dream within it; not until we wake do we know that we are dreaming. Only at the ultimate awakening shall we know that this is the ultimate dream.

Oh great, mused Daniel; like I don't have enough problems.

He put on his jacket, grabbed his cigarettes and headed out into the cool evening, trying to clear his mind, lift his mood, bring some reality, some continuity, back into his increasingly fragmented life, but as he wandered down towards Green Lanes with its hubbub of activity and noisy traffic, all he could think about were Zhuang-zi's words and how Atheenaton, for all its wonder, might just be a dream within a dream.

15

They walked along the beach hand in hand, their bare feet, encrusted now with wet sand, leaving a trail of dissolving footprints in their wake. The sun began its slow ascent over the mountains, casting strange, elongated shadows, tinged with indefinable hues, across the untamed scrub that spread from the foothills down to the strand.

A cool, refreshing breeze swept across the beach, blowing specks of sand into their hair. Daniel stopped in his tracks and clutched Véronique to him tightly. She responded in kind, manoeuvring her body against his so that their shapes coincided: a perfect fit.

They stood that way for several minutes, Daniel breathing in the sweet scent of Véronique's hair and neck, her soft skin still releasing its light, musky scent, arousing him in pleasant and familiar ways.

'Let's do it again. Right here.' He clasped the firm, petite cheeks of her bottom with both hands and pulled her close against him.

'We'll get sand everywhere . . . besides, I don't think

you're quite up to it, hmmm?' She insinuated one hand between them and groped around until she could feel his flaccid penis through his jeans and then started to rub gently with the palm of her hand until she felt it start to stiffen beneath her touch. 'Oh, I don't know. Maybe I was a little hasty.'

Daniel brought one hand to her face, gently clasping her jaw, whilst the other reached down between her legs. They had not dressed completely before going out, deliberately leaving off their shoes and underwear on the pretext of going for an early-morning swim. But now, as Daniel kissed her deeply, impulsively, the immediate sensations of fingertips on naked flesh caught them both off guard, and before he knew it his face had flushed, the sweat was rising on his neck and cheeks and his erection was straining against the constriction of his jeans.

Feeling him hardening against her, Véronique unzipped his jeans with swift, deft movements and prised him out while Daniel's fingertips, with equally delicate motions, fluttered in the thick, wiry hair that nestled between her upper thighs.

Daniel was as excited as he had ever been in his life. He broke away from her and wriggled out of his jeans while Véronique cast off her skirt. She reached out her hands, and when Daniel clasped hold of them and tried to pull her towards him, she tensed her arms and held him away from her.

'What is it?'

Véronique looked down at Daniel's groin and smiled approvingly, a look which raised his blood pressure still further.

'Come on, let's—'

Daniel's Dream

'No. Over there.' She nodded towards the sea.
'What?'
Véronique laughed. 'Don't you worry about a thing. You're in safe hands.' As if to prove the point, she released his left hand and reached down, taking hold of him gently, stroking back and forth.

Daniel could feel the familiar sensations – part pleasure, part agony – running ahead, out of control, and anxious that, far from being unable to perform, he was in danger of sprinting to the finish line before the race had officially started, he withdrew her hand and chased her down to the water's edge.

The water was surprisingly warm and still, and within moments they found themselves in a deep embrace, the water lapping gently around their chests. Véronique clasped her hands around Daniel's neck and allowed the water to take her weight. Lifting her feet off the seabed, she wrapped her legs round his waist. She could feel his erection bumping against her backside, and teased him by resting herself on it for a couple of seconds before lifting herself off. By now, Daniel was in a frenzy of excitement; the gentle caress of the sea-water, far from dampening his ardour, was coaxing him to greater fervour. Suddenly, without signalling his intention, he grabbed Véronique's buttocks and with effortless ease, thrust deep into her. She gasped, as much with surprise as sexual frisson.

Supporting her with his right hand, Daniel lifted his left hand from the water and cradled the back of her head, bringing her face close to his. As she rocked slowly back and forth, with small, tight movements, their lips met. A heightened sexual pleasure, like an electric charge, coursed through Daniel's body, from his groin to his lips and then up through the top of his head where, in a single moment of ecstatic release, he felt his face, neck, shoulders, torso and limbs pulsate with pleasure, a small, controlled explosion, as every synapse in his brain crackled and sparked with an existential vitality, as if a small volcano had erupted inside his head. He thrust hard and deep, and with each movement revelled in the moans of rapture that issued from Véronique's parted lips.

With a final thrust, Daniel was spent. Holding on tightly to Véronique, he felt the last of his strength ebbing away, and as his legs started to tremble in spasm, he just had time to whisper, 'We're going under . . .' before his knees unlocked and he teetered over sideways into the water, taking Véronique with him.

They lay quietly side by side, hands clasped, until, chilled from the damp sand, they decided to continue their walk. The sun had lifted above the horizon, raising the air temperature so that it caressed them like a warm breath, and it was with free, easy movements that they wandered along the water's edge, pausing every now and then to kiss or caress each other.

Ahead of them, scampering across the sand, Daniel spotted an unusual crab racing towards the water's edge. It was quite alone and, with the rest of the beach so empty, looked decidedly lost. By the time they caught up with it, it had stopped moving. He reached down and gently lifted the battered, spiral shell. Nestling deep within its coils was a small yet spirited inhabitant, which actively protested at this interference in its journey.

'I think this one is in need of a new home,' said Daniel, examining the damaged sea-shell.

Daniel's Dream

Véronique looked at him blankly. 'What do you mean?'

Daniel looked at her pensively; he wasn't sure why, but he felt strangely protective of the sad little creature he held in his hand.

'It's a hermit crab,' he said softly, watching the crab's legs wriggle excitedly in its cramped mobile home. He looked up at Véronique, but she still registered nothing more than mild curiosity. 'They're born without their own body armour, so they have to wear cast-off shells – you know, snail-shells and the like. They're also known as robber crabs.'

'More like pauper crabs, if you ask me.'

'Or squatter crabs, perhaps,' said Daniel, replacing the crab on the sand.

'What happens when they outgrow their shells?'

'They have to search for a new one. And if they don't find one, they've more or less had it.'

'But I'm sure they would – find a new home that is. Think of all those empty shells lying around on the sea bed.'

Daniel nodded sadly. 'I suppose so. But moving from one to the next is very tricky. For that short period they're completely naked and exposed. It's very dangerous if any predators are looking on. I suspect they're rather soft and succulent without their clothes on.' He grinned, expecting Véronique to pick up on the silly allusion, but she only looked down glumly.

'It seems rather sad that they should have to wear hand-me-downs. Do you know, right up until my teenage years I had to wear Marianne's old clothes – she's just a year older than I am – and I hated her for it. For years I made her the scapegoat for all my problems, if I wasn't getting on well at school, if I didn't have any friends, if

I was sad or unhappy, it was all her fault, all because I had to wear her stupid old clothes.'

'Ah,' said Daniel, remembering their little spat from the previous evening. 'And do you still blame her for everything?'

'Marianne? No, not any more. Despite what you might think, Marianne is an angel. I love her more than you can imagine.'

Daniel was a little unnerved by this sudden seriousness, which seemed out of keeping with Véronique's usual mood. Clearly there were matters of considerable import concerning her relationship with her sister, things which evidently mattered deeply to her, but rather than pry he decided to leave well alone. If there was something he should know, he had no doubt she would tell him about it in due course.

'I suppose they could always hide for a while,' she said, as the hermit crab scuttled off across the beach, heading for a large pile of black rocks ahead of them. 'If they were squeezed out of their home, I mean. Until they found another one.' She smiled, a touch sadly, and clasped Daniel's arm tightly.

'Come on. Race you back to the taverna!'

And before Daniel had time to answer, Véronique had shoved him away and was sprinting back towards the village.

By the time they reached the Neraida they were both exhausted and thirsty. They found a table in the shade overlooking the water, ordered hot coffee and bread from the ever-present Vangeli, and sat silently for a while, enjoying the view, the peace and the quiet.

Daniel was struck by how familiar everything now

seemed: the beach, the taverna, the particular aroma of the coffee. But there was more, something else, something not directly connected with his surroundings that made him feel comfortable and at ease.

For a moment the sensation wavered about him in the air, like heat haze, and he could not pin it down. Then suddenly it was clear. Wasn't this exactly the way he had felt all those years ago when he first met Lisanne? That intense sensation of desire and longing: a sensation that was simultaneously deeply pleasurable and achingly painful, torn between want and wanting, with the mind ever eager but the body bereft? And that wonderful, bubbling excitement that threatened to overflow every now and then, especially when he looked at Véronique, studied her closely or caught sight of some previously unrecorded movement or mannerism. Yes, it was always that way with love when it was new. Or lust, perhaps. Either way, Daniel could not help but recognise the feelings and, even though in the waking world he would also have had to contend with other responses – not least guilt – here in his dreams he felt free to enjoy whatever experience came his way.

This wasn't the way it had been with Alex. Even at its most intense, his short-lived affair with Alex was, by definition, shrouded in guilt and sinfulness. It was wrong, and he had known it was wrong, though that knowledge did not prevent him from getting involved. But there was no reason – at least, none that he could fathom – to feel guilty in these circumstances.

There were, however, other emotions at play, including something completely new, an emotion which, to the best of his knowledge, had no equivalent in his waking life. Daniel was, by his own admission, in love or in lust or infatuated – it wasn't important which – with a woman called Véronique, who to all intents and purposes did not exist. If he was prepared to consider his predicament, he had to face the fact that he had fallen for a vision, a fantasy, something that could not extend beyond the boundaries of the impermanent, evanescent territory of sleep. Like the crazy old drunk he had seen on the Underground, he was communing with someone no one else could see, who wasn't really there. There could be no 'future' to this relationship, nowhere for it to go, no way for it to exist in any state other than this, this dream, with all its incumbent attributes and peculiarities, that, though it mimicked real life, was not, and could never be, real. And Daniel had absolutely no idea how to handle that.

'What are you thinking?'

Daniel looked at Véronique and shrugged. 'Nothing much. What about you?'

She reached across the table and took Daniel's hand. 'I was just thinking how happy I am, how happy you've made me.'

'Really?'

'Of course. Can't you tell?'

Daniel shrugged again. 'Sure, only . . .' He broke off. Did he dare bring 'reality' into this place, to introduce his queries and problems, all of which probably meant nothing here: questions without answers, problems without solutions? Did he dare risk breaking the spell that kept him here in order to satisfy his curiosity? Hadn't Kate already warned him off once?

'Daniel? What is it?'

He took a deep breath. 'Why are you here, Véronique? I mean, what are you doing in Atheenaton?'

Daniel's Dream

'The same as you I expect.'

'But that's just it. I don't know why I'm here. I mean, I don't live here. This isn't my home. I live in—'

'Don't Daniel. Don't spoil it.'

'Spoil it? How will I spoil it?'

Véronique frowned. 'With questions. Unnecessary questions that can't help you.'

'It isn't help I need. It's answers.'

'I think you'll find you're wrong, on both counts.'

Daniel shook his head. 'Look, there are some things I just have to know, or else nothing makes sense. Is this a dream, Véronique? Am I dreaming you? Or is it the other way round? I mean, where do you come from? And Marianne? I mean, where have you—'

'Daniel, please.'

'But I just want to understand . . .'

'You have to stop.' Véronique withdrew her hand sharply. 'There is no point in asking those sort of questions. They can do no good.'

'But—'

'No, wait. Listen to me, Daniel. Your questions have no relevance here; they barely have any meaning. They just can't be answered.'

'How do you know? How do you know that?'

'Because I've been here longer than you.'

'But surely—'

'Oh Daniel, just stop, will you!'

Daniel was shocked by this outburst. He could see that Véronique was not merely upset; she was actually trembling.

'Your questions have no meaning, Daniel. You want to pigeon-hole this place, to interpret it logically, to label it and handle it and . . . Well it can't be done. All those questions you have, ones that you expect must have answers, answers that someone is keeping from you. Lose them. Forget them. File them away with all those other imponderables like "What is the meaning of life?" and "Why are we here?" The only thing you really need to understand, Daniel, is that this place is real only as long as you believe it is real. Call it a dream if you like, or a vision . . . Call it anything, but doubt its existence and it'll disappear for you.'

Véronique was close to tears, and Daniel was deeply upset to see her in such a state.

'Okay, okay,' he said, patting her hand and trying to calm her.

'You're the best thing that's happened to me since I came here, Daniel. I don't want to lose you. Not yet.'

'And I don't want to lose you. I just . . . I would just like to have whatever level of understanding you possess about this place. It's evidently enough to appease you.'

Véronique nodded. 'It'll come, Daniel. Don't rush it.'

Daniel sighed. He gazed out over the glowing sand and the endless ocean. 'I love this place,' he said softly. 'I hate it when I leave. And when I'm not here, all I can think about is coming back.' He looked at Véronique, expecting some sort of confirmation of this, as if she should feel the same way, but she said nothing. She still looked tearful. Mindful of her mood, he none the less decided to push her on this point: surely she too missed Atheenaton when she wasn't there?

Véronique shook here head. 'My situation is different, Daniel.'

'Different? How?'

Daniel's Dream

'I don't ever have to miss Atheenaton, because I never have to leave. In fact, I can't leave, Daniel. There's nowhere for me to go. Atheenaton is my home.'

Daniel felt his mouth go dry. He struggled to get the words out.

'But . . . but that's fantastic. You're here for good? I mean, you never have to leave? You're here for ever?' He shook his head, decidedly woozy all of a sudden. He had now stayed in Atheenaton for longer than ever before, and as he had stayed awake all night, watching Véronique doze, he suspected that he might shortly be returned to his waking life.

Véronique shook her head. 'Not for ever. Nothing lasts for ever.'

Daniel frowned. 'What do you mean?'

Before she could answer, the edges of his vision became blurred, the sounds around him faded into silence, and suddenly everything was darkness.

16

Daniel replaced the receiver and tried again. Still engaged. He lit a cigarette, paced up and down for two minutes, wandered into the kitchen, switched on the kettle for the sixth time that morning, returned to the living room, picked up the handset and dialled again.

No answer.

He held on. He started counting. Five. Ten. Fifteen. He was still hanging on when it rang for the twentieth time. The thirtieth.

He slammed the handset down.

He dialled again.

Still no answer.

Why am I doing this? he wondered, angered at his own obsessional behaviour. Why am I getting so irritated about making a blasted telephone call?

He wandered back into the kitchen. He was on edge now, pacing from room to room, unsure what to do with himself. Should he try Lisanne's number again? How much of this could one person stand?

In the kitchen he stood against the sink and gazed out of the window. It was a grey day, the cloud hanging thick and low over the rooftops of the terraced houses. A few people wandered gloomily along the streets, caught up in the routine convolutions of their everyday lives. Daniel sighed. Somewhere along the line he had lost touch with the familiar, the regular, the everyday. Now his life was like a badly edited movie, a minor example of fifties French New Wave, with the protagonists jump-cutting from one scene to the next, skipping erratically from one location to another without the usual ebb and flow, the comforting rhythms that gave life its seductive continuity.

To kill time, Daniel decided to make himself a cup of coffee. He felt dozy and befuddled, and hoped the caffeine might stir him from his lethargy. Measuring out a heaped teaspoon of instant coffee into a large green mug, he poured in the boiling water and stirred aggressively, well past the point where all the granules had dissolved. He added the milk and watched impatiently as it spiralled down into the murky brown. And then, focusing intently on the swirling coffee, he tried to relax.

What was the panic? Why the sudden urgency to talk to her now? He'd see her tonight, after all. If only she had answered the phone the first time, then there wouldn't have been any problem; everything would have been okay. He would have stayed calm, reasonable. He would be behaving normally.

But now he was frantic.

I have to tell her, thought Daniel. I have to tell her everything.

He grabbed the coffee and marched over to the telephone. He took a deep breath and dialled again. Engaged!

Daniel's Dream

What was this, some sort of plot? What had he ever done to offend British Telecom? He felt like dialling a number at random just for the satisfaction of actually getting through to someone. He tried the operator instead. No one answered. Daniel shook his head in disbelief. Periodically, he was sure, the cosmos singled you out for special consideration. It conspired against you, not out of malice or aggression – it was just one of those things. If you dared to rally against that contrivance, to defy it or take arms against it, you were asking for trouble.

Daniel sipped his coffee and stared into the middle distance. There were times – times like this, when he moped over a cup of steaming coffee – when it seemed that nothing would ever change.

Even Atheenaton, for all its evanescent delight, could not help him here, here in the real, wide-awake world. And no matter how he felt about Véronique and Kate and Barry and the rest of the spectral misfits that peopled his other world, in the end he was destined, it seemed, always to return to this, to normality, to misery. In the end, he mused, Atheenaton was nothing more than a wonderful distraction, and it wasn't *real*, was it? Because, thought Daniel, if there's an acid test, then surely that is it. Real things, people, events, they're not perfect. They're faulty. And Atheenaton isn't . . . it isn't . . . there isn't . . .

Daniel slammed his hand down on the coffee table. That was the problem in a nutshell. Atheenaton, Véronique, Kate, Barry, Vangeli, Kostas . . . it was all too good, too damn *perfect*. Nothing in real life is that good, ever. Reality is people who interfere, friends who abandon you, wives who don't understand you, telephones that don't work, instant coffee that tastes awful, filthy old drunks on Tube trains who threaten you. Reality is boredom, frustration and helplessness.

And death. Most of all, perhaps, reality is all about coming to terms with death, with the shocking, unpalatable truth that beautiful young people in their prime may have their lives snuffed out without reason, without sense. Reality is everything you despise. And everything else is pie in the sky. Everything else is just a dream.

There had been a time, once, when life was good, a time when he was very happy. If he dared to, Daniel could remember the good times; the small victories, the great triumphs, gained in more innocent days, before the accident, before life had revealed its true character. Daniel had once been foolish enough to believe that life was a miraculous thing, that it was something wonderful. But now he thought differently; now he knew better. Life was not beautiful: it was a lottery, a tightrope walk, a constant struggle against dangers and risks that you didn't even know existed. If you were lucky, you survived. You survived the traumas of birth, the whooping cough and measles that threatened to finish you off before you'd learnt to read and write. If you were lucky, you survived the host of viruses floating around in the atmosphere which could murder you before you'd experienced your first kiss. If you were lucky, you survived the countless accidents that nearly happened, the endless near-misses, the myriad moments when you came within seconds of copping it, but didn't: the flight you missed that crashed into a mountain killing everyone on board, the hotel you should have been staying in that was bombed by terrorists, the ship you should have sailed on that hit a reef and sank. You survived all these, the ones that you read about and

Daniel's Dream

the dozens you didn't even know had passed you by, and you survived it all only to deal with a hundred heartbreaks and disappointments, a thousand day-dreams that never came true, a million wishes left unfulfilled.

If, in between these set-backs and let-downs, if every now and then you managed to succeed, to pull something off against the odds, to create something beautiful or make something happen, then maybe you celebrated. But it was always short-lived. The victories, the triumphs, only ever lasted a short while. Then it was back to the daily grind, back on the survival merry-go-round, cheating death with your ducking and diving, and working and hoping and praying that you'd make it through another day.

But not everyone made it through the day. Alex hadn't. And what had she done to deserve such a fate?

What had Véronique said? That some questions were meaningless? It was beginning to feel as if *all* questions were meaningless. If only he hadn't woken up so soon; if only he had had a little longer to talk to Véronique. Now all he could think about was returning to Atheenaton and being with her; not just temporarily, but for good. If she could stay permanently, why couldn't he? Or was that another meaningless question?

Daniel picked up the handset and dialled again. He heard it ring three times and then . . .

'Hello, Lisanne Cokely.'

Daniel swallowed noisily. Suddenly the inside of his mouth was completely dry, as if he'd been chewing blotting paper for half an hour. He gave a throaty cough before speaking.

'Hello,' he said hoarsely. 'It's me.'

* * *

Lisanne replaced the receiver and stared worriedly at it. She was still staring at it when Jane, her secretary, brought in her morning coffee.

'Lisanne? Is something wrong?'

Lisanne looked up and shook her head. 'No . . . that is, yes, but I don't know what it is.'

'Daniel?'

Lisanne nodded sadly. 'It's getting worse, Jane. I'm at my wits' end.'

Jane put the coffee mug on Lisanne's desk and, seeing she was in need of a confessor, casually sat down in the seat opposite, the one usually reserved for visiting authors.

'He's started talking complete gibberish,' continued Lisanne, picking up a pencil and twirling it between her fingers as if she were hand-rolling a cigarette. 'That's the second time he's phoned me at work sounding completely frantic, only to spout some nonsense at me before apologising profusely and hanging up. You know, on top of everything else . . . He was a total shit last night. I can't tell you. Just unbearable.' Lisanne gave a loud, heartfelt sigh. It sounded like the final breath escaping from some dying animal: it made Jane shudder. 'I'm not sure how much more of this I can take.'

Jane nodded uneasily. 'Why don't you get him to see someone . . . if he's, you know . . .'

'No, he won't do it. It's difficult enough getting him to see Dr Fischer, and even then he only ends up being rude to him. If I suggested that he see a therapist he'd go mad. Oh God, what have I said.' Lisanne sighed again and shook her head. 'I'm beginning to think I'm the one that needs professional help.'

Daniel's Dream

'Don't be daft. You're the most well-balanced person I know.'

'But I'm lost, Jane. I just don't know what to do any more. Do you know, we haven't made love in six months.'

Jane blushed. 'Well, perhaps . . . what with the accident . . .'

'Dr Fischer says there's nothing to stop him from having "an active life". It isn't that he can't; it's that he won't. If I didn't know better I'd think he were having an affair.'

Jane wondered momentarily whether she should ask if this were, indeed, a possibility, but thought better of it. 'Perhaps you just have to give him a bit longer. It can't have been easy for him. After all, he nearly died, didn't he?'

Lisanne frowned and said nothing for a moment. 'That is the line, isn't it?'

Jane shrugged. 'I'm not sure I understand.'

'What we've been saying all this time . . . how he nearly died, how close he came and all that. But you know, it's not really true. Not really.'

'But the accident . . .'

'. . . that never happened.'

'What? But I thought . . .'

'Oh yes, there was an accident. But it wasn't the accident that everyone was told about.'

'You've lost me.'

'Perhaps that's just as well.'

'No, go on. It's obviously bothering you, whatever it is.'

Lisanne shook her head. 'It'll just make me sound like a heartless cow.'

'Well, that's okay; I already know you're a heartless cow. Come on, spill.'

Lisanne took a sip of coffee and pondered a moment. She wasn't sure whether she dared to express her thoughts out loud. At the same time, she feared that if she kept such notions bottled up inside her, then they might fester like an untreated wound.

'Well, it's just a matter of semantics I suppose. There are two accidents, if you like; the accident that did happen – a horrible, tragic affair in which a young woman called Alex was killed – and an accident that didn't happen, in which both Alex *and* Daniel were killed. That was the accident that *nearly* happened, in which Daniel *nearly* died. If Daniel had been in the car when it smashed into the tree, then yes, God forbid, he would almost certainly have been killed like that poor girl. But he wasn't in the car. He was thrown free and sustained some bad bruising, a broken collar-bone and some trauma to his neck and vertebrae; nothing that could be remotely thought of as life-threatening. If he'd been severely injured, rushed to intensive care, operated on, been close to death's door, then made a recovery, yes, then it would be fair to say he'd nearly died. But none of that happened. Nothing like it happened. All I'm saying is . . . well, someone nearly mowed me down today while I was crossing the road opposite Marks & Sparks. A great big Merc, driver not paying attention. Missed me by inches. In an accident that nearly happened, I nearly died. Does that entitle me to go around for the next six months making everyone's life miserable? Does it?'

Jane shrugged. 'Perhaps he feels responsible for her death. Were they very close?'

'I don't know, I don't know! All I know is that it's like living with a fucking zombie! I can't go on with it, Jane. I just can't!'

Daniel's Dream

Jane stood up and walked round the desk, put a comforting arm around her employer, and allowed her to cry bitterly on her shoulder until her blouse was wet through and the coffee had turned stone cold.

'And I think we should tell her.'

Janice looked up from her newspaper. 'It's not our place to interfere.'

Vince reached forward and pulled the newspaper down from in front of Janice's face.

'Janice.'

'What?' she said, irritated. 'Oh for God's sake, Vince, what do you want from me?'

'I want you to phone Lisanne and tell her that her husband is having delusions.'

'But I don't know that he is.'

'I spoke to him Janice. Believe me, he's cracking up.'

'I spoke to him too, remember? And as far as I'm concerned, he's perfectly okay – a bit disturbed, perhaps, but that's no surprise when you consider what he went through.'

'You don't really believe all that guff about the dream?'

'Believe what? That's he's having the dream? Of course I do.'

'No, dummy, believe that this place really exists. I mean you can't . . .'

Janice grimaced and folded the newspaper in two, laying it down on the seat beside her. 'It's not important what I believe. What's important is that it really exists for Daniel, and frankly that's all that matters.'

'And you don't think there's anything wrong with a

grown man believing that in his dreams he goes to the land of Oz?'

'Why do you have to be so dismissive? Just because you don't understand . . .'

'Oh, let me guess what's coming next: I can't possibly understand because I'm an insensitive, unimaginative boofhead and Daniel is Mister Delicate and Vulnerable. Well I don't buy it.'

'How can you be so closed-minded?'

'Because it helps me to keep my head when all around are losing theirs.'

Janice sneered. 'Very poetic.'

'See, not so insensitive after all. Kipling.'

'I *know* . . .'

'Do you like Kipling?' said Vince with a leer that gave credence to almost any accusation of insensitivity or boorishness that Janice might hurl at him.

'Please, Vince, not now.' Janice picked up her newspaper again, hoping it might shield her from his tiresomeness.

Vince pulled a face. 'Just trying to inject a little light humour into the proceedings. So, are you going to tell her or what?'

'If Daniel wants Lisanne to know about it, he'll tell her. *You* suggested he speak to her, *I* suggested he speak to her. I don't think we've any right to interfere beyond that.'

'You're talking about Daniel.'

'So?'

'He's my best mate. I can't just sit around and do nothing while he plans his route to the funny farm.'

'Oh, for God's sake, you make it sound as if he's completely barmy.'

'Darling, just—'

Daniel's Dream

Janice snapped the paper down. 'Don't do that Vince.'
'Do what?'
'Make the endearment "darling" sound like "pathetic female idiot". You always say it when you're about to patronise me.'

Vince smiled, not very pleasantly, then cleared his throat.

'My apologies. All I was going to say, love of my life, is that just because Daniel's wacky dream fits in with some poncey New Age gobbledegook you've read about in one of your—'

'Okay, that's it. I'm not discussing this any further with you.'

'Janice—'

'No. If you want to tell Lisanne, that's up to you, but I shan't condone it and I shan't back you up when Daniel comes gunning for you because you've betrayed a confidence.'

'Gunning?'

'Yes, well, on your head be it.'

Janice reached for her jacket. 'And if, as I strongly suspect, you intend to drive Lisanne to distraction with your half-baked analysis, please make it absolutely clear that you are doing so off your own bat, and that it has nothing to do with me. Lisanne is a good friend, and I'll need someone to stand by me after the divorce.'

'What you don't understand is that I'm just trying to help.'

'I understand the "trying" bit, Vince. I understand that very well.' Janice strode to the door, stepped into the fresh air, and resisted a powerful temptation to slam the door behind her.

17

Daniel searched all over Atheenaton for Kate. He ran from the Pumphouse to the Neraida to Kyma and back again, but there was no sign of her. He stopped to question a few of the villagers, but no one knew where she was. At Kyma he had hoped that Véronique might be able to help him, but she was not in her room, nor at any of the tavernas. Kostas said that he had seen the girls wandering up the beach several hours previously, but he did not know where they were heading.

Frustrated and tired, Daniel eventually found himself back at the Pumphouse. He sat down at the table beneath the gnarled olive tree and searched his pockets for cigarettes. When Barry appeared from the kitchens, Daniel beckoned him over, offered him a cigarette, and invited him to sit down for a while.

'I'm not stopping you doing something important, am I?'

'Not at all, Daniel. There's always time to talk to a friend,' said Barry, apparently pleased to be stationary for a few moments. He fished around in his shirt pocket and eventually retrieved a book of matches. He lit the cigarette, closed his eyes, and inhaled deeply.

'Barry?'

Barry opened his eyes and smiled serenely. 'Uh-huh?'

'Why do you work so hard? Everyone else seems just to potter around and enjoy themselves, but you're always on the go.'

Barry smiled. 'It's what I do best.' He breathed the smoke out slowly, watching the grey plumes spiral up into the pine-scented air.

'But do you have to? Couldn't you just put your feet up for a bit, go lie on the beach? Relax?'

'Nah, that's not my style. I like to be active, to be doing something. If I just sit around, I get irritable and anxious. I've always been like that.'

Daniel decided that, now that he had Barry alone, he should risk asking a few of the questions he was desperate to have answered. If he transgressed some law or other, no doubt he would find out about it soon enough. But he had to know, even if it meant being hurled back to his waking world or temporarily banished from Atheenaton.

'You mean, you were the same at home?'

'Absolutely. It's the cross I bear.'

'And where is home?'

'Well, it was Boston. But Atheenaton has been more of a home to me than Boston ever was. Whether or not I decide to go back there remains to be seen.'

'You don't want to stay here?'

Barry started to tap the table nervously with his long, strong fingers. 'I've been here a long time Daniel. It's been wonderful. I can't tell you how much it's helped me.'

Daniel's Dream

'Helped? How?'

'Aw, you know. Re-established some balance in my life. You know what this place is like, what an effect it has on you. I was crazy when I first arrived, off the wall. Literally didn't know when to stop. You think I work too hard here; you should have seen me in the old days. I was working my way to an early grave. Atheenaton changed all that. It wove its magic and cured me, or at least, it slowed me down. If it hadn't been for this place . . . well, I don't like to think about it.'

'Then why not stay?'

Barry sighed. 'Daniel, you're still kinda new here. Right now I guess Atheenaton seems like some sort of paradise, compared to back home. I don't know what your situation is, but I suspect you, like most of us, have some stuff to work out. Once you're straight, nice though this place is, it'll no longer have the same appeal. Deep down, we'd all like to go home eventually.'

Daniel shook his head. 'I don't understand. When you say "all", do you mean . . . ?'

'We're all here for a reason Daniel; you must have seen that. All I'm saying is, take away that reason and . . . Anyway, for me it'll soon be time to move on. You can't stay here for ever.'

'But Véronique can't go home – wherever that is. She says she can't leave.'

Barry nodded. 'Well, everyone's circumstances are different.'

'I don't understand.'

'It's not for me to explain, Daniel.'

'Please, Barry, just tell me if—'

Barry held up his hand. His expression had changed

slightly, from serene to severe, and Daniel sensed he was overstepping the mark.

'That's enough questions, Daniel. If you want to know more, you'll have to ask Kate.'

'Sure, but I can't find her.'

'Kate's usually busy in the mornings. Why don't you just hang out here for a while? She'll probably be along around lunchtime. I'll get you some coffee.'

Barry stood up to go. 'You know, we're all very fond of you Daniel. We're especially happy about you and Véronique. She's a good kid; it's great to see her so happy.'

Daniel opened his mouth to respond, but Barry was already half-way to the doorway. 'I'll get that coffee to you,' he called over his shoulder before disappearing into the darkness of the taverna.

By the time Daniel found Kate, sitting on the patio outside the villa, his mood had deteriorated from mere impatience to anger and frustration, so he was not mollified by the friendly wave and accompanying smile that Kate gave him as he marched down the garden path.

'I've been looking for you everywhere,' he said petulantly, and was annoyed when Kate did not acknowledge his distress.

'And now you've found me,' said Kate.

'You don't understand; I've chased all over Atheenaton.'

'Oh, Daniel, do calm down. You're getting very flustered, and for no reason at all.'

'But I needed to see you. Urgently.'

Kate nodded. 'And I needed to greet a new arrival. You're very precious to us, Daniel, but you're not the

Daniel's Dream

only visitor here, you know. So, now that your wish has been fulfilled and you've found me, what can I do for you? There's something cold and thirst-quenching in the refrigerator if you're over-heating.'

Daniel tried to ignore Kate's flippancy in much the way that he had refused to acknowledge her gentle but firm put-down, but he had to admit that she had a most effective way of deflating his self-importance, and instead of holding on to his anger – which, he now realised, was going to do him no good at all – he took a deep breath and sat down on the patio beside her.

'Sorry,' he said, embarrassed by his outburst.

'That's quite all right. Anyway I'm *so* pleased to see you: it seems like ages since we last spoke. Actually, it's just as well you dropped by, as I've been meaning to talk to you. About Véronique.'

'Véronique? But . . . that's why I needed to see you.'

Kate made only a marginal attempt to suppress a knowing smile, reminding Daniel of the underlying theatricality that coloured most events in Atheenaton, of the fundamental unreality of the place.

'Well, seeing as you were so anxious to speak to me, perhaps you should go first.'

Daniel paused for a moment. He had been in such a panic about seeing Kate that he had not formulated so much as an opening sentence to explain what was bothering him, and now that he had the chance to address his problems, he wasn't sure how to begin.

'I take it you know about Véronique and me.'

Kate's face lit up with excitement. 'Who could fail to notice? And if it's my blessing you're after, then fear no more. She's a wonderful girl, and it's heart-lifting to see her so happy. You've done something very special Daniel; I hope you know that.'

Daniel frowned. 'Special? I don't—'

'Sorry, I interrupted. Do carry on. About you and Véronique.'

This additional interruption put Daniel completely off his stride. What on earth did she mean, 'special'? Daniel chose to let it go for the moment; he had questions to ask, and did not want to get involved in a discussion that would probably lead nowhere.

'I want to stay with her.'

'Of course. Is there a problem? She has a nice enough room as I recall. Or did you want to bring her back here, is that it? I can easily make myself scarce.'

Daniel could not tell if Kate was being deliberately obtuse, but rather than make any inflammatory accusations, he merely restated the matter in terms that could not be misunderstood.

'I'm in love with her. She's told me that she can never leave Atheenaton. I want to stay as well, with her, for ever. I don't want to go back.' Having finally given voice to his feelings, Daniel felt both relieved and exhausted. He was not prepared for Kate's immediate, unequivocal response.

'I'm afraid that's impossible for a number of reasons, Daniel. Actually, I'm surprised that Véronique didn't say as much herself.'

'How can you say that? Why should anything be impossible?'

Kate looked at Daniel long and hard. 'That's a terribly naive question, if you don't mind my saying so.'

'Oh come on, Kate, don't do this to me.'

Daniel's Dream

'Do what? Did Véronique tell you you could stay here with her?'

'No, she fobbed me off and refused to tell me why.'

'And you're not prepared to accept that and just get on with things?'

'No, of course not. Why the hell should I?'

Kate nodded. 'Because there might be very good reasons for doing so.'

Daniel started to lose patience again. 'Yeah? Like what?'

Kate sighed. 'I have to tell you, Daniel, you're not making this easy on any of us. Most visitors are a lot less bullish than this: they give Atheenaton a chance. They don't make so many demands. I have to say that it doesn't help your case one bit.'

'Case? What are you talking about? All I want to know—'

'Yes,' interrupted Kate. 'I know. You've made it abundantly clear.' She paused a moment, during which Daniel had the distinct impression that he was about to hear something he'd rather not know.

'Very well. I should explain that the information I'm about to give you is usually withheld until a later time, but seeing as you've been so insistent . . .' Kate gave a little cough, which only served to put Daniel on edge. What was all this cloak and dagger stuff? Why was she treating him like a naughty child? After all, he was only after some information.

'It's clear to everyone here, Daniel, that you haven't yet understood why you've come to Atheenaton. That isn't altogether your fault; it is, after all, early days. It is also clear that you've taken to it very strongly, which, bearing in mind your current situation at home, is also not surprising.'

'What do you know about my situation at home?'

'Oh, Daniel, you needn't sound so petulant. It's not as if we don't understand. We all want to escape at some time in our lives, particularly from emotional pain. Don't you realise that we're all here for the same reasons, more or less? We've been unable to cope. We've sought refuge; Atheenaton is our sanctuary.'

Daniel nodded. Although he had not expected to hear it put so unambiguously, especially not from anyone in Atheenaton, everything Kate said rang true.

'I *do* realise that. You think I don't appreciate it?'

'No, no, it's not that. It's just that . . . how can I put this? You have an ingenuous, rose-tinted view of Atheenaton, which is touching but quite misleading. You believe Atheenaton is a paradise, a promised land, some undiscovered holiday spot where you can settle down and live happy ever after. Despite appearances, it is none of those things. You didn't stumble in here by accident, Daniel. You came because you had to. Because you're sick.'

'I'm not sick.'

'Yes, Daniel, you are; you're very, very sick. You're suffering from a debilitating guilt that has robbed you of the will to live. You feel guilty for cheating on your wife, and you feel guilty because the woman with whom you had the affair was killed in an accident, an accident in which you survived. Loose endings, see?'

'Now wait a minute—'

'And you can no longer see good in anyone or anything. You've forgotten how to love.'

Daniel's Dream

'That's not true! I love Véronique!'

'I think not. Your feeling for her may be very strong, very exciting, very potent, but it certainly isn't love.'

'How can you say that? How can you possibly know? That's an outrageous claim!'

Kate held her hands out as if in appeasement. 'Perhaps, but it's what I believe. More to the point, in the matter of Véronique, it is less important how you feel than how she feels. She is, quite obviously, deliriously happy to have met you: it's a turn of events at which we're all delighted. She deserves this last chance of happiness.'

Kate dropped this last comment into the conversation so casually that Daniel, still preoccupied with his own affairs, almost missed it.

'What do you mean? What last chance? What on earth . . . ?'

'She's dying, Daniel. Véronique is going to die.'

'I can't believe what you're telling me; first Alex, now . . . Please, Kate, tell me it's not true.' Daniel's voice was cracked and frail. He had not moved from the patio, and sat with his back against the villa wall, the evening sun drying the tears on his cheeks.

'I know what a shock this must be for you, and believe me, if there were any way . . . You can understand now why I didn't want to answer your questions. I didn't want to upset you this way.'

Daniel shook his head in sorrow. 'How long has she got?'

'No one knows. Atheenaton is Véronique's sanctuary, her retreat from the pain; not just emotional, but physical too. She'll remain here until the end; it's just too painful for her back home.'

'And there's nothing anyone can do? I can't believe that in a place like this there's nothing you can do!'

'It's terminal, Daniel; even in Atheenaton we have to learn to accept death, no matter how hard it may seem.' Kate took Daniel's hand and held it tightly. 'Véronique has been living with the knowledge for a year. Six months ago, the pain became too much, and she found herself wandering, like you, along the beach.'

'And Marianne?'

'Marianne and Véronique – despite all appearances – are very close. When Marianne discovered the truth about her sister, she had what amounted to a nervous breakdown and, in effect, followed her here. It happens only very occasionally. I expect she'll remain for a while, once Véronique has gone.'

Fresh tears rolled down Daniel's face. It wasn't just the terrible truth that hurt now; it was the injustice of the whole situation.

'I did tell you that some things were best left alone, Daniel,' said Kate gently. 'We tried to keep it from you, but you just had to know. And you can't blame Véronique; after all, you're her last chance of any real happiness. We thought it might be good for both of you. We were all counting on the fact that you'd return before . . . well, we didn't expect you to be staying too long. You might never have had to know.' Kate reached across and stroked Daniel's hair.

'Return? To Lisanne you mean?'

'Eventually, yes. Once you were healed.'

'You still don't understand, do you, Kate. I don't *want* to

Daniel's Dream

return. I don't want to leave Véronique. Ever,' said Daniel, aware of the pointlessness of his words. 'I just don't want to. What am I going to do?'

'There's nothing you can do except make the most of whatever time you have left together. Véronique's very special, and she's so fond of you, Daniel. You could be good for each other.'

'It's not enough,' said Daniel, shifting so as to lie back on the patio. He was confused, uncertain of his emotions, his motives, his feelings.

Kate's confession had shocked him deeply. He didn't want to think any more; he didn't want to do anything any more.

'I'm so tired, Kate. I'm so tired of having to deal with all this . . .'

'I know, Daniel, I know. But think how it must be for Véronique. I know this is the last thing you want to hear but, tired as you are, you have to be strong. Not just for you, but for her too.'

Daniel nodded reluctantly. Suddenly it seemed as if the weight of the whole world were on his shoulders. Death did that to you, he thought to himself: it made everything feel so heavy.

He closed his eyes. Sometimes – just sometimes – even dreams, it seemed, were not enough.

18

'Can you put me through to Dr Fischer?'
'Just a moment please . . . I'm afraid Dr Fischer is with a patient at present. Perhaps I can help?'
'No, it's okay. I'll try to catch him later.'
'Do you want to make an appointment to see him?'
'No, no, I just wanted some advice.'
'Well, surgery is very busy today; perhaps you could call tomorrow morning after ten?'
'Yes, thank you.'

Lisanne put the phone down and sighed. Where were they when you needed them, your friends, your advisers? Where were they hiding? Wasn't it always the way?

She stood up and went over to the window. On the streets below thousands of City workers were pouring out of doorways, their coats, umbrellas and briefcases lashing and slicing the air as they jostled for position on the crowded pavements. How sure they all seemed, how certain that their lives were unfolding as they should, according to strict timetables and accepted patterns of behaviour. How uncertain and unsteady her own life seemed in comparison.

Vince's phone call had unnerved her. Not only was she shocked to hear about the contents of Daniel's dream, but she was also highly distressed that Daniel had not seen fit to talk to her about it. Surely she would have been a more appropriate listener than Vince? Why wouldn't he confide in her any more? What had she done to become such an outcast? Lisanne tried hard to recall an occasion – *any* occasion – on which she had betrayed Daniel's trust, but nothing came to mind. She may not have been the ideal partner; no doubt there were times when she behaved selfishly or thoughtlessly, or perhaps even cruelly, but one thing was certain: she was, and had always been, completely loyal to Daniel. It was inconceivable that he could think her unreliable. Besides, if what Vince had told her was true, there seemed to be nothing that warranted keeping the truth from her: after all, it was just a dream, albeit a bizarre and obsessive dream.

At least, this is what she told herself by way of reassurance. The fact was, she had been unsettled by the undeniable tremor of panic in Vince's voice, which, despite his constant assertions that there was 'probably nothing to worry about', suggested just the reverse. She couldn't even be sure that he was telling her the whole story. Whatever, if Vince's reaction was anything to go by, there was reason to be concerned. From what he had said, it sounded as if Daniel was suffering some sort of delusional psychosis – not that she was an expert, hence her impatience to speak to Fischer. Does he know about this? she wondered.

At least it helped explain Daniel's increasingly bizarre

Daniel's Dream

behaviour. If he was living his life only to explore this 'Atheenaton' place in his dreams, no wonder he showed little interest in her or indeed anything in 'real life'. Why bother even being awake if your dreams are so enticing?

This last notion was not something Lisanne believed, but then she had no real idea of what Daniel was experiencing. She could barely envisage a dream that was preferable to reality, let alone this serial affair that had taken over Daniel's life.

But why hadn't he told her about it? Why had he excluded her, especially when it was so clearly important to him?

And then there was the matter of the book. As soon as Vince started to describe Daniel's dream, Lisanne saw the connection: *Greek Idyll*, Robert Jameson's first novel. It was eerie, uncomfortable.

Down below the crowds were swelling, the movements of the anxious commuters, viewed from this distance, increasingly random as queues of matchstick men and women did battle with newspaper vendors, traffic wardens and lost tourists, everyone desperate to get away from everyone else, away from the numberless strangers whose lives meant nothing to them and back to the arms of their loved ones, their families and friends, their parrots and pooches . . . or perhaps just to a cramped living room with a television and a comfy chair. How many of them, she wondered, were heading for anything other than the routine, anticipated dimensions of everyday life? How many of them would arrive home to find that the dog had died, or that the parrot had flown the coop, or that their spouse had, without a warning of any kind, upped and left? Or jumped off the roof. Or gone mad . . .

Ever since Daniel's return from India, Lisanne had been haunted by the fear that his increasingly unsociable and odd behaviour was not just a response to his terrible misfortune, but an indicator of a deeper malaise. Were there types of madness that one just didn't recognise? Were there varieties of dementia that dressed themselves up as lesser complications, disguising their true nature? Or types of lunacy that were so subtle as to go virtually unnoticed, even by close observers?

Lisanne paused for a moment and checked herself. She wished she could be certain that her response was not simply paranoia. Since the first signs of Daniel's aberrant behaviour, she had wondered about the possibility of madness more often than she dared admit, but had never felt confident about pursuing the matter. Besides, what could she do? Daniel was not about to entertain such ideas, and Fischer had never intimated that Daniel was anything more than very shaken and suffering from post-traumatic stress. There had never been any suggestion that he was truly unbalanced.

She stared at the telephone, wondering if she should perhaps call Janice and talk to her about it. Even though Vince had not mentioned her, it seemed unlikely that they had not spoken about this most recent revelation. Perhaps Janice – frequently the voice of reason in Lisanne's increasingly delusory life – might have some words to comfort or console her. Perhaps she could shed some light on the whole subject; Janice had some understanding of these things.

Lisanne dialled Janice's work number, but there was no answer. Rather than drive herself to distraction with endless attempts to contact her, she tried to put all thoughts

Daniel's Dream

of Daniel aside and get on with the work in hand: Robert Jameson's new novel.

She fished the manuscript out from under a pile of papers and, sitting well back in her chair, turned to the first page and started to read.

19

They drove in convoy, two open-topped jeeps cruising up the mountainside, following the winding track past lemon groves and vineyards, higher and higher, towards the peak. Kate, Véronique, Barry and Daniel led the way; Marianne, Kostas, Vangeli and Imogen – a new arrival in Atheenaton – followed.

It was festival time in the mountains; every village they passed through had been suitably adorned for the holiday. People waved and shouted greetings as they drove by, beckoning them to stop for food and drink, to celebrate the feast.

Daniel sat in the back with Kate, assimilating the rush of images and sounds that assaulted his senses from every angle; the sun flickered through overhead branches, birds sang out from the bushes and trees. Everywhere, life erupted in a cacophony of noise and colour. Every now and then the jeep would round a bend in the road, and the views down across the hillside to the coast were breathtaking. The sense of festivity hung in the air like a potent, heady perfume: a sense of celebration tinged with a hint of sobriety, as if there were more to the occasion than just a party.

'What exactly are we celebrating?' Daniel asked Kate as the jeep rounded a particularly hazardous bend.

'Whatever you want to celebrate,' she said.

Daniel nodded. 'And what if I have nothing to celebrate?'

Kate peered at him quizzically. 'There's always something, Daniel. You just have to look for it. How about you, Barry?'

'It's a beautiful day. Sometimes that's enough.'

'Kostas is celebrating his conquest of Marianne,' said Véronique, turning round to look at Daniel.

Daniel nodded. 'And what about you, Kate? What are you celebrating?'

Kate smiled. 'Your return to the fold,' she said softly, then leant forward and tapped Barry on the shoulder. 'Left at the next crossroads, Barry, then straight on till daybreak.'

Daniel gave Kate a look of shocked amazement, then, seeing Kate's cheeky smile, burst out laughing.

'So *that's* where we are!' he said triumphantly, and allowed the tension that had been mounting since early that morning to dissipate.

They arrived at a tiny village in the lee of the overhanging peak as the sun reached its zenith, and piled out on to the gravel and sand forecourt of a dilapidated taverna.

'We've arrived,' said Kate with unusual solemnity.

Daniel gazed around. They were on the northern edge of a square bounded on one side by the taverna. Opposite

Daniel's Dream

where they had parked stood a line of olive trees obscuring some smaller villas. Along both sides, bare wooden tables had been placed, in readiness, Daniel presumed, for a buffet of some kind. In the centre of the square, a huge tree resembling an aged, gnarled oak spread its boughs in a natural canopy. Its trunk had been whitewashed, and dozens of coloured lightbulbs adorned its branches.

As the second jeep drew up, Daniel became aware of the familiar strains of 'Synaxaria' coming from the taverna. He smiled.

'Especially for you,' said Kate, seeing his smile.

'Time for drinking!' boomed Vangeli as he leapt out of the jeep and headed through the door of the taverna. Barry and Kostas grabbed a table and placed it underneath the central tree, while Marianne and Kate hunted for chairs.

'We must be early,' said Daniel, looking around him for other signs of life.

'Just wait,' said Vangeli returning with four ceramic carafes and eight glasses on a large wooden tray. He put it on the table and started to pour the retsina. By the time the eighth glass had been filled, the chairs had been arranged and everyone was seated.

'To us!' toasted Kate, lifting her glass without spilling a drop.

'*Yamas!*' chorused the others, each grabbing a glass and downing the contents in one.

'To a day of celebration,' said Barry, refilling his glass. 'It sure feels good to be free.'

Free? thought Daniel. Free from what? Surely he can't mean the Pumphouse?

Imogen, the newcomer, raised her glass timidly and smiled. Daniel thought she looked pale, and far younger than the others seated around the table. What's your problem? he wanted to ask, but thought better of it.

The music from the taverna swelled and filled the square. Villagers started to emerge from their homes carrying plates of food, jugs of wine, baskets of fruit, which they placed on the bare tables. They greeted the party by the oak tree with friendly shouts of *'Yassu!'* and various benedictions that Daniel could not understand.

Within an hour, the square was bustling with crowds of olive-skinned, dark-haired locals. A group of musicians – the local bouzouki band – had gathered to the right of the taverna and were busy setting up their instruments. More food appeared on the tables, more retsina materialised in their glasses, and more laughter began to echo around the square. Children, each dressed in what Daniel imagined were 'Sunday-best' clothes began to mill about among the adults, and soon the lively shrieks of kids at play were added to the melange of festive sounds. They were the first children Daniel had seen in Atheenaton, and though it was heart-warming to see children racing around and having fun, he could not help but be concerned. Were they there because they too had problems, illnesses, things they could not cope with? Or were they just part of the background, the infrastructure, of this extraordinary place? He had to concede that he would never understand the mechanics of Atheenaton, and that any attempts to do so would only end up tying him in knots.

Daniel's Dream

The musicians started to tune up. One of the children brought a tray laden with glasses of wine for the band, and they all abandoned their instruments to toast themselves and the assembled crowd, before launching into a rousing *syrtaki*. Daniel became aware once again of the smell of pine needles and the atmosphere of ease and goodness that he had first encountered in Atheenaton. He felt Véronique take his hand beneath the table.

'What are you celebrating today,' he whispered as he leant over to kiss her neck.

'Meeting you,' she said softly, returning his kiss.

Daniel watched in delight as Kostas and Barry walked into the square, stood side by side, an arm's length apart, reached out to grab one another by the shoulder and began to dance. A space cleared immediately, and everyone began to clap their hands in time to the synchronised display. It was apparent to Daniel that they had done this many times, such was their finesse, and yet there was a freshness and naivety to their movements that endowed the dance with a sense of freedom and childlike wonder.

Some of the young men of the village joined in, and soon there was a line of seven, all dancing perfectly in time. A couple of old-timers cleared a space on one of the tables and matched the youngsters move for move. Everyone cheered and yelled, raising their glasses to the dancers. Wine flowed liberally, generously, into empty and half-filled glasses as the bouzouki band played on.

Marianne and Vangeli grabbed a few bystanders, formed a chain and started a different dance, an apparently simple set of steps that everyone could do (although Daniel had difficulty mastering the rhythmic changes), and the whole village linked up to dance in an ever-increasing spiral round the tree. The band played faster, the happy villagers twisted and turned to the syncopations of the bouzouki, some falling over in mild hysteria and drunkenness while others rallied round to help them to their feet. The spiral broke and reformed many times during the dance, until there were two independent chains dancing around the tree in opposite directions. Daniel found himself between Marianne and Kate at one point, having lost Véronique in the shifts and changes.

'Daniel! Isn't it wonderful?' bellowed Marianne as she twirled beneath his arm.

'Wonderful!' yelled Daniel, beaming. The wine had enlivened him considerably.

'Have you decided what you're celebrating yet?' shouted Marianne.

'Not really. How about you?'

'Life, Daniel, I'm celebrating life and living. I think it's what Véronique would want, don't you?'

Daniel nodded, a touch seriously. The chain broke once again, and he found himself linked up between two local women, who blushed when he smiled at them.

They danced and drank, ate and sang. The never-ending supply of food and drink kept spirits high and appetites lively. The sky darkened into night and the lights on the trees bathed the village in a warm glow. During a brief respite from the dancing, Kate took Daniel aside and, as he was decidedly tipsy from the

Daniel's Dream

retsina, supported him as she led him up towards the peak.

'Where are we going?' said Daniel, his words greeting the warm evening air like a troupe of circus tumblers entering the ring, tripping up and falling over each other.

'Trust me. I want you to see something.'

They walked in near-darkness away from the village, up a narrow dirt track. Despite being unable to see anything other than shadows, and even though his balance was not all it might be, Daniel felt quite safe. He allowed Kate to guide him up the steep incline until they emerged on to a bluff of rock. Down below Daniel could see the fairy-lights of the bustling village and the crowds of people milling around without apparent purpose or direction. It was an enchanting sight.

'Look Daniel . . . no, not down there, over here. Look.'

Steered by Kate's gentle pressure on his arm, Daniel peered out into the darkness.

'I can't see anything,' he said, perplexed.

'Wait,' said Kate softly. Daniel peered into the black space ahead of him. As his eyes grew accustomed to the dark, he began to recognise shapes floating in the void. Slowly he identified the gentle, faint flicker of lights as each shape metamorphosed into the silhouette of an island set against a blue-black sea. He gazed in astonishment as the lights grew brighter. Before long he could make out thousands of tiny islands, all glittering in the night. He turned slowly; from every angle, stretching out into infinity, lay countless islands.

'I don't . . . Are they all . . . ?'

'Just like us, Daniel. And all of them are celebrating tonight, dancing and drinking with abandon. And on every island you'll find an Atheenaton with its Véroniques and Kates and Daniels, each consumed with their own grief, each surrendering their sorrow for one night.'

Daniel watched in silence. Below him the musicians had resumed their playing, but the music was barely audible on the peak. He clasped Kate's hand tightly. He knew that he had had too much to drink, and that he was therefore prone to sentimentality, but even so, the sight had moved him deeply, and he found the words he wanted to say caught up in the back of his throat.

'I didn't realise . . . So many islands. So many people.'

'Everyone needs sanctuary now and then, Daniel; you're not alone.'

'Are they – the islands – all like Atheenaton?'

'Each person comes to the place that is most suited to their problems. You chose Atheenaton.'

'I did?'

'Certainly.' Kate smiled. 'So, have you decided yet?'

'Decided?'

'What you're celebrating?'

Daniel looked down at the ground and breathed in deeply. He stood there for several moments, just gazing at his feet. Suddenly he was overwhelmed by emotion, by the thought that he might one day have to leave Atheenaton, to say goodbye to Kate and Barry and Kostas. And Véronique. The thought that his departure would, in some way, be his reward for having solved whatever problems had brought him here in the first instance, was of no solace at all. If being healed meant leaving Atheenaton, he wasn't at all sure that he *wanted* to get better.

Daniel's Dream

Daniel peered into the deep, dark night. Eventually he looked at Kate and shrugged.

'I'll let you know,' he said sadly, and then, still staggering, started back down to the village.

20

When Lisanne got home she found Daniel fast asleep on the sofa. Her immediate response was to wake him up; the knowledge that he was off somewhere in his own little world, happy and presumably without a care, was about as much as she could stand. How dare he escape like that, running off into his own pathetic little fantasy, leaving a trail of destruction behind him? Didn't he have any idea of the misery he was causing?

She took her jacket off and hung it on the end of the banister, then walked over to where Daniel was snoring contentedly. She stood over him for a moment, wondering whether she dared to disturb him. She knew that for many months Daniel had had to contend with nothing but demons in his sleep. She had lost count of the number of times since the accident that she had had to stroke his brow to calm his torment. Knowing this – and despite the misery he had put her through – she could not bring herself to wake him. She looked down at him and sighed. He would put her in an institution at this rate, she was sure.

She was just about to tiptoe away when she noticed the book lying face down on the carpet beside the sofa: it was *Greek Idyll*. Lisanne felt her heart skip a beat. She leant down and picked up the book; an old Underground ticket acting as a bookmark confirmed that Daniel was two-thirds of the way through. An icy chill gripped the back of her neck like a steel claw. Had she been asked why this small discovery so disconcerted her, she would have been hard pressed to find a rational explanation. All she knew was that there was something wilfully perverse – deranged, perhaps – about this choice of reading matter.

Was it possible that Robert's book was having some subliminal effect on Daniel? Was he replaying the events of the novel in his subconscious, with himself as hero? It was too strange to contemplate. With a shudder, Lisanne replaced the book on the floor, but as she did so Daniel awoke with a start and, seeing Lisanne bending over him so closely, yelled out. Lisanne leapt back in astonishment.

'It's only me,' she said hastily, unable to hide the hurt in her voice: Daniel had screamed when he saw her; if ever there was an ill omen . . .

'Oh God, what are you doing? You frightened me half to death!' Daniel sat up swiftly and swung his legs off the sofa. He took a deep breath and sank his face in his hands.

'Sorry,' said Lisanne pathetically. 'I've only just got in. I saw you asleep and . . . I'm sorry.'

She turned to leave. Daniel's outburst had shocked her. She could feel her hands shaking and felt close to tears, but she was damned if she was going to let him see her cry. She strode over to the staircase and paused for a moment on the bottom stair.

Daniel's Dream

'Just one question, Daniel. Why are you reading that book again? Just explain that, will you?'

Daniel turned and stared at her. 'What do you mean, "again"? I haven't read this book before.'

'Oh yes you have. Robert's one of my authors. You read it in manuscript – or at least, you tried – last year. I can't believe you don't remember. You hated it.'

Daniel shook his head. 'You're wrong.'

'Don't tell me I'm wrong, Daniel! I *know*! I brought the book home to read. We even discussed it. I remember you saying that it read like a parody of *The Magus*, which, incidentally, none of the reviewers seemed to pick up on. You tore it to shreds. I can't believe you'd want to give it a second look. Well?'

But Daniel did not answer. He picked the book up from where Lisanne, in her panic, had dropped it, and gazed at the cover.

'And another thing,' said Lisanne, now emboldened by her anger. 'Why on earth didn't you tell me about this dream of yours?'

Daniel looked up at her, clearly shocked.

'How . . . ?'

'Vince told me about it. Why did I have to find out from Vince? Why don't you trust me for God's sake?'

Daniel's mouth went dry. He tried to clear his throat, but the shock and the embarrassment of being found out had unnerved him. 'I didn't want to burden you. You've got enough troubles.'

'But I could have helped you.'

'I don't want help, Lisanne. Don't you see? I don't want to be helped or healed. I don't want to be released or absolved or any of those things. I just want . . .'

Peter Michael Rosenberg

Daniel did not finish his sentence. Lisanne watched with growing unease as he stood up slowly and, deeply absorbed in his own preoccupations, dragged himself across the room to the bottom of the stairs. 'I'm tired,' he muttered as he shuffled past her. 'I'm just so tired.' Without further explanation, he headed straight to the bedroom.

21

Daniel wandered into the Pumphouse. It was dark inside, save for a single candle flickering on a table near the back. Through the gloom he could make out the silhouettes of several people huddled together; if they were talking, they were doing so not much above a whisper. Daniel walked over slowly. He couldn't understand why the lights weren't on, why there was no music. Had there been a power cut?

'Hi,' he called out. 'What's going on?'

'Hello, Daniel.'

He recognised Kate's voice. 'Come and join us,' she said.

As he neared the table he made out the familiar faces of Barry, Kostas and Imogen. Imogen was playing distractedly with an empty glass and staring at the table; she didn't look up when Daniel sat down. Barry was smoking a cigarette; his legs were crossed and he leant back in his chair, blowing the smoke out slowly so that it spiralled up into the rising heat and light of the candle. Kostas was tapping his fingers rhythmically on the table and looking at the floor, his face half-shadowed in the wavering light of the candle. It took a few moments for Daniel to realise that something was wrong; save for his own moods and tantrums, everyone else in Atheenaton always acted as if life was one long party; he rarely saw a long face.

'What's up? Is the electricity down?'

'Nah,' said Barry softly. 'Let me get you something to drink, Daniel. How about a scotch?' Barry sounded tired, very tired, as if he had been awake for several days; Daniel felt suddenly uncomfortable.

'Sure, scotch would be fine,' he said, pulling a chair up to the table beside Kate. 'Does someone want to tell me what's going on?'

Kostas got up and went over to the bar. Imogen looked at Kate, then looked away again. Daniel felt a chill creep into the room.

Kate spoke. 'It's Véronique. She's gone, Daniel. Véronique is dead.'

22

Lisanne wandered into the travel shop. It was still early and, save for the staff, she was the only person in there. It made her feel conspicuous.

She had left Daniel fast asleep, as usual. Following the previous evening's disastrous confrontation she had decided to do a little detective work herself. If Daniel would not tell her what was going on, she would find out for herself. And she would start by finding out about the origins of this ridiculous dream world of his.

Feigning nonchalance, she headed over to the racks of brightly coloured brochures, picked one up at random, and flicked through it absentmindedly. Most of the travel agents in the area were run by Greek Cypriots: if anyone knew about Greek islands . . .

'Can I help you?'

Lisanne looked over her shoulder at the young woman behind the counter and smiled uneasily. 'I'm not sure.'

The travel agent glanced at the brochure in Lisanne's hands. 'You're interested in Greece?'

Lisanne nodded. 'Yes, I . . .' She hesitated, fearing that her prepared question would yield nothing but blank looks. 'Do you know of a place – it may be an island, I'm not sure – called Atheenaton?'

The young woman's polite expression turned to one of sly amusement, and Lisanne's creeping discomfort erupted into full-blown dread. 'What?' she said. 'What is it?'

The travel agent leant across to her colleague, a handsome young man with sleek black hair and deeply chiselled features, and rattled something off in the language that Lisanne heard every day in the shops and stores of the neighbourhood, but of which she understood not a word. The young man burst out laughing. Lisanne felt her face redden. What had she said, for God's sake?

'It's not a place,' said the young woman, giggling. '$A\delta\eta\nu\alpha\tau o$: it's a Greek expression. It means "impossible". You want to go to an island called "Impossible"?'

Lisanne felt her heart explode in her chest. As she ran out into the crowded street, she could still hear the woman laughing.

Daniel was still in bed. Lisanne had had enough. She was determined to have it out with him once and for all and did not care about disturbing him.

'Daniel?'

Daniel did not stir. She sat on the bed beside him, and touched his arm. He did not respond. She grabbed his arm and shook him roughly, but Daniel remained fast asleep, and try as she might, she could not wake him.

23

Daniel recognised the place the moment he came round the corner: the empty sand, the same azure sea; the branches of the olive tree that intruded into the scene were the same shape as those on the cover of *Greek Idyll*. And there on the sand, its pages fanned open, was a book which cast the shadow of a face on the sand.

Daniel stood for several minutes staring at this extraordinary sight. He wondered where the owner of the book had gone, and why it had been left open. With a hint of trepidation, he wandered across the sand until he stood just a metre away from the book. He looked along the beach in both directions, and even peered out to sea, but there was not a soul to be seen. He knelt down and picked up the book; he turned it over and examined the front cover. There was no pictures or photos on the front, just the name of the author, and the title: *Daniel's Dream*.

Daniel sat down on the warm sand, opened the book at page one, and started to read.